2 /

DARK
WATER

PART TWO OF WILD WATER

JAN RUTH

My son; for his patience with all matters technical.

John Hudspith Editing Services;
for super sharp crossing and dotting.

JD Smith Design; for beautiful insides and outs.

FOR PAUL

CHAPTER ONE

Jack

As Fridays went, it was the worst Jack could ever remember. The plan had been simple enough: finish in the office early and escape for half-term with Anna and Lottie at the farm. His daughter was already excited and expecting Jack to collect her from school. Anna had arranged pony rides, dressed Benson the labrador in his party outfit – a musical dicky bow – and had made an elaborate birthday cake. Everyone was looking forward to it.

His ex-wife put a stop to all of this.

On the point of leaving the loose ends of the day in the capable hands of his staff with his son pretending to be in charge, Jack was stopped in his tracks by a phone call from Patsy. 'Don't bother going to the school for Lottie, I had to collect her at lunchtime. She's covered in spots.'

'Spots?'

'Yes! Chickenpox.'

Jack perched on the edge of his desk and rubbed his eyes. 'Right, put her on the phone, please.'

Lottie's tearful voice came on the line. 'Daddy, I've got a chicken disease.'

'Do you feel poorly, sweetheart?'

'Not really, but it looks a bit like syphilis. There's funny marks where the feathers are going to come out and my feet are itchy where the claws will grow.'

'I see. Put Mummy back on, please.'

He could hear the phone being passed to Patsy, although Lottie's weak voice continued in the background.

'What in God's name have you told her? *Syphilis?* She thinks she's got a poultry disease! What sort of mother are you?'

The phone was dead because, of course, she'd disconnected. Jack slammed the receiver down and looked up to see his junior receptionist, Tabitha. She eyed him nervously as usual, dumped some files on his desk, and scuttled out. Sometimes it was hard to believe his divorce was nearly four years ago. The animosity rumbled on, complicated structures of control hiding the real fear. Even below the surface, Jack's life was filled with good things but the thorn in his side – of sharing parenting with a woman he'd grown to despise – was increasingly tough. He logged off his computer and poked his head round to the back office to give last-minute instructions to Oliver.

'Right, I'm off. Make sure you lock up and *don't* turn up with a hangover in the morning. The diary's pretty full and you need a clear head.'

His handsome son turned his head with a know-it-all expression towards Jack. 'Like you've never worked with a hangover, eh, Dad?'

'Not recently. Anyway, it takes years of experience to get away with it.'

He acknowledged the staff on the front desk and made his way outside, annoyed to find the pool car yet again dumped at an odd angle across the forecourt. Since Oliver had finally passed his test, the long-suffering vehicle had been backed into every available post, bollard, and low garden wall in the Redman Estates area. It had even managed a flying leap into the middle of the roundabout on Prestbury Road.

Surviving this, it had gone on to experience other mysterious mechanical issues which suggested it had been driven through deep water at some point. Jack had been patient for the first few months. 'If that car ends up in the crusher, then it will *not* be replaced, get it?'

'You want me to catch a bus to do viewings? Not a good image, Dad.'

'No, Ollie, you'll be grounded in the office while someone who respects the highway code does the viewings – someone with spatial awareness, someone who knows the difference between the brake and the other pedals.'

He could sense the puppet hand and hear the sniggering as he walked away.

Jack climbed into his new car, something he swore he'd never drive – a Range Rover Sport – and inched around the battered Fiat and into the traffic. He still missed his Aston Martin but if he was honest, the more rugged vehicle was the better option for his lifestyle. Living half the week with Anna at Gwern Farm had worked out better than he'd anticipated. Anna liked it because she got her own space for a few days. Oliver liked it because he got the big flat above the office to himself. Jack kept meaning to move out, but what was the point when he only lived there for three or four nights a week? The only downside was the constant driving back and forth. It didn't help that ex-wife Patsy lived on the north side of Manchester, in the opposite direction to the north of Wales, where he wanted to be *right now.*

Friday night rush hour, but there were no cars rushing anywhere – it was standing or crawling traffic in every lane. A miserable combination of sleet and heavy rain cascaded down the windscreen and Jack wondered if it was a good idea to insist that Lottie spend February half-term at the farm if she was poorly, but then, he had more patience with her than Patsy, and besides, he actually wanted to.

Forty minutes later and struggling to find a parking space, he pulled up outside Patsy's rented house. It looked more run-down than ever, with an old pram abandoned in next door's front garden. Despite this, her Mercedes languished kerbside, looking old and out of place. Lottie snatched the front door open, wearing a pair of her mother's Louboutins, a flapper style dress with dozens of necklaces, and waving an ostrich feather. So much for being ill. But Lottie was a law unto herself; theatrical, full of clever nonsense, and utterly beguiling.

On closer inspection, she did have a few spots behind her ears and very pink cheeks, although that could have been stage make-up.

'Daddy, I'm highly infectious.'

'It's just a virus, you'll be fine.'

She smiled sweetly. 'I know. I looked up poxy on the Internet. It means rubbish, or someone who had bad syphilis. I wanted you to think I was scared so you'd come and get me. Guess what?'

'What?'

'I had a test at school. I had to pretend to be a Chinese chimney sweep and sing "Ching-Chimney Poo". Shall I do it now?'

'Maybe later.'

Patsy materialised in a green tracksuit the same shade as her eyes. Her chestnut hair had grown long again and she wore it pulled into a ponytail. Stripped of her preferred gloss with two small children at her feet, she looked more like the girl he'd married nearly thirty years ago, but that wasn't the case, he reminded himself. A lot of dirty water had gushed under the bridge since then.

The toddler was clinging to her leg, red-faced and bawling.

'Jack. I need to speak to you,' Patsy said. 'Lottie, *please* go and pack a bag if you want to go to the farm, although I don't think it's a good idea.'

'She seems fine to me,' Jack said, watching Lottie thump dramatically up the stairs. 'More to the point, why are you letting her look up all sorts of stuff on the Internet?'

'We looked *together*, she wanted to know all about chickenpox. You know what she's like! Please don't jump down my throat.'

He followed her into the dismal front room, where she lifted James onto her hip and wiped his snotty face, and Jack looked away. This small child caused no end of resentment, but whenever he came face-to-face with James, the overriding feeling was one of pure shame for still not having had a DNA test. Patsy's affair and her pregnancy had been discovered at the same time. Somehow – and he knew it wasn't rational – but the collapse of his marriage, including the loss of their beautiful Cheshire home and Patsy's business, and the devastation it had wreaked on their children all seemed to be epitomised in the existence of this toddler.

The man Patsy had given up everything for, who'd caused all of this volcanic destruction, was serving time for fraud. Jack felt like they were all serving time *with* him.

Lottie dragged a case down the stairs. It burst open in the hall, spilling a dazzling array of dressing-up clothes, shoes, and glitter.

'Clear that up,' Patsy snapped.

'Don't take it out on her,' Jack said quietly. 'Look, it won't do any harm for her to come back with me for a few days, give yourself a break.'

'A break?' she sighed. Her answer was to shove James into his arms and help Lottie clear up, but at least she seemed resigned to the original plan and took their daughter and the case back upstairs. Sounds of arguing ensued as to what represented sensible clothing, and Jack was left holding the baby. The child's heaving sobs settled and he began to explore Jack's face with sticky fingers. Dark blond, slate blue eyes, the Redman stamp. But he used to think his eldest daughter was his too, and look what revelations had come out of the woodwork there! At least Patsy had given up her relentless insistence that Jack was the daddy this time, but rather than make him feel assured, it was beginning to balloon into an uncomfortable tourniquet of guilt. The child was three for Chrissake, and starting to wonder why he only came for Lottie.

While his daughter was occupied with dragging a bewildering array of possessions and bags down from her room, Patsy took James from him and indicated he take a seat. 'Now that you're here, I need to discuss something.'

'You'll have to make it quick, I'm already running late.'

Knowing he was cornered, Jack slumped into a chair cluttered with plastic toys, aware that his mobile was buzzing with missed texts and calls from Anna. He began to compose an apologetic reply, something about being caught in traffic.

'I'm desperate to move out of this house, out of this neighbourhood,' Patsy said, her voice catching. 'It's not nice for the children to grow up here, and I think there's some *weirdo* following me.'

Jack grunted in agreement and sent a text, then slipped the phone into his pocket. Patsy's address was another area which caused him considerable discomfort but he continued to store it in the same compartment as unwanted children.

'Are you even listening?' she said.

'A stalker? You need to go to the police.'

'And say what? I've got a *feeling* I'm being followed?'

'What do you want me to do about it?'

'You're an estate agent. Really, Jack, do I have to spell it out?'

The baby began to grizzle again and something delved into Jack's subconscious. He focused his attention on that of the dark, poky kitchen beyond the sitting room and the cheap furnishings. He used to think it was what Patsy deserved, but had she paid the price, and more to the point, why should the children suffer?

'I suppose you want something in Prestbury or Wilmslow, do you? Somewhere you can show off to your old Cheshire set?'

'No, I don't,' she said, then met his eyes with cool determination. 'I want to move to Wales.'

'Not a chance.'

'So you don't want to give Lottie a chance either?' she said, glancing into the hall as Lottie announced she'd forgotten something and trotted back upstairs. Patsy leant in and lowered her voice. 'She's won a scholarship. It's a school in St Asaph. I haven't told her yet because if we can't sort something out, she'll be heartbroken. You'll be able to see more of her, be involved.'

'I see. Emotional blackmail, again.'

'No, Jack! It's all about Lottie. Come on, we've had this conversation before; she doesn't fit into a mainstream school and what the hell do we do next year when she has to go to secondary? Have you *seen* that school on the sink estate?'

He knew all of this and of course it bothered him. If

there was enough money in the pot he'd have sent Lottie to a private school a long while ago, but thanks to Patsy and her locked-up lover, they'd more or less stripped him of everything he'd worked for.

'I was wondering about that cottage down on the quay in Conwy, the one that used to belong to your parents?' she said. 'According to Move-On it stands empty most of the time.'

Jack sprawled back and closed his eyes. He'd been planning on loaning the cottage to Anna's son, who'd managed to get himself a local bar job in between his university course. The lad was desperate to move out of the farm. With no car at his disposal, living in a rural idyll was a series of complicated lifts and sporadic public transport. Unlike Oliver, his stepson worked every minute of the day and half the night. It seemed unfair that even when he became a fully qualified teacher, the starting salary was so low that he'd have to stay at the farm for the medium to long-term. It seemed he and Anna would never get some space for their own relationship.

Above all, he didn't want Patsy living anywhere near Conwy, encroaching on this life he'd built with Anna. The farmhouse they'd restored together had evolved into a place of deep love and security. Both in reality and in his mind, it was a sanctuary of epic power, and after years of heartache, he was loath to disturb the equilibrium. He hated to think how Anna might respond to the suggestion that Patsy was moving into town.

Patsy handed over a copy letter of confirmation from Cymru School of Music and Drama. He shoved it in his pocket.

'Have you nothing to say? Aren't you proud of her?'

'I've always been proud of her. That's not the issue.

I'll think about it.'

'Don't take forever, they need to know soon. She may never get an opportunity like this.'

'I said I'll think about it.'

A couple of hours later, Jack pulled off the narrow mountain road and took a sharp left. Fully dark by now, the jagged outline of the mountains were just visible as a grey mass. As Gwern Farm came into view, the windows were throwing warm pools of light into the black wilderness, and his mood lifted. The labradors heard the vehicle and barged out, full of hellos and how are yous? Lottie, bleary-eyed and wrapped in a pink blanket, hunkered down and made a fuss of the dogs. Jack grabbed her bags and paused to take a few lungfuls of fresh air, scents of wood-smoke mingling with the pungent, sleet-cold air. He dropped the bags in the hall, kicked the door shut behind him, and went to find Anna in the kitchen as she moved from Aga to table.

'Sorry we're late, love.'

Lottie took centre stage to begin with, desperate to tell Anna about the syphilis epidemic at school and show her the spots on the back of her knees. Anna, used to Lottie's stories, managed to keep a straight face and caught Jack's eye with a raised eyebrow.

'So I'm not very hungry,' Lottie said.

'How about soup and birthday cake, can you manage that?'

'Maybe. So long as it's not chicken.'

'Where have you been anyway?' Anna said, mostly to Jack. 'I've been worried. This food won't last much longer.'

'Ah, longish story.'

'It always is,' she said, her hands busy with several pans and a loaf of homemade bread.

He slid his arms around her and kissed the back of her neck where a small area of skin was just visible. Most of her hair was piled on top of her head in a riot of long curls and tendrils like a wild briar. 'You smell amazing.'

'Fried onion? There's nothing like it when you're starving.'

'Nope, you smell of wholesome country woman.'

'Uh-huh, as I thought, fried onion.'

'No, it's more like snow, and sky.'

'Nice.'

'I'll just get out of this suit,' he said, and she flashed him a smile.

Upstairs, he put Lottie's bags on her bed. In his own room that he shared with Anna, he took a moment to reflect on Patsy's conversation, then removed the letter from his pocket and scanned it. He could hear Anna and Lottie laughing, a faint sound of something musical, Benson barking. Happy, family sounds. He stopped reading for a moment, lifted his eyes, and looked at himself in the mirror. There were two strands of hair on his lapel. Fine toddler hairs. He pulled them off carefully, dropped them into the envelope, resealed it, and folded it over.

Later, relaxed in old denims with the dogs strewn in slumber at his feet, Jack wondered whether to show Anna the letter and the hair, but he'd put off decisions about James and Lottie for long enough, so another day or so wouldn't make a difference. Besides, if they argued it would not only spoil the holiday week but possibly wake Lottie, and she needed the rest. She'd willingly gone to bed and taken her medicine, her arms clamped around a patient Benson. Jack had hovered on the landing for a moment, listening as she related a complicated story to the dog. He knew she was asleep when Benson padded back into the sitting room to take his rightful place in front of the fire. Jack slid an arm around Anna and she nestled into him.

'So, what's the longish story?' she said. 'There's always something with Patsy.'

'Oh, just that she didn't want Lottie to come, so she wasn't packed or ready, and then the traffic was bad.'

Her dark blue eyes settled on his, searching. 'Not like her to be so concerned. She's always got rid of Lottie like a shot, poorly or not.'

Jack swirled the wine round in his glass. 'She's changed quite a lot. Mellowed, I think.'

'You mean she's changed tactic?'

'No, I think she may have learnt a lesson. I honestly don't think she's got an agenda, not this time.'

She twisted round to look at him. 'Not this time … what do you mean?'

When he made no reply, she sighed and got to her feet but Jack caught hold of her hand. 'It's nothing, she made a deal of the chickenpox and I lost my rag, mostly because you'd planned stuff.'

'I had it planned for much earlier.'

'I know, my fault. Thanks for doing the cake. The food and everything.'

'You don't have to *thank* me, Jack. I rather you'd let me know if you were going to be two hours late and that Lottie only wanted to eat icing.'

He grinned, prompting her features to crease into an exasperated smile and he was reminded how much he loved her. He pulled her towards him again and she relented, returning his kiss.

'I'm sorry about the cottage pie,' he said.

'Oh well, you and the dogs ate well.'

Love the second time around was certainly sweeter, despite the baggage it attracted. Well, it was mostly his

13

own baggage. They'd known each other since they were teenagers, then when Patsy had erupted onto the scene, separated. It was pointless thinking that this was all a mistake and that they should have stayed together. Jack had stopped beating himself up about it and besides, then he'd not have had Lottie or Oliver in his life. And of course he'd not have had the pleasure of his eldest daughter, Chelsey, although technically her father was Simon Banks. When Jack had found out the truth about this on Chelsey's wedding day, he'd been disgusted by the years of silence, not only between Patsy and Simon, but the way Anna had kept the suspected facts from him too.

The minute he'd discovered Patsy was pregnant, Simon had been off the scene like the real waster he was, happy to disappear with some cash in his pocket. Although when Jack thought about the hair in the envelope, he was reminded of a few hard facts. Was he really any better? It was all very well making sure Patsy, Lottie, and baby James didn't actually starve, but what if James really was his son? Since the child had grown up a little, he certainly didn't look anything like the slimy French bastard Patsy had had an affair with. He claimed to have had a vasectomy, and although in truth he couldn't actually imagine anyone as cunning and ruthless as Philipe getting caught out with an unplanned pregnancy, it had been easy to blame him for the mess at the time.

'I know there's something on your mind,' Anna said, lying across his lap.

He rubbed his eyes and yawned. 'Just work.'

'What happened to the promise you'd only be in the office three days a week?'

'I was, until two key staff went at the end of last year.'

'You need more staff.'

'Easier said and all that.'

'You're too conscientious!'

'And that's a bad thing? I used to get this argument from Patsy all the time, but my business is what's holding everything together.'

'I know, I'm sorry, it's just …'

'We don't get enough time alone? I *do* understand and I feel the same, but what can I do?'

'I don't know. I don't *know*, Jack.'

She moved off his lap and went to climb the stairs. Calling the dogs, he flung an old coat around his shoulders and let them out the back door for a last stretch while he sat on the wooden bench. It was sheltered by a pergola attached to the stone farmhouse walls. In the summer, it was covered with a riot of old roses, vines and honeysuckle, but even the brown winter version afforded a reasonable windbreak. The rain and sleet had abated, leaving a sharpness in the air that sobered his mind and focused his thoughts. There would be snow on higher ground and the velvet lake beyond the garden would be rippling in the keen breeze. They called it the garden, but really it was a semi-tamed area of hill farm. Not that it was farmed as such, not since Anna's grandparents had been alive. Hens and ducks just about covered it, and sometimes the ragged wild ponies wandered down to crop the dry grass and lie in the heather. Bleak, and yet rich beyond all comprehension, it was fiercely beautiful.

For the first time in years, Jack rooted around the pockets of his coat and lit a squashed cigarette.

The scrap of hairs in the envelope played on his mind, mushrooming into a big cloud of doom. On top of this floated the letter about Lottie. Of *course* she must go to drama school, how could he deny her that? She was born to act, to dance, to sing! She'd be a caged butterfly doing anything else. The discipline would be good for her, as well as being with other like-minded kids – some healthy competition. The fact that it was free was just the most amazing gift, like it was meant to be. He'd checked it all out, looked at the website. They were holding auditions at schools across the country. The Welsh location was pure fluke, it had to be. There was no way Patsy could have engineered it just to piss off Anna and himself.

The cottage on the quay was his other conundrum. It was his property, so there would be no rent to find and no extra travel when he wanted to see Lottie. Or James. His mother would be over the moon too, a couple of miles away. It would be good for Lottie seeing more of her, and it would be good for Isabel. Since the death of his father, she seemed isolated at times. Lottie would be beside herself with joy at all of these changes, too. The only person who wouldn't be thrilled was Anna.

He stamped the cigarette out in the wet grass and called the dogs. They came to him, silken heads and cold noses pushing into his hands, tails thrashing against his legs. Once inside, they slumped down into a row of beds by the Aga. It was late, after midnight by the time he'd checked on Lottie, and showered away the stress of the day. He slid into bed alongside Anna and she shuffled across and nestled into his body.

'Where have you been?' she whispered, then sighed. 'I shouldn't have snapped before. I'm sorry, I didn't mean to give you a hard time.'

He kissed her hair, her face, her shoulders, and she responded, sliding her long limbs around his. Her skin felt clammy and her face was damp.

'Jack, I'm –'

'I *know*, now stop talking. I want to give you a hard time.'

In the morning, Anna answered the landline phone, rolled her eyes, and passed the handset to Jack. It was Clare, his right-hand woman in the office, complaining that Oliver had not turned up 'I don't want to give you a hard time but I can't split myself in two,' she went on. 'The viewings diary is full.'

'I know. Where is he?'

'I've no idea! He either didn't go back to the flat last night or he's passed out drunk up there. I've been hammering on the door, phoning, shouting. This is a regular thing most Saturday mornings, and I'm getting tired of it.'

'Me too. I'll ring round, see if Tabitha can work. If Ollie turns up, tell him to call me.'

Jack sorted cover for the day, then after lunch, went through his mobile for numbers of Ollie's friends, all of which drew a blank. Clearly there was a cover-up operation in progress. Oliver's strange on-off girlfriend though, picked up after one ring. Amy, usually clad in tight animal skin of some description, always made him feel uncomfortable, even over the phone. She'd had a crush on Jack since she was fifteen but despite telling himself it was all in his imagination, it never seemed that way the next time around. His imagination had nothing to do with it.

'Oh … *Jack*.'

It sounded like she was panting, but her enunciation could extract something sexually charged from even the most innocuous of words. He paced up and down the kitchen trying to sound brisk and business-like.

'Hi, love, is Ollie there?'

'Um, no … why? Wait, has he been a bad boy again?'

He ran a hand through his hair, deliberating over

what to say. 'Just tell him he's on a very sticky wicket this time.'

'You sound so cross.'

'Damn right I am!'

'Oh, *yeah*, baby!' she squealed.

Jack almost dropped the phone. He spotted his mother gesticulating through the window, but concentrated on the conversation. 'Look, if you see him or hear of what he's up to, tell him I *will* find out.'

A long sigh. 'Bye, Jack,' she whispered.

He snatched open the door for his mother and she did a double-take. 'You look agitated. Don't tell me, it's something to do with the Wilmslow office? Unless you're coming down with something?'

'Like what?'

'Your father used to be exactly the same at the weekend. All twitchy.'

This was true. His parents had semi-retired to North Wales, leaving Jack running the main office. It all had an uncanny ring of inevitability – history was repeating itself, or trying to. Of course, his father hadn't completely given up buying and selling property and at the first sniff of something lucrative, had purchased the lock-up premises in Conwy. It was jokingly referred to as The Redman Estates Taffy branch, but Jack liked it. The small-scale operation was far from the madding crowd, and the rural properties and seaside hotels on the books were a welcome change from some of the snobby stockbroker belt in Cheshire. And then a chance meeting with Anna had changed his love life too.

'It's Ollie,' Jack said, throwing the switch on the kettle. 'He's on a second warning.'

'He's too young for that kind of responsibility.'

'Mum, he's nearly twenty! Clare's in charge of the branch, all Ollie has to do is turn up on time and do the viewings.'

She gave him a perplexed look and pulled out a chair. 'You were the same at that age. I despaired of you, and now look.'

'Still despairing of me, yeah, I get it.'

Isabel shot him a benevolent smile. She'd really arrived to see Lottie, with promise of a trip to the puppet theatre in Rhos-on-Sea followed by tea at the Pancake House. 'I'll keep her overnight, give you a break,' she said, patting Jack's arm.

Jack knew full well it was his mother who craved the company, but it was the perfect opportunity to have a serious conversation with Anna. He was resigned now to discussing the resurgence of old problems. Whichever way he looked at it, he had unfinished business with Patsy, and before he threw himself into the fray, he needed to be straight with Anna. Well, not *too* straight, but he couldn't go on with his head in the sand forever.

Lottie shuffled into the kitchen wearing a pair of huge fairy wings. She was listless and pasty-faced, but perked up when she saw her grandmother. She was of course, thrilled with the idea of the puppet theatre. Not well enough for pony rides in the rain at Hilly's trekking centre, she'd passed the morning making inedible cakes and producing stage shows with the dogs. Anna's black labrador did his best to accommodate, sporting an array of customised outfits, until eventually he'd whined to go outside. The old dog wasn't quite as tolerant in his old age. Hands on hips, Lottie had given Benson a bossy stare, reminding Jack very much of Patsy.

'Daddy! Me and Benson are *trying* to get married, but he won't sit-stay!'

'Universal problem,' Anna quipped, trying to clear up some of the mess. 'I think in this case though, it's

19

not a lack of loyalty, more likely a resistance to wearing pink tulle.'

'I'd marry you in a heartbeat,' Jack said, catching hold of her hand.

'In pink tulle?'

'Maybe not pink. But you know I'll sit *and* stay.'

She'd given him the usual brush-off – a roll of the eyes and a lopsided smile.

CHAPTER TWO

Jack

The following day, he took Anna to the King Edward Hotel in Conwy. They were busy with Sunday lunch but his parents had been loyal customers for years, and a table was quickly made available. Once seated, he studied her rather than the menu. She was wearing a black velvet dress with a green suede coat and brown boots. She didn't do conventional fashion, she was very much her own woman and her taste in clothes, usually vintage or casual, reflected her artistic personality. There was a good deal of ochre paint under her nails and her hair was wilder than ever. This is what he loved about being with her – the whole package was a severe contrast to the other half of his structured life in Wilmslow.

She snapped the menu shut and met his eyes, and Jack could swear she could read his mind.

'Don't tell me ... you want a plain steak with a salad. No onions.'

'You know me so well.'

They ordered and ate, then Jack couldn't hold off any longer. 'What you said the other day, about me having slipped back into working more in the office, you know it wasn't the original plan.'

'I know, and I know it's difficult. It doesn't help that everything else is so far away from here.'

This was his cue on a plate. He told her about

Lottie's drama school scholarship.

'Oh, that's fantastic!'

'There's a snag. It's the one in St Asaph.'

'I see,' she said slowly. 'So, let me guess. Patsy wants to move to St Asaph and wants you to pay for it?'

'Not exactly, no.' He paid out some more detail regarding the cottage on the quay, and her face fell but he carried on anyway. 'I don't want the kids growing up where they are –'

'The *kids?* Jack, only one of them is yours.'

An uncomfortable beat. 'I'm going to send off some hair for a DNA.'

'I see,' she said, pushing her plate away. 'Go on. It feels like there's a ton I don't know.'

'Not really. It's just, well, I should have done the test years ago, shouldn't I?'

'And does the result of this determine whether Patsy is entitled to the cottage for free?'

'To be honest, it's more about Lottie. Whatever the outcome, if they all stay in the cottage then it's not going to cost me anything.'

'Maybe not financially.'

'I'm thinking long-term,' Jack said, ignoring the chill of her response. 'I won't be needed in the Wilmslow office forever, not once Ollie gets a grip on stuff. I can get out of his hair a bit and cut down on the travel as well. I can maybe oversee the Conwy office instead and go once a week into Wilmslow, if that.'

'I think we're several years off Oliver managing the branch, don't you? *Seriously?*'

'He'll grow out of messing up.'

'Have you heard from him?'

'No. But I'm not worried. If it was bad news I'd know by now. He's in serious trouble though, make no mistake.'

She re-filled her glass and waited till the final drops of wine left the bottle. 'There's a problem with all of this, Jack. Something you've overlooked.'

'Yeah?'

She leant across the table and her voice was low, succinct, and menacing. 'I don't want *that* woman here, in my space. Ever.'

Before he could respond, she drained her glass, grabbed her coat off the back of the chair, and marched out through the restaurant. It was so out of character that he sat motionless for a full thirty seconds when he should have been chasing after her. He was still staring at the table when his mobile pinged with a text from Oliver. Jack read the short message then tried calling the number. It rang the whole time he was paying for the meal and finding his way out to the car park. Anna was leaning against the door of the Range Rover with her arms folded. He snapped his phone off and waved it in his fist.

'Ollie's turned up. He was detained in the bloody police station all Friday night.'

'What for?'

'I don't know that, but I'm going to find out. I want to know what the hell's going on.'

She sighed and squinted at the bright sun. Jack took hold of her hand. 'Come on, let's walk.'

They wandered around the small town, busy with tourists for half-term school holidays. On the square, he peered through the darkened window of the Taffy branch, pleased to note that several people were glued to the window. This was partly down to Anna's paintings. It was an idea which had proved advantageous to them both. An artist's impression of a property was a unique way to sell it. The owners, past and present, usually wanted to buy the painting as well, so it was win-win situation. Taking centre stage was a magnificent portrayal of a hundred-acre hill farm set high above the Conwy valley. Jack had seen it many times, but his eyes were constantly drawn to the way she'd captured that unique blend of stone, sky, and earth. Somehow she'd made it look alive with a hundred shades of grey and translucent water, highlighted by a handful of grubby sheep in the foreground. Despite the lack of colour and the strange sepia sky, the whole scene was uplifting. He shot Anna a smile and pulled her along, his fingers threaded through hers.

On the quay, the breeze was freshening with the incoming tide. It was noisy with seabirds looking for scraps, children throwing crabbing lines over the sides of the jetty, and a guy with a loudhailer announcing trips down the river. The sun slid behind a huge bank of rolling cloud and it was suddenly cold. He put an arm around her shoulders, heartened when she kissed the side of his face and he pulled her in tighter, unable to find the right words to allay her fears and frustrations. He didn't blame her for feeling the way she did. Patsy had caused no end of pain with her behaviour in the past, but he couldn't escape his parental duties. In fact, had no intention of doing so.

Towards the end of the walkway, the old fishermen's terrace sat well back, protected by the town walls to the rear but affording far-reaching views to the front, across the mouth of the Irish Sea to Deganwy. Quaint and deceptively spacious inside, the cottages were worth a fortune and rarely changed hands. Most were lucrative holiday lets. With a busy pub at one end and endless events during the summer, it was a prime tourist trap. The town had its problems, but for Lottie and James it would be a playground paradise, with parks and beaches. Where his sophisticated ex-wife might fit in to this scenario, Jack wasn't too sure, but what choice did any of them have?

They walked until Anna directed him to a lopsided bench set into the tiny shingle beach.

'I seem to keep saying sorry,' she said.

Jack looked straight ahead to the outline of the castle against the sky. 'I need to know if James is my son, surely you can understand that?'

'Yes, I do. And if I'm honest, I'm ashamed at how we've both ignored it. It's just that ... I don't want to face it.'

'This opportunity for Lottie. Can you think of any other way around it? I mean, would you consider her staying at the farm during term time?'

'You mean be a part-time mother to her? I don't think so, Jack.'

'I knew you'd say that. But it would never work, it's way too complicated.'

'I like things the way they are, that's all.'

He pulled out a packet of cigarettes and she shot him a dismayed look, but his desire for nicotine had resurfaced with a vengeance after three years of semi-abstention. 'Thing is, *things* don't stay the same, do they?'

'No, I guess not.'

The guy with the loudhailer started up again, and a procession of families began to make their way along the jetty to the River Queen. While he was smoking and thinking, Jack was aware of the proximity of the cottage windows, like unblinking eyes. He wondered if this is how it would be, that feeling of being watched. 'I've found a bedsit for Josh, called in a couple of favours. I can get it cheap. I'll pay, give him a head start.'

'I see. So this is the deal? My son gets a couple of grotty rooms in return for me agreeing to Patsy having the cottage?'

25

'Think of the fuel you'll save and the extra sleep you'll get. He can jump on a train or a bus to get to uni, *walk* to his bar job. And anyway, I'd like to help, he works so bloody hard.'

This was the absolute truth. Unlike Oliver, Josh had a healthy work ethic. He was serious and determined, where Oliver was the ultimate party boy. The frustration was that Ollie had such gifted abilities and opportunities to go far, but chose the wine, women, and song route too many times. He got on well with his step-brother though, as did Lottie. Lottie adored Josh, and having him live somewhere accessible to her felt like a good spin-off.

'And Lottie won't need to stay over as much. I can see her without the sleepovers,' Jack said.

'You've thought it all through.'

'I'm *thinking* it all through, with you. That's different.'

She sighed, folded her arms, and agitated the shale at her feet. 'Where's this flat, then?'

'It's a one-bed over the Spar shop.'

'Handy. He'll end up living on two-day old pies and stale bread, like the seagulls.'

Jack laughed. To his relief, she laughed with him and rested her head against his shoulder.

The drive back to Cheshire on Sunday afternoon was a huge irritation. Traffic was busy due to the half-term holiday and the vague promise of some sun the following week. Oliver's evasive behaviour necessitated a one hundred-and-fifty-mile round trip just to find out what was going on. No doubt his son had engineered the timing in the hope that Jack wouldn't bother driving all the way back, but since he wouldn't pick up the phone, Jack planned a surprise appearance instead.

Isabel had been all too happy to hang on to Lottie, and Anna was looking at the rooms over the Spar with Josh. 'That's brilliant,' Josh had said on hearing the news. He'd dumped a huge backpack and a myriad of folders in the hall, and hugged Jack awkwardly.

'Don't get too excited, it's a trip down memory lane,' Jack said.

'I don't care about that. This is a mega deal for me, I really appreciate it.'

At least one family member was happy.

A couple of hours later, Jack pulled onto his office forecourt then walked round the back, ran up the steps, and let himself into the flat. The staircase smelt of curry or some sort of takeaway food. When he opened the door to the living room, it was to see Amy prancing about in a zebra-print jumpsuit with a pink bow on her head. Under normal circumstances this would be distracting enough, but then he saw Oliver's face. One eye was practically closed up, with a huge purple bruise swelling over his brow. He had a slash across his cheek, like the cut from a bottle.

'Hey … Dad. You should have seen the other guy.'

'He got beaten up,' Amy said rather unnecessarily.

Jack saw her coat and bag thrown over the arm of the sofa and passed them to her. He watched in fascination as she snatched the animal tail off her backside, and discovered he was holding his breath – although goodness knows why, as he knew it wasn't real, but the rip of the Velcro had him cringing. She stuffed the thing into her bag, then struggled to fasten her pink coat. As she made to pass Jack she lowered her eyelashes and touched his jacket.

'I swear I only just found out what happened,' she said, then fixed her Bambi eyes on to his. Her perfume was rich and spicy, the sort an exotic safari princess might wear.

27

'Right, OK,' he said. *Stupid.*

He watched her sashay down the stairs in high heels, the tufted end of the tail trailing from her handbag. At the door, she turned and gave him a foxy wave and he actually waved back. More stupid.

Jack sank into a chair, threw his car keys down and studied Oliver's face. 'That looks painful. Have you had it seen to?'

'Yeah.'

'Is that all you've got to say? You've got some talking to do.'

'I don't feel up to it, just leave it, Dad.'

'This is serious, Ollie.'

'I got jumped.'

'Where?'

'Coming out of the Dirty Duck.'

'Try again. They don't have that kind of customer.'

'They were waiting outside, alright?'

Jack went into the kitchen and poured a whisky, then called Anna. 'I can't come back tonight, love. He's been in a fight, he's a right mess. There's no way he can work tomorrow. I need to be here.'

The news went down like a lead balloon. The whisky went down easier. Eventually, the story came out when Oliver realised Jack wasn't going anywhere. The fight was over a woman, and as usual, drink was involved.

'I can picture her now,' Jack said, getting into his stride. 'Blonde, tanned legs up to her arse, and a pout still fresh from Botox.'

Oliver frowned. 'Do you know her?'

'I don't know yet!' Jack said, then stabbed his finger on the chair arm. 'I want names, *details.*'

'It was Rupert Harrison-Smith and his mates, they did it.'

This didn't surprise Jack. The Harrison-Smiths

were not an especially pleasant family. They were new money and enjoyed pulling rank in the most obnoxious ways. The tricky aspect was that the old man had done a bunk with a younger woman and their humongous property was on the market – with Redman Estates.

'So, this was all about his sister, Melody, was it? I was right about the blonde, the legs, and the Botox.'

'Kind of. No, not *exactly*. I was showing some people round the property and when they'd gone, she locked me in the bloody bedroom!'

'Who did? Melody?'

'No, her mother.'

It took a few minutes for Jack to catch up, and when he did, his brain wouldn't connect to his mouth for a few seconds. He got to his feet and tried to breathe evenly. In fact, he surprised himself when he finally spoke, because his voice was so much lower and calmer than he actually felt. 'Please, *please* don't tell me you slept with Clarissa Harrison-Smith.'

Oliver set his good eye on his. 'Just the once, twice, tops. She wouldn't let me out, Dad. And yeah, blonde, legs, Botox.'

'It's not funny. Of course I *know* her – she's a fucking client!'

'Alright, keep your hair on!'

'She used you to get back at her old man.'

Oliver shrugged. 'Probably. She's just a sad old cougar.'

Jack stared and raked his hair back. 'And where does this professional conduct leave us with the sale exactly, huh?'

'Well … I think it's still OK, but can you do any viewings? You should be safe enough.'

Jack felt a flare of anger, as if a naked flame has been dropped into a box of petrol-soaked tissues. He covered his face with both hands in an effort to calm down but instead found himself digging his fingers into his scalp. It was impossible to contain. He let rip, aware that he sounded uncannily like his father. Oliver simply closed his eyes and leant his head back and Jack saw the full extent of Rupert Harrison-Smith's handiwork. Throughout his tirade, his son showed no sign of remorse, just a lot of sighing, coughing, and throat-clearing.

'You're such a hypocrite,' Oliver said once Jack had run out of steam.

'*What?*'

'You. You're a hypocrite! Not so long ago you were locked up for fighting at Chelsey's wedding and left the bloke for dead.'

'That was different.'

'How? You never did tell me what that was all about, beating up Mum's boyfriend like that. I mean, I know he deserved it, but you were lucky not to get done for manslaughter.'

Jack sank back down into the chair. It felt like a brick wall had come hurtling out of nowhere and he'd walked straight into it. He couldn't tell Oliver that Chelsey wasn't actually his sister, could he? At the wedding, Jack had been pushed beyond the realms of sanity. Philipe had been taunting him, strutting about like a peacock and threatening blackmail with the information. To explain all of it now would dig open a wound that needed to stay firmly sewn up – for Chelsey's sake more than anyone else. If anything, its resurgence made him all the more determined to sort out the issues surrounding James.

He went back into the kitchen, topped up his whisky, and, as an afterthought, poured a small one for Oliver with plenty of ginger ale in it. God knows what sort of painkillers he was taking, he was already starting to look spaced-out. Despite this, he managed to occupy himself with some frantic activity on his phone before finally admitting defeat and going groggily to bed. Jack simply zoned out; another large glass of whisky and a cigarette by the open kitchen window was not how he'd envisaged his Sunday evening. Three, possibly four children with a woman he despised. The eldest was not his but blissfully unaware, the middle two were hard work probably through no fault of their own, and the youngest … was at the mercy of two strands of hair in an envelope.

Monday morning was cold and wet. He left Oliver in bed and hunted through his wardrobe for work clothes, realising that he'd left all his decent suits at the farm and had to resort to smart casual. He wasn't very organised with transporting clothes to and fro, but he'd had some major distractions recently. Downstairs in the office, Clare looked at him askance.

'Coffee?'

'Do you need to ask?'

She busied herself with the machine. 'So, where's Oliver? I presume he turned up safe and sound?'

'Well, he turned up.'

'Ah, right.'

She placed a large cup of Italian in front of him and began to go through the post. Her eyes flicked to his from time to time, but he kept himself busy with Oliver's work; organising contractors to deal with maintenance issues in rented houses and updating various spreadsheets – including the payroll. He docked two days' pay from Oliver's salary. He'd never done it for sick days in the past but this time, Oliver really needed to learn a sense of responsibility. His absence posed a multitude of problems, mostly with viewings because it had always been Jack's policy, from a safety point of view, to have male viewing staff only. Fat lot of good that had done.

He watched Clare move efficiently from phone to computer to deal with enquiries. When Tabitha arrived, they twittered and laughed for a while then went about the daily routine of running his business. He'd be in a deep mire without them. Since he'd lost two key members of staff at the end of last year – the part-time company secretary to full retirement, and then his lettings manager to a big operation in London – Jack was beginning to feel their absence. It was building to the busiest time of the year for property sales, and he hadn't managed to replace either of them.

'What viewings have we got on?' he asked Tabitha.

She pulled up a screen on her computer. 'A couple of the new houses on the Prestbury estate … Oh, and a second viewing for Alderley House. Oliver must have done something right, they want another look.'

'Sell that one and we can all book our holidays,' Clare said.

Jack looked up sharply. 'The Harrison-Smiths' place?'

'That's the one.'

'*Shit.*'

Tabitha exchanged a glance with Clare, then turned and studied him for a full five seconds. 'Clearly I still haven't quite grasped how all this works.'

'Yeah, yeah, ignore me. Monday morning and all that. Second viewing, brilliant.'

For some reason, Tabitha always brought out the worst in him, saw him as some kind of idiot a lot of the time. Mention of staff holidays had him in a sweat though, and he called the job centre to talk about hiring another sales negotiator, preferably male. Apparently he wasn't allowed to stipulate this, even after he'd explained the famous Suzy Lamplugh case, when Clare had been sexually assaulted.

'You'll be wasting your time sending me a woman,' he said, turning round on his swivel chair, just in time to spot Tabitha creeping past his door en route to the coffee machine. 'I want a young, up-for-it fella with some lead in his pencil.'

'I'm afraid I can't put that in the job description,' Mrs Jobsworth said.

'I don't want a pile of CVs on my desk either, I'm not interested in a list of qualifications or a degree in the history of Outer Mongolia.'

There was a long sigh on the other end of the phone. 'Mr Redman, we've been through this before. I'll do my best to get a shortlist together but I'm afraid some of your desired skills are not coming up as an option on the database.'

Sometimes, Jack felt he had very little option as to how he ran his business and sometimes, it seemed there were too few options on that database called personal life. As he drove to meet the prospective purchasers of Alderley House, with Tabitha in the passenger seat reading up on the Cheshire pile with its tennis courts, swimming pool, and six en-suite bedrooms, his mobile began to flash with Patsy's name.

'Where the hell are you?' she said. 'I've just called the farm and Anna says you're back at work! What's the point of having Lottie?'

'I'm only back at work because Oliver has a problem. Lottie's with Mum, she's fine.'

'What problem? Look, the drama school has been on the phone wanting an answer. They don't keep places forever, you know.'

'I'll discuss it with you later.'

Patsy disconnected just as he pulled in to the circular drive and parked behind two oak trees. Tabitha unclipped her seatbelt while Jack sat motionless.

'Are you not coming with me?' she said, mildly disconcerted.

'Hell no. Any problems,' he said, looking furtively at the ivy-clad façade between two tree trunks, 'you call me on the mobile. Three rings. Don't go in any of the bedrooms, stand on the landing or something.'

He couldn't quite read her expression, but she climbed resignedly out of the vehicle. Jack slunk low in his seat, watching her make her way to the Georgian front door, turning at the last minute to no doubt see only the top of his head at the wheel. To his relief, she had to use their set of keys, so there must have been no one home.

The viewing passed without incident and Jack roared back down the drive and out through the gates in a flurry of gravel, Tabitha hanging on to the edge of her seat.

Maybe he was over-anticipating trouble. The mess his life had got into around Christmas just over four years ago had left him with a touch of paranoia. He'd had a good run of settled times but maybe that was because his head was half-buried in quicksand. At the end of the working day, Jack let himself back into the flat to hear Oliver on the phone, laughing in his familiar infectious, derisory way. Not so ill, then.

'You're moving where?' he was saying. 'Above Spar?' Jack crept up the stairs. Another burst of laughter. 'No way! Anyway, look, I'm thinking of starting up the band again. You up for it?'

By the time he'd reached the top of the stairs, his patience had evaporated. Oliver tactfully ended the call and went about chopping onions and peppers on the kitchen worktop, still in his dressing gown and tracksuit bottoms. 'I'm doing steak, want some?'

Jack leant against the doorjamb. 'What's this about

starting up the band?'

'Oh, yeah. One of the other lads is in, but we need Josh on vocals.'

'Josh is *busy*. If he isn't working, he's either studying or helping his mother.'

'That's not what he said. The place he serves at nights, well, the manager reckons we can do a gig at some festival.'

Jack desperately wanted to yell. Instead, he went to his room and changed into an old pair of Levi's with the pockets hanging off and a fisherman-style sweater. Scruffy, out-of-work attire always made him feel calmer. The smell of fried onions wafted into his room and made him think of Anna. Stuffing a few items into a bag, he went back to the kitchen, decision made. 'Get yourself down into the office tomorrow, 9 a.m. sharp.'

'Looking like this?'

'Yep, looking like that. I'm sure you'll think of something.'

'Where are you going?'

'Back to the farm, I'm on holiday this week, remember?'

Jack ignored the deflated look, the clatter of a spatula thrown down in resignation. 'Dad, *come on.*'

'I did think about arranging for you to work over at Conwy, but then I'd have a problem here.'

'At the Taffy branch? No way, I hate it there!'

'That's settled then. Get an early night. Clare's in charge and in my absence she has the power to hire and fire. Might be worth remembering.'

The muttering and scowling followed him down the stairs, but Jack felt fired with determination. Tough love had just gone into overdrive.

As he pulled out into the traffic towards north Manchester, Jack felt like it was almost a repeat of

Friday night. *Groundhog Day*. He parked outside Patsy's house and she got to the door before him, finger on her lips. 'James is in bed so please don't shout.'

'Who says I'm going to shout?' he shouted. 'Sorry, I'm wound up over Oliver's behaviour.'

'What's he done?'

She ushered him into the living room and listened to the details, a slight frown creasing her otherwise perfect complexion. 'Should I go and stay at the flat while you're away? It sounds like he may need help, I mean with his wounds.'

This threw him for a moment but the idea of her sleeping in his bed turned his stomach. Jack raised a hand. 'No. I'm tired of picking up the pieces. He has to learn some responsibility, some respect.'

'Jack, he's still a teenager.'

'That's no excuse!' He tried to think back to when he was nineteen, but he couldn't recall sleeping with any of his dad's clients. Leo would have annihilated him.

'We made mistakes too,' she said, in a low voice. 'I deeply regret a lot of things I did. Simon Banks, Philipe.'

'Let's not do this, it's history. The damage is done.'

'I know, but I want to say it. I need to say it to you.'

'Oh, so this is about you feeling better?'

She stared at him, blinking rapidly. He knew her well enough to know real tears and when she looked heavenwards, felt the urge to change the subject. He really didn't need an emotion overload, and especially not from Patsy. Normally under these exchanges with his ex-wife, he'd have a cutting reply, but there was something disturbingly different about her demeanour today. With a jolt, he realised it was genuine remorse staring back at him. Four years too late, but maybe it had taken that long to realise what she'd lost. 'I'm sorry, that was uncalled for,' he said. 'I accept your apology, but it doesn't change anything.'

'I know. I just wanted to say something and you're right, it is about me. I have a lot of time on my own, you see. I think about how we used to be, what an amazing marriage we had –'

'*Stop*. Our marriage was a sham thanks to you.'

She considered this for a moment, then lowered her eyelashes in defeat. They glistened with tears. The whole scene was alien, so unlike this once fiery, passionate woman he used to share his life with. He almost wished she was back to hating him because the barbs were so much easier to deal with. Chelsey had said something about her going through a period of deep depression when the baby had been born, and she'd pleaded with Jack to go easy on her. She was, after all, the mother of his children and nothing could change that. It was irksome that this meant he had a vested interest in her general state of mind but he'd proceeded cautiously, just the same.

He needed to change the subject and when she began to wipe her eyes, turned to look out at the dark street. His attention was immediately taken by a shadowy figure, hovering near his vehicle. He banged on the window and Patsy leapt to his side. 'What is it? Is it a man?'

'Kids messing about, probably.'

'God, I *hate* it here. I want you to put a better lock on the back door. Can you, Jack? That weirdo has been nicking washing off the line.'

'Seriously? Er, yeah, I might have something in the car, from the farm. An old bolt.' He pulled the curtains across and turned to face her. 'Right. This placement at drama school, for Lottie.'

Her head shot up. 'Yes?'

'It's only free for the first year, after that it's a crazy load of money.'

'Oh. I did think that if you agreed to the cottage I could work again down there? I'd like to help, financially.'

'Let's not get ahead of ourselves, Lottie might hate the idea.' They shared a rueful smile, knowing how absurd his statement was. 'Alright, look. I agree in principle to you having the cottage –'

'Really? Oh! Jack, *thank you.*'

'Hold on! You need to talk to Lottie about this school first, make sure she understands what it's about before we discuss any move. I don't want her getting carried away with the idea of living down on the quay instead of the main issue. Then, if she's OK with all that, *I'll* tell her about the cottage. You'll have to give a couple of weeks' notice here anyway.'

Patsy looked as if the tear banks were going to burst, and Jack was about to pick up his car keys when she moved awkwardly into his arms, like driftwood caught against something safe before it was hurled down the rapids. Her sobs reverberated through his chest, and it wasn't in him to walk away and leave her. The clingy, weepy version of Patsy was new, and although the alarm bells were girding their loins, he held on to her until she'd stopped crying. After a moment, she slid her arms around his waist and looked up at him, her green eyes glittering.

CHAPTER THREE

Anna

Anna kept telling herself it was fine. Fine that Jack's ex-wife was moving into town.

She tried to concentrate on the painting of an old miner's cottage, squashing the last blob of Parchment White onto a wooden palette. She worked quickly, adding highlights to a dark sky but her concentration lasted barely minutes, before she cleaned off the brush and poked it into an overstuffed jar.

Benson looked up enquiringly. He knew her every move, the subtle signs of her body language.

'Come on,' she said to the dog. 'I'm not getting anything done here.'

Outside, there was a change in the air, altogether softer, intoxicating. After a miserable damp weekend and a thoroughly wet Monday, Tuesday had the promise of spring well and truly in its stride. Under normal circumstances – whatever those were – her spirits would be empowered by this. Down by the lake, snowdrops, narcissi, and coltsfoot were beginning to flower through the brown debris of winter, a mass of dormant bracken and bramble, although the hawthorn was full of tight pink buds. Then it would be primroses, stitchwort, and bluebells. The still mostly leafless trees looked silver against a bruised sky. Despite the lack of foliage and the promise of a heavy shower, the branches and hedgerows were full of birds.

This was the next most noticeable difference, the return of birdsong. Nesting had begun.

She found her usual sitting place beneath the leaning oak, where its roots erupted out of the ground like coiled snakes. At her feet were the remains of last year's leaves, some just skeletal membranes outlined with an early frost. The dogs explored the lake. Hooper, the partially deaf chocolate labrador, and Benson, swam like sea lions, nostrils high above the water, legs paddling away, fat tails flayed behind them and leaving a stream of ripples. During a sudden heatwave a couple of summers ago, she and Jack had swum there too and it had been magical, if not the most romantic, odour-wise. They'd even made love outdoors, on the banks of the lake and the earth had been warm, even after sunset.

She'd tried calling Jack but either his phone was switched off or it had run out of battery, so she resorted to a text, presuming he'd get the message sooner or later. The phone infuriated her. In fact, all technology infuriated her and she went out of her way to avoid using it. Jack had bought her a mobile, then became cross when she left the house without it or failed to charge it. Most of the time, it never worked properly at the farm anyway and any calls that did get through usually resulted in a lot of disjointed shouting and a fair bit of walking to and fro, confusing the dogs.

Jack hadn't called since Sunday evening. She'd overheard Josh on his phone the previous day talking to Oliver, telling him all about the flat. The call seemed to end abruptly but then Oliver had called back on the landline and the conversation quickly turned to guitars and amplifiers. Anna had happily zoned out, convinced any emergency must have passed. In fact, this was further confirmed when Josh said afterwards that Jack had left Oliver to it, just stormed out of the flat, and Oliver wasn't very pleased. Anna was *very* pleased, and fully expected him to walk through the door, tired and hungry, but when ten o'clock came, she'd tipped his dinner into the dogs' bowls, threw the bolts across both doors, and gone to bed.

The landline was ringing as she approached the house. It stopped abruptly and switched to the message service as she paused to remove her muddy boots and stop the wet dogs from barging into the sitting room. When she listened to the playback, she was slightly dismayed to discover it was Isabel, wanting to know when Jack was going to collect Lottie because she had appointments in the afternoon. Anna arranged to go over there herself just as Jack's car pulled on to the drive.

'Oh, at *last!* He's back,' she said to Isabel.

'Come for lunch, both of you. And we won't let him talk business.'

Within seconds, Jack was striding into the hallway and throwing his bag down. By the time she'd moved fully into his arms and looked into his blue-grey eyes, her list of irritable questions went on the back-burner. Being in his arms after an absence, no matter how short, felt practically life-changing. He was a great hugger, kisser … *lover.*

'Sorry I didn't call, time just got away from me,' he said.

'Well, where have you been, all night?'

'Crashed on Patsy's sofa.'

'What the hell for?'

She followed him into the kitchen and watched him move around the space, filling the coffee machine and raking a hand through his hair. It was always slightly too long, and as a teen he was always in trouble for it, but that was more than thirty years ago. She half-listened to his explanation. Something about waiting for a peeping Tom to reappear and a new bolt for the back door. Then it was a chase over back gardens and empty streets when the offender ran hell for leather over walls and hedges. This was typical of Jack.

'That was a really stupid thing to do. You've already got a police record. What if he'd had a knife, or brought friends?'

'I know,' he said, stirring a mug of coffee. 'Gave him a shock though, he wasn't expecting a chase, and then it took me ages to fit that bolt on the back door with no power tools.'

'Heroic.'

He took a slurp of coffee and looked at her over the mug. 'Look, I couldn't leave her like that, not with a child in the house. And actually, we talked about a lot of stuff. First long conversation we've had in years without arguing.'

'Cosy.'

'No. Ulterior motive from me. I wanted to be sure she understood all the boundaries. I've insisted *we* tell Lottie about the cottage after she's sounded her out about the drama school. And after the night I've had on that bloody sofa I know I've made the right decision about this. I want my kids out of there.'

'I wish we'd talked it through a bit more.'

'I'm sorry, love. It all happened like a pre-determined chain of events, like a row of dominoes going down. I've read Ollie the last rites as well. He's been shagging one of the clients.'

This didn't entirely surprise her, Oliver had always been a handful. Integrating him into the business had seemed a good plan three years ago. He was an exact split of Jack and Patsy's personalities, but he had all the right credentials to be successful in the agency. Her own son was his opposite, dark and sensitive, creative and musical. Too serious at times. She told Jack about the resurgence of Utopia.

'I've told him that's a bad idea,' he said.

'Maybe it isn't. Josh could do with some fun.'

'Ollie's had enough fun for the year already.'

Isabel had made a quiche and three different salad dishes. Lottie had recovered from her mild bout of chickenpox and came readily to the table, although she still refused to remove the giant fairy wings until Jack told her their special powers would be reduced if she wore them all the time. Jack and Isabel held all the magic touches when it came to Lottie. Even Patsy lost patience with her and Anna found her hard work at times, although their relationship had slowly improved over the years. She put it down to trust, and who could blame her? When she thought about the trauma the little girl had suffered when Jack and Patsy had separated, she could forgive any sort of behaviour. This was when she was ashamed about giving Jack a hard time. He was such a good dad, a provider and protector. A real alpha male, she just wished all their respective children were theirs, and not subject to some irritating third party.

'I don't want those big round beetroots, Daddy. They're the Devil's balls,' Lottie said, and Jack stopped dishing out the salad with a barely disguised grin.

'Who told you that?'

'No one.'

'What about the radishes then?'

'Jack, please!' Isabel said, 'At least *try* and set an example.'

When Jack and Lottie were in the garden with Isabel's dog, Anna expressed her fears about the latest developments to Isabel. She liked and respected Jack's mother, and felt secure in the knowledge that the respect was mutual. More importantly, Isabel was no fool where Patsy was concerned. She didn't mention the DNA test because that felt exclusively Jack's prerogative and the right words wouldn't form in her mind. Isabel listened to the news about the drama school and Quay Cottage with a bewildered expression.

'Am I to express surprise when Jack tells me any of this?'

'Oh, I don't think he'll mind me spilling some of the beans.'

'Well, I hope Jack's right about Patsy learning a life lesson. Leopards don't change their spots though, do they?'

'That's what I'm worried about. I know Jack is acting in the children's best interests. But I can't help feeling depressed about it. I mean, I don't *want* to bump into her in the butcher's, or be looking for her around every corner,' she went on, a slight catch to her voice. She took a deep breath, surprised by the emotion bubbling up, but she couldn't stop. 'I don't *want* her standing at the bar when we go for dinner, observing everything we do and say. And then every tiny excuse for a problem will have Jack running down to the cottage. Oh … I'm sorry.'

Isabel frowned and patted her hand, then fetched the leftover wine from the lunch table. They took their refilled glasses and wandered out to the long cottage garden, pulling out the patio chairs and sweeping them free of leaves.

'Josh is moving into the flat over the Spar,' Anna said in an effort to regain her composure. 'I hate to think what he's going to do with all the pots and pans he's taken.'

'Oh, I remember that feeling. Bittersweet, isn't it? Danny was the last of mine to move out. I remember thinking, thank God for that, no more exploding meals in the microwave and scantily-clad women at odd hours.' Anna must have nodded. Her mother-in-law was too astute. She went on, 'In time, Patsy will find something, or more likely *someone* to fill her time with.'

'I guess so. Jack says she wants to work, so maybe she's turned a corner.'

'Well, then. I think we should at least give her a chance. Jack won't stand for any messing about, mark my words.'

They both looked to where he was playing with Lottie and Isabel's young collie, but despite the warmth in the sun, Anna felt a chill.

Towards the end of the week, Lottie seemed fully recovered, and begged to go to Hilly's trekking centre. Since it wasn't Jack's scene, Anna offered to take her while Jack, intent on moving future plans forward, wanted to make a shortlist of possible works down at Quay Cottage. He'd already spent the morning on the phone sorting out problems with sales at the Wilmslow branch and checking up on Oliver, and then Conwy office wanted him to call in and sign something. Anna reckoned he may as well carry on working.

'I'm not really *working*,' he said. 'I'm only available as a last resort, or for big decisions.'

'Alright, go ahead, it's not a problem. I could do with a catch-up with Hilly. She's been a bit mysterious lately.'

'How do you mean?'

She watched him pulling on a pair of tatty denims and pushing his feet into a pair of paint-splattered trainers. She tried not to assume it was because he couldn't wait to have his ex-family installed, but rather that he was short on time and his work ethic usually came before everything else. He loved to be busy, and not always behind a desk or sealing a deal, either.

'It feels like she's avoiding me,' Anna said.

'Probably just busy. Half-term at the stables means a load of kids. Isn't she getting married next year as well?'

'Hmm. To the farrier.'

'Got to hand it to her, she knows how to cut costs. What did she say the other week, I'll never pay for another pair of shoes again?'

'Something like that.'

Lottie burst through the bedroom door wearing a pair of baggy brown corduroy trousers, a horrible wig kept in place with a headscarf, and bright red lipstick. This was likely due to her latest obsession with *National Velvet*. In her mind, she was Velvet Brown in 1944 and she was off to ride the future Grand National winner. It was, of course, totally unsuitable for an afternoon at the trekking centre, but Lottie's imagination always won out over simple logic – she couldn't help herself.

Jack pulled her onto his knee. 'Sweetheart, you have to wear a crash hat, no arguments.'

'No one wore them in the film.'

'That was before health and safety. Hilly isn't allowed to let you ride without making sure you're going to be safe if you have a tumble.'

'But Daddy, Hilly's helmets look like bald heads. It will go on top.'

'Well, that's kind of true, they've all lost their original covers,' Anna said, and Jack exchanged a look of amusement with her. 'Well, see what Hilly thinks.'

Anna could hazard a guess as to what Hilly might think. They set off in the old Land Rover, Lottie giving her a bullet point account of Elizabeth Taylor's life story while holding on to Benson's collar so he paid attention. When she got to anything sad or embarrassing, she'd lift the dog's ear and lower her voice to a whisper and Anna had to pretend not to hear.

A short diversion into the town centre for cake, then they travelled along the mountain road before pulling onto the only space available on the grass verge. Hilly's Trekking Centre was a small yard, mostly kept going by tourists, although Hilly had them down as Public Enemy Number One. February half-term was the first full week of the year she was fully operational, and the place looked manic with children, busy with a long line of hairy ponies tied to the picket fence. Hilly, trying to keep track of everyone, was centre stage with a clipboard.

'A bit of sun and the whole world wants to ride out!' she shouted to Anna. Lottie ran happily into the tack-room, holding onto her wig and the waistband of her trousers.

'Can't blame them,' Anna said, looking at the duck-egg blue sky.

'What's with Miss Lottie Loops today?'

'Don't ask. She's Velvet Brown. *National Velvet*?'

'Oh! She's an odd one.'

Anna agreed and they made small talk until Lottie re-emerged with the wig strapped over the top of a crash hat. The parents waiting about stopped dead in their tracks, probably thinking it was fancy dress and they'd messed up. Most of the other children thought she was either funny or they made fun of her. Lottie took it all in her stride, commanding attention with some wild story about her appearance being due to a near-death experience from a deadly chicken disease.

Hilly was open-mouthed to start with. 'That child, she's born to be an actress.'

'Now that you've mentioned it, any chance of a natter?'

'What, *now?*'

'I have cake.'

'Why didn't you say? Let me get this lot mounted up and out of sight for a couple of hours. You go and put the kettle on.'

Bryn was in the hall, pulling his boots back on. He grunted and nodded at the cake box.

'Alright for some, yakking all afternoon. Some of us have work to do.'

In Hilly's mess of a kitchen, Anna cleared a space on the table and washed two mugs. She slid Welsh cakes and half a lemon drizzle onto a plate, then stared through the kitchen window. She could hear Hilly shouting and the clatter of hooves as the long line of children trotted out along the mountain road. Lottie's freaky headgear, bobbing along behind the hedge, made her smile.

Hilly burst through the door and collapsed into a chair and it was like old times. She missed old times. Hilly was hardly ever available these days, or so it seemed. Maybe it was Anna that had changed, and not so much everyone else.

Before Jack she'd been engaged to a man she didn't love and her beloved farmhouse was falling to bits. Jack had fixed all of that. Not only had she fallen back in love with him, but he'd gifted a massive injection of his own cash into the farm to reverse the decay and transform it into a beautiful home. It was still solely in her name, he'd made no demands on her. But she had no need to struggle to make ends meet, like the years before with difficult Bed and Breakfast guests, or trying to sell her paintings. Yet there was something missing for her.

Since she'd lost both parents, suffered an uncomfortable relationship with her son's father in Italy, and led a generally independent life, it was only since she'd stopped *needing* to be independent that she realised it was more about her personality as opposed to a set of forced circumstances. She'd never felt comfortable being so beholden to Jack, but this seemed more acute now by the sudden realisation that she was virtually in the same position as Patsy. Even her son was in debt to him now. She'd always been her own woman, never defined by a man, but this latest development with Patsy just added to her vulnerability. Was that because she'd taken Jack from her in the dark and distant past? Maybe she was scared history might repeat itself.

'Well, I hope you found a racehorse for Velvet,' she said, pouring tea for Hilly.

'She got Billy Buttons. Never won a race in his life. Oh, hold on, I tell a lie. Egg and spoon last summer on the beach. So, go on, what's on your mind? Judging by the amount of cake you've brought, it must be serious.'

'Oh, it might be me. I think I've lost my identity.'

Hilly frowned but listened to her fears with no interruption, her mouth bulging, and occasionally nodding or wagging her head. On the face of it, it all sounded a bit puny when she'd got it off her chest. Hilly cut another wedge of cake.

'You're not listening, are you?' Anna said eventually.

'I am listening. More tea?'

They moved on to round two: buttered Welsh cakes. She even talked about the DNA test and Jack spending the night on Patsy's sofa. Hilly raised her brows.

'Well?' Anna said, irritated by her general lack of response.

'I'm *thinking*,' Hilly said, still chewing and slurping. 'Look, I know it's a mess – it's always been a

49

mess – but like I keep saying, you've got Jack. In fact, you've got the best of Jack; he's out of your hair a lot of the time. Are you saying it's not enough?'

'Now you're making me sound spoilt.'

'No, not necessarily. You do sound a bit premenstrual though, or maybe perimenopausal.'

'I can't be both.'

'Mid-life crisis? Empty nest syndrome?'

'Why are you trying to label me? You know what, just forget it!'

Hilly's mouth dropped open.

Anna stormed out of the kitchen, gripped by a huge wobble of emotion. It lasted until she reached home, to find Jack sat under the pergola reading the paper, his long, denim-clad legs propped across a chair, a pint of ale and a cigarette next to the old plant pots from the herb garden. The dogs fussed around her, and the normal domesticity of the scene made her feel especially ashamed of herself.

'Hi, love,' Jack said. 'Where's Lottie?'

'She'll be ages yet. They're riding over Conwy Mountain and across part of Tal y Fan. Back about five.'

'I thought you were having a pow-wow with Hilly?'

'Oh, we did, a bit. She's busy.'

'I'll go and get Lottie later. Get yourself a drink,' he said. She took a bottle of ale from the fridge and pulled out a chair, wondering whether to tell him about her childish spat with Hilly. Although it didn't feel very childish. In all the years they'd known each other she couldn't recall Hilly behaving quite so insensitively. It felt like she'd spilled her guts and Hilly was poking them with a self-righteous stick. In fact, she'd been on the verge of tears, not a common condition for her. All she'd needed was a vote of confidence and instead, she'd got something that felt like chilly indifference. As she poured the gold liquid into her glass, she ruminated on another tense relationship; her very own personal Public Enemy Number One, Patsy Redman.

'How was the cottage?'

'Needs a few cosmetics, I can do that. Main job is the central heating system. Needs replacing, really, it's shot.'

'Sounds expensive.'

'I can get a trade job no problem,' he said, his eyes still on the *Financial Times*.

'Jack ... I've had an idea. Why not sell Quay Cottage and buy something in St Asaph instead?'

'Thought of that. It would cost and it could take too long. I honestly can't be bothered spending any more time or money on this. Patsy can live in it until the kids have finished their education, then that's the end of it so far as I'm concerned.'

'But that's years!'

'Of course it's years!'

'So, wouldn't it be worth doing? To sell it and buy something near the school?'

'No, it wouldn't. There's no school there for James. At least I can enjoy the benefit of less driving about if the kids are here. Anyway, there's another problem with selling the cottage.'

'What?'

'It's in my will, and I'm certainly not changing all that again.'

'Well ... who are you leaving it to?'

He folded up the paper and slapped it down on the table. 'To my bloody kids! It's virtually all I've got left. Oliver will get the business if he shapes up, the rest of them will have to share the cottage as a holiday home or something. At least it'll keep its value, and I can't see any of them wanting to go for a long weekend to St Asaph, can you?'

'What about the farm?' she said, her heart banging.

'What about it? It belongs to you, then it will go to Josh. That's how it should be.'

It all made perfect sense, was all perfectly reasonable. She couldn't fault his logic or his integrity. Despite this, controversial words came tumbling out of her mouth. 'If – *if* – we were to get married, would any of that change?'

He squinted at her for a full ten seconds. 'No.'

'I'm sorry, I just needed to know.'

'Anna, I'm not going to marry you so we can own the farm as a joint asset, sell Quay Cottage, and blow everything else out of the water here. I want to marry you because I love you. There's no strings to that and I hope there isn't from your point of view.'

'Of course not.'

He picked up his smouldering cigarette and she almost asked him why he'd started smoking again, but of course she already knew the answer. The women and children in his life were putting pressure on him again. When she called up the dogs and made to walk down the garden, Benson struggled to get his hind legs moving, then gave up and chose to lie down again. Jack caught up with her.

'I understand how you feel, I really do. I'm not over the moon about it myself but I really want this for Lottie. Can you please just try and find the advantages in the situation instead of working against me?'

She held him to her, hooked her thumbs into his belt, and pressed her face against his grubby T-shirt. His lips grazed the top of her head and his hands travelled around her shoulders, pulling her in tightly. He felt like a warm, safe harbour in an endless sea. They must have stood there for long minutes, listening to the evensong of the birds, their chatter stilled when a red kite passed over, circling and watching. She tried not to think of it as a doomed prophecy.

The spring weather continued and the remainder of the weekend passed without incident. She busied herself with cooking and gardening and painting a magnificent sky full of migrating birds. Jack played with Lottie, caught up with his tax returns, and fixed the duck pen. They laughed, made love, and got drunk on homemade sloe gin from the previous year. They watched Lottie's solo performance of Elizabeth Taylor's life in film, featuring Benson (bribed this time with homemade liver dog biscuits) in a variety of hats, waistcoats, and scarves.

Ignoring the more obvious problems looming on the horizon, the only real blot on the weekend was her spat with Hilly. She'd tried calling to apologise but either Hilly was just too busy or was deliberately ignoring her, which hurt. In all the years she'd known her, they'd supported each other like sisters. She was the only person who knew all her business with Jack, even down to the secret about Chelsey and Simon Banks. She'd always had the feeling that Hilly wished she didn't know, and the constant speculation was something they never agreed on. Anna had always said it would implode and Hilly said not if everyone kept their word and stayed quiet.

Of late, all this had reared its ugly head again and sat like a small stone in the corner of an old, comfy shoe. When Jack had gone to the stables to collect Lottie, Bryn had demanded payment, something which had never, ever happened. For years, they'd had a loose arrangement where Anna provided the occasional equine painting and an endless supply of organic duck and hen eggs, hay, and straw when she had a glut in return for either herself or Lottie to ride.

'I can't believe he charged you!' Anna said when Jack grumbled about never having any cash.

'It's not a problem, they're trying to run a business. I just wasn't expecting it. Felt a bit of a twit, standing there counting out loose change.'

'And he let you? Good grief, all the work you've done for Hilly, selling that land and not charging her a penny!'

'Yeah, did cross my mind. Have you upset her?'

'No! More the other way around.' She'd thrown the bread dough hard at the board, then punched her fist into it.

'OK, well, just be sure to start charging if that's the way she wants to do it.'

'Oh, she can go buy her own eggs from Spar.'

Jack had said nothing more on the subject. He packed the car on Sunday afternoon and Anna made sure he took the five suits he'd left draped over chairs and hung on wardrobe doors, plus two loaves of her tomato and basil bread.

'Try not to worry,' he said. 'About anything. Promise me?'

'I promise.'

'And don't worry about expenses either, it'll all work out.'

Lottie put her arms around her neck, kissed her cheek, and whispered next to her ear, 'My mummy has very expensive knickers, but they scratch.'

'That's the price of beauty.'

'Are yours comfy, Anna?'

'They certainly are. I think being a nice person counts for more.'

'I'm going to be a nice person *and* have expensive knickers.'

She laughed, smiled, waved them both off. When

the car was almost lost to sight, just a dust cloud trailing down the bumpy track, she stopped smiling and breathed a sigh of relief.

CHAPTER FOUR

Jack

He didn't feel as relaxed as he normally did after a few days at the farm, but there was too much going on in the background. On the way back from dropping Lottie home, his mother called, something about him looking after Anna because she was feeling insecure and was he sure about letting Patsy live in the cottage after everything she'd done?

'I know what you're saying, but this is about an opportunity for Lottie. You'd be pretty horrified if you could see where they live now. She's done her time, I reckon she's learnt a lesson and the kids need good schools.'

'Well, I suppose so, when you put it like that.'

'You'll see more of them.'

'Yes, I know. What are you doing about that little boy?'

'I'm dealing with it.'

'Good. Don't take her word for anything.'

'Mum! I'm not wet behind the ears. And why are you and Anna discussing all of this anyway? *I* only found out about this drama school a week ago.'

'Oh, it's what women do, we talk about our feelings. And anyway, I like to think she can talk to me about anything.'

'Did she mention Hilly? They've had some sort of falling out.'

'No … Oh, Hilly's changed since she took up with

that Bryn Hopkins. He comes from a long line of dodgy horse dealers.'

'What's that got to do with anything?'

'I'm just *saying*. I think she'll give up the trekking after this season, she looks worn out.'

Jack grunted. 'Right, well, keep an eye on Anna for me, will you? She's a bit down with everything.'

Isabel chuckled. 'I've just called you to say the same!'

'Well, it's your turn now, I'm back at the office.'

'And don't be too hard on Oliver, he must feel very foolish.'

'That's not been my impression so far.'

He pulled in to the office forecourt, parked up, and struggled up the stairs with an armful of suits, his overnight bag, and a carrier bag full of baked goodies including Lottie's black cupcakes. Who'd pick pink colouring when there was black to choose from? As he neared the inner door, he could hear the buzz of conversation and sniggering. 'What's she like then, Big Mummy?'

'Proper rich. She's kinda weird though, reads books like *Knitting with dog hair* or *Make your own sex toys*.'

'No way!'

All eyes swivelled to Jack as he barged through the door. The flat was full of male bodies, feet up and drinking from cans. 'Right lads, party over. Take this rubbish with you and sling it in recycling.'

At least Oliver couldn't roll his eyes, they were still every colour of the rainbow. Clare had kept him up to date with his movements, and so far so good, although she'd been horrified at his appearance. 'Keep him in the back office and keep him busy,' he'd told her. But the punch-up and the possible reasons for it were all over Facebook and Twitter in no time. So much for keeping it low-key.

'Still bragging about it, then?' Jack said, knocking Oliver's feet off the coffee table. 'I hope there's no charges involved. Is there?'

'No. And they just keep *asking*.'

'It might help if you took those bloody pictures down from Facebook.'

'They're not mine, I've been tagged in them. Some of them aren't even me, they're photoshopped. Harry Styles and Joan Collins.'

'Well, get untagged. Better still, close the damn thing down! And stay out of the Dirty Duck. A lot of my business connections drink in there and you're slowly eroding our reputation with your stupid behaviour.'

'Don't start, Dad. It's always about your precious reputation.'

'Of course it is! How do you think we stay ahead of the game? I'm tired of spelling it out to you.'

'Then don't.'

'Right now, if someone came along with a pot of money for this business, I'd sell it in the blink of an eye,' he said, then realised what he'd said, but of late, Jack felt like he was working for nothing. The goals he used to have had either been surpassed or disappeared from his agenda, melted away by a changed set of values. He'd been treading water for the last few years, probably because there was little choice. He imagined himself living full-time at the farm, popping in to the Taffy branch now and again. Isabel, Lottie, and James would be just down the road. Chelsey, her husband, and his grandchild would visit regularly. He saw himself taking James and his other grandchildren fishing on the jetty, playing on the beach, exploring the farm.

Redman Estates of Wilmslow would be taken over

by a bigger chain, still employing his loyal staff but Jack would have no responsibility for it, just a stash of money in the bank. Oliver would either have to perform under new management or find another job.

The problem with this rosy vision of the future was Anna.

He understood her totally. His family were overpowering, and there were plenty of them, all with big personalities. None of them were the quiet retiring sort, except maybe for Chelsey but there was a damn good reason for that. Anna might be the balm to his soul, but her strength fed from solitude and self-preservation. She loved and wanted him, but she didn't always need him. He always knew this, even when they were teenagers her philosophy was 'if you love something, let it go'. At the time, her looks of indifference had struck him as uncaring. Patsy had stepped in easily and his schoolboy naivety had let her.

Now he was older, and wiser, but maybe he just needed to convince Anna of that.

Monday morning, and Oliver stood before his desk. Smart, in a familiar dark blue shirt, his bright blond hair slicked back, designer stubble covering the worst of the bruising along his jaw, and enveloped in a cloud of Jack's Armani Code. Ray Bans completed the look.

'Sorry, Dad.'

'What for? Using my stuff or sleeping with the clients?'

'Both.'

'I see, boxing clever.'

'I am sorry. You're not going to sell the agency, are you?'

'Depends on whether you keep tempting me. What have you learnt from this last caper? Anything?'

A shuffle, a long beat of consideration, and a half-hearted shrug. 'Yeah …'

'Right, back on viewings then. And if I find any more dents on the Fiat, it's coming out of your salary.'

'I think the wheels needs rebalancing.'

'Lunch hour.'

Jack sighed, restacked the files on his desk, and logged onto the day's diary. The first item was a meeting with Mrs Harrison-Smith. Big Mummy herself. Jesus, what did she want? After that, it was a long list of interviewees. The job centre had excelled itself. Amongst his email was something from DNA Online. He was interrupted from opening it by Clare announcing the arrival of his first appointment.

'Shall I bring some coffee?' she said and Jack nodded sagely. It hadn't gone without notice that Oliver had shut himself in the back office, quite possibly with a chair under the door handle. Clarissa bustled in with a sense of over-importance, doe eyes, fake boobs, and blonde hair, the works. He had to hand it to her, she looked mid-thirties rather than mid-forties.

'Mr Redman, *Jack*. Can you help me? I'm utterly desperate.'

For a wild moment, he imagined Clarissa pregnant with twins or some other such atrocity.

'Desperate?' he said carefully. 'How?'

'The house! I'm going mad in there, it's the memories, you see. I want to sell to the Bentleys. They made an offer last Friday.'

Jack flicked onto the property screen and read through the details. 'It's way too low. No one takes the first offer. At least wait till they come back –'

'That's just it, I *can't.*'

He played with the computer mouse on his desk. Normally, he'd advise against looking desperate but if she wanted to spend money, so be it. 'Well, you could move out into rented, if you're desperate.'

'Oh! You clever man. Can you arrange that?'

'Yeah, give some details to Clare and we'll get a shortlist together, arrange some viewings for you.'

'I'd rather you dealt with it.' She lowered her voice and her eyelashes. 'It's the entertaining, you see.'

'I beg your pardon?'

She leant across his desk, giving him the full benefit of her enhancements. They rested like two perfect globes on top of the printer. When he pushed his chair back, he couldn't miss the view beneath the desk either. Legs crossed in a short leather skirt, a triangle of satin knickers on full show.

'I need somewhere with full insulation,' she went on.

'Loft insulation?'

She laughed at this, her head thrown back to show her perfect teeth. 'No, Jack. Sound insulation. Oh, you know what I want.' She flicked her hair, threw up her bejewelled hands, and rummaged in a copious handbag for her car keys. 'I'll leave it with you, get back to me.'

Normally, all of this would have struck him as pretty funny and the whole office would have got plenty of mileage out of it, but he couldn't wait for this woman to leave his office so he could forget all about her; she clearly had too much time and cash on her hands, preying on teenage boys and pumping herself full of steroids. He entered the lettings details into the system, then allowed himself to be distracted by the usual daily grind. Through the front window, he saw Oliver ease himself into the Fiat, looking every inch like a drug dealer who'd fallen on hard times. He reversed over the kerb so fast he must have at least grazed the front spoiler as the car bounced down and roared away, smoke and beeping cars in its wake.

His brother rang. He knew it was Dan before the call got put through to his office because he always managed to keep Clare talking for an age, flirting, laughing. Eventually, the extension bleeped on his desk and Jack picked up.

'Jacko. How's it going?' Dan said.

'Alright, you?'

'Yeah. Got a bit of news for you. Getting hitched. Best man duties up for grabs.'

'You are? Fucking hell, who to? How many months gone is she?'

'Ha bloody ha. I'm in *lurve.*'

'Ha bloody ha.'

'No, seriously. Ellie Jones.'

'Which one's that?'

Jack knew full well who Ellie was, but they were always teasing each other over the women in their lives. His younger brother was like a honeypot to the opposite sex, and he'd played the field for years with amazing success. On good authority his allure was down to his cocky sense of humour and a sexy backside. These were Daniel's prime assets, according to more than a handful of extremely intelligent women. Now he was a fully-fledged lawyer, Jack wondered where this sat on the scale of eligibility, before or after the amazing arse?

'Oh, good one. When's all this happening?'

'August. Get this, she's got rellies in Wales, and since most of my family are down there now we thought we'd do the serious bit at the King Edward.'

'In Conwy?'

'Yeah. Problem is, there's a lot of hanging around after that; before the reception, and she wants some *nice* photographs, so we were wondering if we could use the farm for some drinkies and piccies?'

'Oh, right. You'll have to ask Anna.'

'I'll phone her.'

'OK, and congrats, Dan, I mean it.'

'No embarrassing stories in the speech. I'm willing to pay for your silence.'

'Ha bloody ha.'

The job hunters began to arrive. He tried to list some pertinent questions but decided to trust his instinct instead. It was depressing how many people were out of work, hopelessly over-qualified, and trying to impress him. He should have made Oliver sit through it all with him, then a few pennies might drop. By lunchtime, he was glad of a break and took over from Clare on reception. Tabitha kept frowning at her screen.

'Jack, what's this rental request on the system? An insulated room … do you mean loft insulation, or cavity wall?'

'No, more like a padded cell with handcuff rings on the walls.'

A long beat, eyes front. 'I see.'

She didn't though, not really.

Patsy called to say she'd discussed the drama school with Lottie. 'So, can I call them and confirm now?'

'Go ahead.'

'The thing is, Jack, she's not stupid. She's already asking how she's going to get there.'

'Just tell her we're working on it.'

He wanted to save this part for Anna and himself, mostly so Anna felt involved and had some kind of input, although when that was going to happen was anyone's guess.

'How's the cottage looking?' Patsy said.

'Not bad. You should be OK to come over at the start of the school summer holidays. July is it?'

'I'll give notice here, then. And Jack, I can't thank

you enough. It's changed my life, all of our lives.'

He ended the call abruptly. Patsy acting and speaking normally freaked him out far more than Patsy set on the path of destruction ever had. When he'd spent the night on her sofa, it was largely an exercise to see how long she could keep up playing the Good Mummy and Reasonable Ex-Wife. He already knew she was an amazing actress – ironic that this trait had manifested itself in Lottie and was now the subject of a massive shift in the order of things. While he'd been waiting for the Peeping Tom to show up outside, he'd utilised the time to impress a few rules on her.

'Unless it's something to do with the children, we still lead separate lives, yes?'

'Of course. Oh, unless there's a maintenance issue.'

'Then you call the number in the cottage, *not* me.'

Then it was Lottie on the phone, wanting to tell him all about her audition and the drama school he was meant to know nothing about. The second Clare put the call through and her tinkly, excited voice came over the line, the utter joy at being the best daddy in the world surpassed just about everything else going on in his life.

When Clare and Tabitha had gone home and Oliver had gone out for Chinese food, Jack flicked off the office lights and nudged the computer back to life. He clicked onto his emails and opened the correspondence from DNA Online. His eyes dropped to the bottom line and the words *probability of paternity* and *inconclusive* stared back at him.

So much for doing it on the quiet. In the accompanying notes, it explained that an inconclusive result usually meant that the samples were rubbish and they needed to do a re-test before confirmation. He leant back in his leather chair and closed his eyes. Mixed in with the tension of this was frustration and shame. Shame that it had taken him years to come to terms with the fact that he may have fathered another child with his ex-while she was having an affair with another man. The financial burden meant nothing, he was obliged to pay a hefty figure to Patsy as a matter of legalities and he'd never deny food and clothes to a toddler under the same roof no matter the circumstances.

Anna said she had him playing into her hands at every turn. If it wasn't money, it was the emotional screw.

He called Gwern Farm on the landline. Most of his life seemed to exist on the phone during the week, but he still felt pathetically relieved when he heard Anna's voice.

'You did what? An online DNA test? I had no idea they even existed.'

'It was inconclusive.'

'That means please send more money.'

He grunted. 'You could be right.'

'So, is Lottie all clued-up about the new school?'

'She is, she's very excited. Look, I'm hoping to move them over in July.'

There was a noticeable intake of breath. 'Have you told them about the cottage already?'

'Only Patsy. I thought we'd tell Lottie together.'

'Oh, well, OK.'

'We can take her to see the inside next time she's over. Maybe you could help choose bedroom colours with her or something.'

'Bedroom colours? Right.'

He threw a chewed biro across the desk. 'Just what else am I supposed to do here?'

'I don't know, Jack! Patsy always seems to land on her feet. This time it's a smartened-up, all expenses paid, grade-two-listed cottage in my home town. And all I know is how that makes me *feel.*'

'I'm not over the moon about it either but we need a united front, otherwise Patsy will lap it up.'

'I'm sure she'll lap it up anyway *somehow.*'

Although it was half expected, it wasn't a good conversation. By the time Oliver returned with the Chinese, his appetite had diminished and most of it was scraped into the bin. Was he doing the right thing? If the cost was serious damage to his relationship, then no.

Anna called him back and apologised some two hours later. 'Look, go ahead and tell Lottie about the cottage. I'm sorry I snapped, but I honestly don't mind if I stay out of it. In fact, I'd rather it was nothing to do with me. Everything I emotionally invest in seems to come back and slap me across the face these days, so I'm going down the self-preservation route. Sorry if that sounds cowardly.'

'No, it's not cowardly.'

He said a lot of placatory things, but in his heart of hearts, he was bitterly disappointed. Instead of helping him blend the boundaries of his two families, she had effectively drawn a hard, black line between them, deeper and wider than ever before.

The new prospective member of staff turned up for a trial run. Tony was in his thirties, with a wife, one small kid, and one enormous mortgage. He was over-qualified, something in computing, which certainly wouldn't go amiss. Jack took him out on a variety of appointments to see if he could think on his feet. Two market appraisals, and then it was on to collect Clarissa to show her two possible properties for rent. If he could handle Big Mummy, Jack reckoned the job was his. Jack filled him in on Oliver's role so far in the proceedings, mostly to save any further speculation, and to see if he flinched when Jack suggested he look after Melissa in his absence. 'Anything to do with negotiation of the sale though, that's me.'

'Got it. Wow, this is some place,' he said, on seeing Alderley House. 'Wow, that's er ... some woman,' he said on seeing Clarissa materialise in tight leather trousers, her breasts bouncing beneath the fabric of her silk shirt. She climbed into the passenger seat, bracelets jangling, her big mouth going ten to the dozen.

'*Two* handsome men! Where are you taking me? Oh, I do love surprises, drive on.'

She struggled to get the seatbelt across her enormous chest then twisted round to speak to Tony. 'Are you the new boy? I'm Clarissa.'

'That's me, bit of an old new boy, but pleased to meet you. Tony Burgess.'

'Lovely smile, Tony. You'll do well in this game, I bet you'll sell lots of houses.'

'I hope so. Still learning the ropes.'

'Oh, *ropes!* Yes, it's hard learning new things as one gets older.'

Jack stole a glance at Tony through the rear-view mirror but his expression was unreadable. Mrs Harrison-Smith was not an unusual client, plenty of rich Cheshire wives were of the same inclination. Drugs, sex, and money was a common enough undertone in an area as rich as the Cheshire stockbroker belt. Footballers, retired actors, ageing rockstars, they all had too much time and money on their hands. Jack cashed in when they wanted a change of scene.

Clarissa placed a wandering hand on his thigh. 'Jack, I feel I should say something about Rupert's behaviour.'

'Go ahead.'

A shriek first. 'He's such a red blood! Well, he's in Switzerland with his father. A good dose of fresh air on the slopes will sort him out. And he isn't going to press any charges, so don't worry.'

So Rupert got a holiday and Oliver got his smashed-up nose pushed onto the grindstone. For a wild moment, Jack had stupidly expected some sort of apology for Oliver being beaten up, but of course Clarissa had a different take on the world. In truth, he pitied Rupert more, but how to respond? He was saved when Clarissa took a call on her mobile and began a loud conversation – one of Jack's pet hates.

'Bunny, is that you, darling? Yes, it's *tonight!* I told you the time. Come for eight. EIGHT. EIGHT O' CLOCK. CAN YOU HEAR ME? That's better, yes … I'm cooking the spatchcocks. Oh, for goodness sake … SPATCH. COCK. What? What's still sore?'

Irritated by the lack of signal, she ended the call, perched a pair of reading glasses on the end of her nose, and began to text, making vicious stabs at the keypad with long red nails. 'Stupid man. *Stupid.*'

Jack risked a glance through the rear-view mirror. Tony was staring out of the side window, watching the Cheshire fields zip past.

'Mixed signals?' he said. 'Fellas need clear signals, right from wrong, black from white.'

Oh yes, matey, you got the job.

Employing Tony meant that weekends could be staggered better between the staff, something Oliver was very pleased about. Planning took place immediately.

'Yo, Dad. Me and Josh have got a gig in Taffy Town. Can me and Amy come down with you to Conwy next weekend?'

Jack stopped mid-shave and sighed. He'd been

hoping for a long weekend alone with Anna, to simply enjoy some peace and quiet. Oliver practising riffs and Amy prancing about in an animal-print outfit was the last thing he needed. 'Can't you do it another time?'

'Not really. Josh's boss in the bar said we could have a twenty-minute spot for some music festival thing, so not much point doing it any other time.'

Fuck. 'Right, well, I'll have to ask Anna.'

'Anna's totally cool, she won't mind, she's made up about the gig.'

'I mean about you bringing Amy.'

'What's the problem?'

'It's manners to ask, it's not my house.'

'You live there half the time and pay for nearly everything, don't you?'

'It's Anna's home, it's called respect,' he said, rinsing the razor. He sluiced water over his face and fumbled for a towel. 'Why do I have to spell everything out all the time?' No reply. He flicked the towel over his shoulder and went back into the sitting room. Oliver had departed, the flat's door slightly ajar, no doubt happy to roam the wine bars again knowing that Rupert Harrison-Smith was enjoying his après-ski elsewhere.

Around five, Jack set off to meet Patsy and Lottie for an early dinner. Patsy had insisted on driving halfway across Cheshire to meet him in order to tell Lottie about their future plans, and Jack had readily agreed. Not only would it save him from the rush hour traffic across north Manchester, but the location of a child-friendly pub-restaurant in the countryside was infinitely more desirable as a meeting place, especially on a warm spring evening.

Her car was already there when he pulled in to the Cheshire Cat at Prestbury, close to where they used to live. He spotted them the second he walked through the door and it was like going back in time. He remembered the place now; they used to bring the children here when they were young. Chelsey would have been Lottie's age now, Oliver a toddler, and Lottie still a baby. Happier times. Amazingly, ten years on and Patsy didn't look that much different. She'd always been slender with a natural eye for style, something which had spiralled out of control when he'd been at the peak of his earning power and before she'd blown their life to smithereens. She'd gone through an aggressive stage, both in looks and manner. Now though, it seemed a period of austerity had helped her regain a natural beauty.

Jack hoped it was another sign that she'd come to her senses, learnt some hard lessons, and softened with maturity, but then her green eyes locked onto his and it was difficult to understand what he saw there – a mix of remorse and gratitude, certainly. The other more disturbing thing was that old disruptive friend, sexual attraction. He bought some drinks and headed over to the table. She half rose and kissed his cheek with a soft, lingering pressure. Her hair brushed his face and her hands rested on his shoulders.

'Looking good, Jack. You still have those swimmer's arms. No sign of a beer belly either, and those Levi's are –'

'Let's keep to the agenda in hand, shall we?'

Lottie was a good distraction throughout their exchange, chattering about some incident at school and clearly pleased to have her parents together. For a moment he wondered if perhaps this was sending the wrong message. They ordered food and Jack got straight to the point with the school and the loan of the cottage. Obviously, his little girl was beside herself with excitement but he was careful to tell the absolute bald facts to Lottie before her mother could fabricate anything or drive him in a corner. Patsy let him do all the talking. They ate a distinctly average meal – burgers for him and Lottie while Patsy picked at a salad – but Lottie enjoyed it with gusto, then begged to go out to the play area.

This was his cue to go, but somehow he found himself still sitting there while his ex-wife told him all the latest gossip concerning old friends. Jack found himself talking about Oliver's escapades with Clarissa Harrison-Smith.

'Our son's a handful, isn't he?' she said. 'But I trust you to do the right thing. You're a good dad, always were.'

Jack drained his glass and flipped over a beer mat. 'Where's James tonight?'

'Mum and Dad have him. They don't blame you any more, you know. I think they regret coming down so hard on you.'

'Right, good.'

'I er … after you'd gone the other night, I thought about what you'd said, about starting with an honest, clean slate.'

'Yeah?'

She rummaged in her bag and brought out a plastic folder containing swabs and a child's dummy. He knew instantly what it was, his eyes never leaving hers as she passed it across the table to him. 'I've paid for it myself, all you need to do is a mouth swab and send it off. It's really fast, a couple of days or something.'

'I did one, but it failed.'

'On the quiet, trying to catch me out?'

After what seemed an eternity, he picked up the packet and shoved it into his jacket pocket. When he stood to go, she remained sitting, looking up at him. It should have been awkward, but it wasn't. It felt natural to kiss her goodbye. It was a chaste, two-second peck on the cheek, the same sort he gave his sister. He paid the bill and kept on walking, stopping to speak to Lottie on the climbing frame outside. She was hanging upside down like a bat, ankles crossed and arms folded.

'It is all real, isn't it? The drama school and me and Mummy and Jamie living by the seaside?'

'Course it is!'

'Daddy …'

'Yeah?'

'I've had the best idea. You could come and live at the cottage as well.'

Jack hunkered down, close to her cold face. 'No, Lottie. I'm with Anna. You know that, sweetheart.'

'I know. It was just a dream. Sometimes they come true.'

He kissed her goodbye then got into his car and floored the accelerator.

They left for Conwy on Thursday evening, for a long weekend. Oliver took a few days' holiday to do the music festival on the quay, so it was fortunate Tony was around. 'I feel like I'm throwing you in the deep end a bit,' Jack said, tidying his desk.

'Best way to learn.'

'Clare's in charge. Any negotiations over half a million go through me. Any problems, I'm on my mobile. Don't hesitate.'

'That's straightforward.'

'Yep, that's the way I like things.'

'Me too. Have a good weekend.'

'That might be a challenge, but I'll try.'

On the forecourt, Oliver was busy loading the 4x4 with guitars and what looked to be enough cabling and electrical items to supply the National Grid. He let out a whoop when an old banger drew up, an amplifier strapped into the boot. This was manhandled out of the car and rested on the back bumper of Jack's vehicle while Amy shifted everything round to make room for it.

'Watch the bloody paintwork!' Jack yelled. He stuffed his small holdall in the passenger footwell since there didn't seem to be much room elsewhere, with all the musical luggage and Amy's sizeable zebra-striped case already in situ. Jack climbed into the driver's seat and cringed as the amp dropped into place. The suspension seemed to plummet with it. Oliver slammed the hatch down with equal force and Jack closed his eyes.

'Dad, can Spider come as well?'

'Spider?'

'He used to be in the band.'

A grubby-looking teenager gripped the top of Jack's car door and leant in through the open window. 'Alright?'

His greeting was presented as a bland statement rather than a polite question. Jack sighed with irritation. He tried calling Anna but there was no joy. He texted her to say that he was sorry, but he was bringing three weird teenagers with him.

'*Get in*,' he said to Spider. 'You pay your own way.'

'Nice one.'

'Have you not got a bag or anything?'

'Nah, be alright.'

Amy moved up on the back seat to make room. Her travelling outfit was a skin-tight, black velour catsuit, mercifully tail free but with a hood complete with ears, and a sparkling diamond collar and lead. It was difficult not to stare when she pressed the lead into Oliver's hands. He grinned and gave it a discreet tug.

CHAPTER FIVE

Anna

She laughed at the text, something about three crazy teenagers and a lot of apologies. Given the phone calls between Josh and Oliver over the last few days about the music festival, it was all expected. Josh, who still hadn't moved out from home properly, was looking forward to his friends coming over. There was plenty of room at the farm, the weather was set to be fair, and the town was buzzing with activity.

She'd made a huge pan of chilli con carne with homemade cheese bread and thrown some duvets across the spare beds, although there was little point assuming that Oliver's female companion would sleep alone. And then they were late, because the music equipment had to be dropped at the venue first. Jack was in an irritable mood due to shifting the amp up a flight of stairs and into a lockable practice room. She pushed a beer into his hands the second he stepped through the door, then waited till he'd drank a good half of the bottle.

'The boiler's playing up, there's something nesting in the gutters, and the duck house roof has come loose again.'

'I love you too.' He wiped his arm across his forehead then put the bottle down and kissed her properly, with deliciously cold lips. His hands felt good on her waist and she couldn't wait to get him to herself. Jack looked his best when he was out of his business suits. She'd never known a man look so alluring in a pair of old Levi's. Much of this was down to his lack of vanity and his sense of humour, although he did look after himself these days. Since he'd had the ulcer scare four years ago, he was careful with his diet and kept himself in shape.

Anna remained the same shape whatever she did: voluptuous.

Dinner was fun. Amy politely explained she was a teetotal vegetarian but she was happy with bread and salad, whereas Oliver and Spider ate and drank like pigs. Jack made the boys clear away and do the washing-up. She was surprised at the state of Oliver's face and rooted about in her herbal cupboard for arnica and St. John's wort. Amy was impressed with her grandmother's antique drawers full of herbs, and studied the collection with curiosity and a lot of questions.

The remainder of the evening passed in a not unpleasant blur, with sporadic guitar practice from Oliver and Spider, singing from Josh, and once she'd applied the arnica to her satisfaction, imaginative dancing from Amy. At least it kept the conversation light between Anna and Jack, although she really wanted to know if he'd met with Patsy and Lottie. Since she'd told him she wanted nothing to do with all of that, she had little choice but to wait for the information to materialise.

'What do you make of Amy?' he asked when they were alone in their room.

'Seems quite sweet.'

'*Sweet*? She has a caseful of animal outfits.'

She laughed at his incredulous expression and draped her long skirt and underwear over the back of the chair. 'Bit dreamy, but at least she's clean and polite. Not like Spider. I hardly recognised him, wasn't he your neighbour's son from when you lived at The Links?'

'Yep, one and the same.'

'Looks like he's been living rough.'

He ignored this, choosing instead to pull her against his hardening body, her breasts pressed against his chest. He pushed her gently onto the bed so her mass of increasingly wild hair lay in a mess across the pillow. They didn't bother pulling the curtains, preferring the blue-black illumination from the moon. Enveloped by the softness of the old brass bed and taken to another, safer refuge in her mind by their lovemaking, she allowed herself to forget about Patricia Redman.

As a result of clear skies through the night and into the early hours, there was a sugary ground frost in the morning. The water in the lake looked like frozen ink. But by the time they'd breakfasted, the chill was already surrendering to the rising sun. She dropped Amy and the three lads into town and walked the dogs, while Jack re-set the boiler and did farmer-type tasks. He loved the contrast to his office job. It slowly developed into a sparkling spring day for the music festival. The town was buzzing with the first event of the year, the kindness of the weather being the main topic of conversation.

Although it had started as a low-key event, commercial opportunity had muscled in. Since tourism was generally viewed as a necessary evil, no one seemed to mind when residents set up market stalls in the streets selling home-grown plants and cakes and bits of second-hand furniture. The council wagged their finger to start with, then closed off the streets to traffic, strung out the bunting, and charged table room instead. To keep the purists happy, they offset all of this by providing historical interest; flags, men in chainmail walking the castle walls spouting bits of history, and long-haired men carrying birds of prey. To keep everyone happy, there were hot-dogs and chips as well as an *olde worlde* hog roast and gourmet food tent.

People still complained – they said it wasn't one thing or the other.

By early evening, no one cared either way. The atmosphere was settling into party mode and fairy lights competed with a dramatic light show projected onto the castle. It was busy, the town a myriad of buskers, street processions, and pavement artists. They gravitated towards the quay where the real ale marquee was being run by Josh's boss. There was a staged area where various acts entertained an increasingly noisy crowd. Like everything else it was an eclectic mix of Welsh folksingers, rock bands, Irish dancers, and mime artists.

'Lottie would have loved this!' Jack said. He had a plastic glass of beer in one hand and a hot roast beef sandwich in the other. 'Shame I couldn't bring her as well.'

'She'll be here next year, won't she?'

He looked at his beer instead of her eyes. 'Yeah, she's excited.'

'Well, I hope she isn't counting on riding through the summer.'

'Still no joy? Mum says this Bryn Hopkins comes from a bad lot.'

'Hmm, there's rumours but … Oh, I don't know.'

She linked his arm and inclined her head against his shoulder. A terrible childish ache began to stir deep in her soul when she thought about the horses. She *adored* Hilly's Arabian mare, Blue. After six years they had a bond. She'd once nursed the animal all night when she had colic. It's true what they say about not really knowing what you have till it's lost. She recalled February 1st, the Pagan festival of light. The day had been true to its name, with washed-out skies and a rolling sea. Normally, she and Hilly rode along the Roman roads to the druids' circle above Penmaenmawr, but they'd not managed it this year. Hilly had been in Ireland with Bryn. Anna had looked forward to it for weeks, but when she'd called in to the yard, the horses were all turned-out in distant pastures and everywhere was locked up with chains and padlocks. She could never admit, not even to Jack, how it had made her feel, although he knew her so well it was difficult to hide. He had picked up on her despondency straight away.

'You know what? We'll just buy a bloody pony. How much are they? We've got the land. In fact, we'll buy two, then you and Lottie can ride together.'

'That means acres and acres of fencing. We haven't got horse pasture, Jack, it's scrubby hill farm. I can't begin to think what it would cost to treat. And I'm too big for a pony, which means getting a horse. That means expensive.'

'Get a cheap horse or a really big pony. I can put fences in, not a problem.'

She smiled at his logic. He didn't really understand the care and commitment of a horse, but why would he? If Jack could find solutions with physical actions he was always happy.

'It's not just the riding, it's the loss of something precious,' she went on. 'I've been friends with Hilly for a lifetime. It's mixed up with that.'

He took a big bite of his sandwich, then looked beyond her shoulder. 'Isn't that them over there?'

Anna spun round and Hilly caught her eye with a

moot expression, but at least she lifted a hand in greeting.

'Invite them over for drinks,' Jack said. 'Let's see how the land lies, see if it's fixable.'

'Alright. In a while.'

Utopia came on stage, and tuning-up put paid to any further conversation, but that was fine. She wanted to think. In a way, she'd rather Hilly admit that Bryn just didn't like her, instead of the prospect of future put-downs. She felt sure he was behind it. All she'd wanted was a vote of solidarity when she'd felt vulnerable. Given the current developments moving at a smart pace with Quay Cottage and Hilly giving her – not the cold shoulder exactly, but a lukewarm one – it was difficult not to brood and feel down, even when she reasoned herself out of it. She knew how lucky she was, but some things still hurt as if she were a child. Even with the gifts of hindsight, grown-up perception, and Jack's loving influence, she couldn't help but feel insecure. Jack thought he had a handle on it all, but women could outthink men easily when it came to emotional matters, and not only did she not trust Patsy, it seemed that her best friend was no longer an ally. Areas of her life which had once nurtured her were now denied.

'Hey, they sound alright, don't they?' Jack shouted.

She smiled and looked across to the stage, at her son and his second-hand keyboard.

Maybe she should sell Gwern Farm and downsize, give Josh his inheritance when he needed it the most. After all, it was unlikely he'd ever live there comfortably on a teacher's wage, not even in the distant future. The house was a bottomless pit for money. Not so long ago, the thought of selling her beloved piece of paradise would have left her distraught. It was the prospect of this which had broken her relationship with Alex, and now here she was contemplating the very same idea. And yet, this time, the thought was almost a comfort, perhaps because it was the only remaining control she had. Jack had made it plain it was all completely hers and with Josh almost gone, the idea refused to let go. It was like a laser piercing through the shadow of darkness. If she bought something smaller, away from here, they could own it in joint names and everything would go back to how it was – *better* than it was. She wouldn't feel quite so beholden to Jack, and they could start this new phase of their lives on neutral ground.

Things change, he'd said. Things don't stay the same.

Utopia's set finished and the crowd roared. Jack was laughing, clapping. Could she could do that to him? All the time and money he'd invested in it? Could she do it to herself? Was she cutting off her nose to spite her face or was it a case of paradise already lost?

She watched him beckon Hilly and Bryn over and they came with an older woman in tow who was introduced as Bryn's sister, Heather. She looked like she needed a good wash. She didn't smell too good, either. Leggings and a leather biker jacket was not a good look on a scrawny sixty-year-old woman missing half her teeth. They'd all been drinking since lunchtime and Bryn looked unsteady on his feet. Despite this, Jack went to the bar and they dragged some chairs round a plastic table full of screwed-up chip papers.

They talked about the wedding. A date was announced, sometime next August.

'That's your busiest time,' she said, surprised. 'Will you close?'

'Only for a couple of days. Maybe forever. To be

honest I hate August on the yard, the bloody kids and the flies, can't tell them apart sometimes.'

Jack slid a tray of beers onto the table and straddled a chair the wrong way round. 'Well, a drink to the happy couple,' he said, a tad sarcastically she thought but they managed a half-hearted toast.

'You sound fed up with it all, Hilly.'

'The yard, you mean? You know how it is when you run your own business. There's no escape, no one you can trust to run it in your absence. It becomes a bloody ball and chain.'

'Yeah, I know what you mean, actually.'

'For us, it's the physical work in all weathers,' Bryn cut in. 'We're not getting any younger. You don't know you're born, sitting in that nice warm office. I bet you got a coffee machine as well, am I right?'

Anna flicked her eyes to Jack, willing him not to respond, then said to Hilly, 'It must be a help having Bryn around.'

'Oh, yes. Sometimes I can't believe how I've struggled on my own all these years. Even so, I'm thinking of retiring.'

'Part-time you mean, like Jack?'

Jack made a derisory grunt. 'Doesn't feel like part-time to me. It feels like full-time squashed into three or four days.'

Bryn shifted uneasily in his chair. Hilly said, 'I'm going to do livery only, pack in the trekking.'

'No money in it,' Bryn added. 'No one wants to pay. They just want to ride something a bit flash then sue you for compensation when they hurt their little finger. The paperwork mountain is bigger than fucking Snowdon.'

Heather cackled and took out a tin of tobacco and rolling papers.

'So if you just do livery, how will that change

things?' Jack said.

'Private-owned horses, see? We offer grazing, stabling, and shoeing. But that's where the buck stops. Everyone responsible for their own, pay their own way. We get all of the money, none of the work.'

Jack nodded and drank some more beer. 'So, Anna and Lottie could keep their horses there?'

Heather homed in. 'You're buying a horse?'

'She might be,' Jack said, looking steadily at Hilly. 'Doesn't seem to be any other option.'

'I can get you a good one, proper Irish stock, cheap,' Heather said.

'Is that right? How come?'

'In the trade so to speak, been in the family for generations.'

'Actually, I was thinking of offering to buy Hilly's horse. If that's an option? Or on a shared basis? I mean, from what you've just said I think it might work for both of you.'

'Jack, can we talk about this another time, *please?*' Anna said, realising it was probably too late because he wasn't paying attention to her. He'd got the bit between his teeth.

'Not even for cash? No strings, name your price.'

'Throw some money at it, eh?' Bryn said. 'That's how you lot deal with it.'

'My lot?'

'Yeah, you capitalist sorts.'

'Deal with what, exactly?'

'When you can't get what you want.'

'I'm offering to buy half a horse from Hilly, that's all. If it's a no-go we'll look elsewhere.'

'I'm sorry, but Blue is on loan to Meredith Edwards,' Hilly said. 'She went last week. I'm hoping she'll buy her. Most of the time she stood around doing nothing, waiting to be ridden. For nothing.'

Anna watched her walk away, push through the crowd, and disappear without a backward glance. Bryn slammed his empty glass down on the table. 'Got that? You see, I don't like middle-class twats with a wad of cash trying to buy into some rustic fucking lifestyle.'

'I was just trying to find a solution here.'

'We don't need a *solution*. Because there is no longer a problem.' Bryn leant in across the table and pushed his face closer to Jack. 'Is that loud and clear? Or can I get it across another way?'

'Are you threatening me?'

'You think a bit of banter's a threat?'

'Not especially. But if you want to be rude about the way I earn a living then you need to understand that it cuts both ways. You don't seem able to see the bigger picture. Maybe that chip on your shoulder's obscuring it.'

'I could knock you down like a pack of fucking cards.'

'Go on then. Sometimes violence *is* the only solution. After all, it's more universally understood.'

'Are you taking the mickey?'

Throughout most of this exchange, Anna had sat motionless with her eyes closed. She only opened them fully when Bryn scraped his chair back and made after Hilly.

Heather laughed and nodded in Bryn's direction. 'He's pissed, take no notice. I don't care where your money comes from, love. You can buy me a drink anytime.'

'Cheers. It's your round,' Jack said, getting up and leaving the table.

Anna slid her untouched drink in front of Heather and followed Jack out into the night air.

It was a silent journey home. They couldn't find Amy and the boys anywhere, but Jack reasoned they could either crash at Josh's flat, find a taxi, or walk. Back at the farm, Anna threw her bag onto the kitchen table and made a fuss of the dogs. Benson didn't get up from his basket, although his tail twitched in greeting.

'Well, that was a bloody disaster,' Jack said. 'I hope Hilly realises what she's getting into there.'

'You made it all ten times worse.'

'How?'

'By rubbing him up the wrong way. Now I'll end up avoiding *him* as well as Hilly and Patsy.'

'So *I* have to be careful not to upset him because *he's* got a temper? Anyway, what's Patsy got to do with this?'

She threw the switch on the kettle. 'I won't be able to walk the streets without wondering which one is going to pop up, ready to take aim.'

'You've *nothing* to be ashamed about, what have you done wrong?'

'Jack. It's a small town. It's not a question of right or wrong,' she went on. 'People here won't remember the issue, but they won't forget the animosity.'

'So all those years of friendship mean fuck all? It's like she *used* you till Bryn came along. I don't like the way she walked out of that conversation while he carried on insulting us. It was cowardly.'

'Hilly?'

'Of course Hilly! Actions speak louder than words. What she did condones everything he was saying. It makes me wonder if it's what she really thinks of us. She didn't even come after us – or you, to be precise.'

'I know,' she managed to say, then burst into tears.

'Oh, love, come here,' Jack said, 'I'm sorry for going on. I'm just frustrated with the situation.'

Within seconds she was enveloped in a bear hug, her face crushed against his chest. All she could think about was how grateful she was that they were alone. There was no one to see her pathetic behaviour. A middle-aged woman sobbing over a childish spat about a horse. It was insignificant in a world of war and starvation, but in that moment it was *her* world, and it was crumbling at the edges.

They were woken in the night by Amy and the boys crashing through the front door. She heard Hooper bark a couple of times, claws clattering across the stone floor, then a lot of whispering and giggling. Footsteps creaked on the stairs and across the landing. One of the dogs had followed them, sniffing under all the doors. Then it was running water, thumps, and stifled laughter. Jack stirred next to her. He was a light sleeper at the best of times and she wasn't surprised when he sighed with irritation and made to get out of bed.

'There's no point losing your rag with them,' she hissed. 'They're drunk, they think they're being quiet, like we used to. Don't you remember your dad standing at the top of the stairs in his undies and wielding a golf club? He thought we were burglars.'

He sighed and dragged the duvet back, then settled around the curve of her back. 'Yeah. Happy days.'

'Although we didn't realise it at the time, did we? We moaned about everything, how unfair life was.'

'And here we are, older and …'

'Still moaning about how unfair life is.'

'I thought when we reached our age you got all the answers. Is it just me or does everything seem even more complicated? I don't mean failed relationships, I mean those old-fashioned traits like honesty, loyalty, and respect. All that stuff that got drummed into us as kids, what happened to it? I don't see it in other people.'

'Maybe it's not there.'

'I can see it in you and Mum. I can see it in Josh and Chelsey.'

She smiled into the dark. She remembered her grandparents complaining that life had sped up to the extent that no one had time to be kind or to think about their actions. Laughable at the time.

'Do you think people pretend to be kind on the surface, but maybe it's just another way of getting what they want? Maybe that's why it's so complicated; there's no real trust anymore in what people do or say. And don't get me started on the Internet or the phone. If you can't see someone's face, aren't the boundaries horribly blurred?'

'That's depressing,' he said, and rolled onto his back, an arm strewn across his eyes, 'but I think you might be right.'

The best cure for a hangover and a disturbed night's sleep – in fact for a lot of other ills as well – was a long walk in the hills. Jack, and three of the dogs, agreed that this was a good idea. The younger residents of the house looked dead to the world. Benson, the eldest resident, ate his breakfast and pottered around the garden but then as Anna pulled on her boots, a sure sign a long walk was on the cards, climbed back into his bed by the Aga. She was slightly concerned about it, but Jack said it was just old age, the chilly spring weather setting off his arthritis.

The air was sharp, the wind chill increasing steadily as they headed up the winding grass tracks across Pensychnant, but they were soon warm from the climb. The land flattened towards the top of the rise, affording views across the Irish sea, the land before them falling away to the valley of Maen Esgob. The tracks were rough stone, frequently crisscrossed with running streams. It was hard going against the wind and they didn't speak for a good while, but it was a companionable silence, punctuated only by the bleat of new lambs and the wind tearing through the grass.

'I had a weird dream last night,' Jack said as they scrambled over a stile. 'You and Heather. Bridesmaids.'

'Oh ... what am I going to do?'

'You? Nothing! If she wants you to be there she can send a proper invite or call round and ask.'

She ignored this, choosing to walk on, to fill her lungs with the clarity of the air. 'Sometimes I think I'd rather enjoy being a hermit. It wouldn't bother me, being called the eccentric dog woman.'

'Don't they call you that anyway?'

They began the descent into Capelulo, along the edge of a deep gorge. Sunday lunch at the village pub was basic, but she had neither prepared nor cooked it, and it was bliss to leave all the dirty plates on the table.

'Not as good as yours,' Jack said, spearing an errant parsnip from her plate.

She smiled and sipped her sparkling water, aware that she was preoccupied as well as tired but seemed unable to shake herself out of it. Jack could read her mind.

'It'll settle down with Hilly. And don't worry about Patsy, I've told you, I've read the riot act there.'

It was on the tip of her tongue to snap at him that his words would make no difference. It felt as if he was trying to placate her. What had he said not hours before – actions speak louder than words?

'Did Dan phone you about his upcoming nuptials?' he said.

'Oh, yes, I forgot to tell you. It's great news, a bit unexpected though, isn't it? I've told him we'll decorate the trees with white balloons.'

They prepared to depart on Tuesday morning, taking their noise and chaos with them. Jack was interrupted a dozen times by phone calls from the office. Then he was on his laptop, tapping away at the keyboard, landline phone scrunched under his ear. His conversations made no sense to her. It was all about mortgage rates, survey fees, and negotiations with landowners. He was still wearing his washed-out denims but he was showered and shaved, a faint whiff of Armani Code about his person.

Phone calls finished, he began scrolling through emails, his expression suddenly grim. He told Oliver, Amy, and Spider to go and wait for him in the car. When they were alone, he asked Anna to sit next to him then angled the computer screen towards her.

'What is it? I need my reading glasses.'

'It's a DNA result.'

'Oh. I didn't know you'd done another.'

'Patsy set it up and paid for it. It's just come through.'

'She paid with your money?'

He sighed. 'That's not the point really, is it?'

'Well? And?'

He ignored her question for a moment and began tapping away again, but she could see the answer in his gloomy reflection.

'Seems I owe her an apology,' he said.

Anna could hardly believe her ears. Patricia Redman was the mother of all conniving bitches, and here he was wanting to *apologise*. He must be owed a thousand apologies from her.

'How do you know this is accurate? She could have swabbed Lottie for all you know!'

'Lottie would have told me,' he said, then looked

up at her. 'Why are you so angry with me?'

'I don't know,' she said, knowing full well why she was angry. She hadn't wanted it to be true. She'd wanted the child to be someone else's responsibility.

'How do you think I feel? I've practically ignored the kid for three years. I feel a right bastard.'

She shrugged, out of words. 'I just don't know, Jack.'

He collected his papers, logged off his computer, and closed the lid with a definitive click. Although she knew she was being unreasonable and unsupportive, another smaller, more powerful set of thoughts had begun to control her feelings.

He kissed her, a brush of the lips, a hand on the small of her back. 'I'll call you later.'

She watched his vehicle nose down the driveway, avoiding the potholes. An odd silence descended on the house like a cloying, wet blanket of wool. They'd left their mess behind, but Anna was used to that. Soon, even more of Jack's mess would be left here on a frequent basis while he went back to his other life seventy miles away. Soon, there would be toddler mess in her house, and an emotional, less tangible mess elsewhere as Patsy enjoyed her freedom in the town – while she and Jack no doubt looked after the two youngest children, their relationship on hold again while they dealt with the fall-out. It just kept coming.

She wandered through the rooms, considering her grandmother's furniture: the sewing box, the bookcase, the bureau. She left the forgotten trainer, the earpieces and cables, and the dirty plates and mugs festering where they'd been left, then stood at the door to her son's room and heaved a deep sigh. While they'd been out on the hills the previous day, Josh had borrowed her Land Rover and Oliver and Spider had helped him move some furniture and his personal belongings into the new flat. Where the bed used to be, there was a fresher section of carpet, a few errant pieces of Lego, and a deep border of ingrained dust. Everything changed, nothing stayed the same.

Through the rain-streaked window, the seasonal circle remained constant. Snowdonia was coming back to life with a faint green flush. Downstairs, Benson met her eyes with a telepathic stare, then lowered his head to his paws.

CHAPTER SIX

Simon

It was people watching, that was all. Lots of people did it. There was nothing in it – it wasn't like he was some sort of weirdo, stalking women and having sexual fantasies. It was nothing like that. He did like to make notes though, a log book. It was just the way he was, meticulous with detail. Maybe he should be a private eye or something. He'd be good at that.

It started the day he came across Patsy Redman in the dentist's waiting room. He'd held an old magazine across his face, terrified she'd recognise him and his cover would be blown. Not that he was undercover as such, but he didn't want to talk to her. She was stunning, always had been. Even in her forties she had the natural gloss and grace of a woman much younger. Her eyes, cat-like and green. Long, shiny hair and she was in good shape.

'Patricia Redman,' she'd said at the desk. 'Can someone see me straight away? I can't wait for long.'

He'd know that voice anywhere. Typical of her to try and queue jump.

Once he'd got over the shock of seeing her there in that shabby room in north Manchester, he began to wonder what her backstory was. He always imagined that she lived an expensive executive lifestyle in Cheshire, married to Jack Redman. The only information he'd come across was a piece in a local glossy, funnily enough in the doctor's waiting room. The magazine was about three years old, but on the back pages he'd seen his daughter's wedding. Chelsey Redman. He'd torn it out, folded it over, and stuffed it in his pocket, then walked out of the surgery and kept going, even missed the appointment about his rash. He'd felt shocked to see her like an adult. He'd given life to her, but he didn't know her. She didn't know *him*, and he was thrown by how that made him feel. A couple of days later, when he felt calm enough, he unfolded the shiny sheet of paper and scanned the words.

It looked like a proper society do, Oxford Hall or somewhere. Very nice.

On the day he saw Patsy in the dentist's, he hung around outside then followed her. If she got into a car he was done for, but she walked all the way down Highcroft Street, through a housing estate, and eventually, into a two-up two-down on Stretford Road. Well, well ... how the mighty fall! A few visits watching the house from across the road in the bus shelter confirmed two younger children and no one else at the property. After that, he watched Patsy most days to establish a routine. She took the girl to school, the little boy to pre-school. She went running. Liked to keep in shape, did Patsy. He kept up with her easily – he was no slouch in the fitness department. In fact, his job demanded it. A serious walker-climber, he was a survival expert in any wilderness except the city. Humanity was the most dangerous predator.

He found it hard to believe she wasn't in a relationship.

He'd slept with her when they had shared a house as teenagers. Christ, that was nineteen seventy something – more than thirty years ago! He was usually stoned and she was usually naked, clad in just heels and suspenders. Every boy's dream. She was a tiger in bed and the fact she was seriously chasing Redman added a different sort of spice to it. He could let rich Jack do the boyfriend bit with the hearts and flowers and keep her in posh panties while he enjoyed her liberal state of mind. It all fizzled out when Jack's hippy ex-girlfriend, Anna, caught them at it and they cooled it for a while. Williams was a right pain in the backside, interfering and judgemental.

Then Patsy declared she was up the duff. Every boy's nightmare.

'How do you know it's mine?'

'The dates? Jack's careful, you're a waste of space in that department.'

'Bit random that, isn't it?'

'Oh, piss off.'

'Fine with me. Not interested in any sprog, I'm going places I am.'

'Like where? The drop-out centre?'

After that, he *forced* her to make an appointment at an abortion clinic but she bottled it at the last hour and broke down. The tears, the fighting! Jesus, he'd not wish that on anyone. She might seem hard on the surface but there was no way she was giving up that bunch of cells. Maybe she was enjoying the attention, who knows? Not long after that, she got engaged to Redman, which was not much of a surprise and if he was honest, a fucking amazing relief. They didn't see much of each other for a long time and he missed the sex. Actually, he came to realise that he missed more than that. Anna Williams had a rough time as well if he recalled; ditched by Redman and failed all her exams. She was a stuck-up cow though, kind of supercilious and untouchable. It's a pity they couldn't have got it together but she looked at him and Patsy as if they were the bottom of the food chain.

When he bumped into Patsy a year later, he managed to convince her they should carry on.

'I think we're pretty good together,' he said, and the bitch rolled her eyes! The first time he'd confessed his feelings to a woman and she mocked him. The anger came out of nowhere. He panicked, plucked at her underwear, and pushed her onto his bed. 'Lie down.'

'Such a sweet talker. You're going to have try harder than that.'

'Mess me about and I'll tell Redman everything.'

She laughed. So he hit her. She listened, and then they'd had rough sex. In truth, he wasn't sure what had happened. She liked it like that sometimes, she made no secret of it, but he may have gone a bit too far and in truth, it was a breaking point of sorts. He made Patsy do a blood test with him and the kid. They were both curious but in hindsight, for very different reasons. She was probably hoping it was Redman's after all and she could tell poor little simple Simon to shove it, but it turned out he *was* the daddy. He felt nothing. The only satisfaction was the possible hold it might mean over Patsy. He even boasted about it to that stuck-up cow Williams when he was drunk in a club and she read him the riot act. That was a laugh! Sanctimonious cow. Patsy could stay married to Jack for all he cared, he didn't have a problem with that, but he knew he'd blown the extra-curricular activity with his dumb behaviour.

Patsy paid him to clear off and keep his gob shut. Classy. That was a low point in his life, but the money came in handy with a mild cannabis habit and boozing all day. He didn't touch any of that shit now. He had a hobby instead.

He acquired a pair of powerful binoculars. At first he was amused by how much he could see. If he climbed round the back of the houses onto the allotments and lay flat under the shrubs, he could get a close-up on her tits when she was hanging the washing out. Every time she bent down to the basket to grab her Janet Reger knickers, they fell forward and hung there weightily. Not quite so pert but he could imagine holding them again. Next door had a better pair, but her washing was cheap and nasty. Patsy's stuff was all lace and rosebuds. Very girly, very nice.

The really interesting thing happened when Redman turned up in a white Range Rover Sport and stayed the night. He nearly got caught out having a good look at his swanky car. The shock when the door flew open and he came flying out! For an office boy, the guy could fucking run. Adrenaline pumping, skimming over walls and fences, he only got away because he knew the back streets and managed to crawl under some broken fencing and escape through the allotments, stumbling over turnips and spuds. It was crazy, but he was laughing by the end of it.

When he got the money it was like a sign. £220,000: not bad for a mountain guide with a couple of rooms and a row of boots to his name. His parents had died within six months of each other and he'd wasted no time getting the house on the market. It was unsettling in there, looking at his old room and all the tat his mother used to collect, but it brought a few quid in, getting the place cleared. It was cathartic in a way. Not that he'd been abused or knocked about. No, his mother had simply been neglectful, a depressed drunk.

He packed in the job and acquired a car and a laptop. This opened up all kinds of opportunities to feed his obsession. No, it wasn't that, he was re-training; Private Eye Banks. His daughter was out there somewhere, and either Jack or Patsy would eventually lead him to the pot of gold. The thought of seeing Chelsey had him in a lather of anticipation.

Every time a car pulled up outside Patsy's house, his hands shook and his bowels turned to water. But it was never her. Maybe she lived abroad or in London, she could be anywhere.

He followed Jack for several days. This guy's life was seriously *full-on*. Office, swimming pool, office. He swam something like fifty lengths at any one time. He watched once through the glass till the attendant tapped on the window and mouthed something unsavoury so he had to sit in the car and wait. Redman would eventually come out, towelling his hair, phone glued to his ear. 'Tony? Yeah, if the vendor's happy with that, go ahead. Get on to the solicitors, will you? Don't want to hang around with this one.'

Big hot-shot deals in the car park. Then it was Patsy's house to collect the little girl. He never picked up the toddler. Had the dirty bitch played away again? Was that behind the divorce? There was no big Cheshire house anymore, but Redman had family coming out of his ears and a thriving business from the looks of things. And then he'd belt down the A55 to North Wales every few days. What was that about?

Yeah, Redman had it all, whereas his own middle-age was empty, more so than his life had been as a teenager, because at least then, his parents had been around and he'd had a few mates.

The more he discovered, the more his frustration grew. There was another son, he had a brother, a sister. It wasn't fucking fair. Some of that family was *his*. He used to think Redman had got the raw deal, laughed behind his back for years. He smoothed out the society news page and read it over and over. His daughter, holding on to Redman's arm. Looked like she had a kid as well. A grandchild ... he was a fucking granddad! He'd never thought about it before. Paternal love, commitments, and responsibilities were not concepts he understood or was ever really comfortable with. But things changed, they *could* change.

The weather improved, better for stake-outs and watching. Not that the grimy streets around his flat were any indication that the seasons were changing. He preferred the countryside, he just couldn't afford to live there. Redman could though. Over a couple of months, he'd established that Gwern Farm was his luxury weekend retreat. Very nice. The day he saw Anna fucking Williams walking two labradors and a collie, he nearly had heart failure. He'd know her anywhere – tall with big tits and loads of hair. They held hands and went for walks. Very touching, childhood sweethearts back together.

The gundogs were a bloody nuisance, he had to make sure he was downwind all the time.

He took his tent and his camping stuff. When he wasn't exploring the hills, he was finding new hidey holes to lie and watch. Conwy was teeming. He bought a selection of hats and grew a beard. With a pair of dark glasses, he could wander anywhere and no one was any the wiser. Even if he bumped into Redman or Williams, there was no way they'd recognise him. Like a proper private eye. Simon Banks, private investigator. Jammy rich bastards a speciality.

For some reason, Redman started collecting the boy, just for short periods of time to start with, then it was with the girl and over to the farm. There was some sort of family get-together, a birthday maybe. The older son was there, a good-looking blond with an interesting piece of Cheshire totty dressed a bit like a rabbit with a white tail. Very nice. These toffs knew how to pick the right playmates. He'd seen plenty of action around the Dirty Duck in Wilmslow and when he got the chance, he intended to spend a bit more time in Cheshire, just to see how the other half lived.

He knew it was Chelsey before she got out of the car. Tall, slender, strawberry blonde. The binoculars were glued to his face, pressed into his eye sockets, not wanting to miss a second.

'Dad?' she shouted. 'Is it alright to let the dogs get wet?'

He nearly shouted out. Redman's reply was muffled from inside the house, but she carried on walking with the little one, a boy in dungarees. The kid had something glinting in his hand, like a necklace. The dogs bounded ahead and slid into the lake, and the toddler laughed and pointed. It touched something he'd never felt before.

'I'm here, love,' he said to himself. 'Daddy's here.'

It was emotionally exhausting. Sometimes he had to stop watching and lie on his back and look at the clouds instead. He'd imagined it would be enough just to see her, but in less than twenty-four hours, he was itching to speak to her. When Redman picked up the little lad in the garden, his frustration bubbled up like lava. In fact, watching Redman's life made him feel like a kid again, looking in the toy shop window at all the things he couldn't have. A feeling that real life was happening elsewhere and he was behind a thick pane of glass, banging on it with his fists.

Chelsey went home after a couple of days, and he was torn between following their car and watching Williams hang clothing on the line. It was a proper old-fashioned washing line with a wooden prop, like his mum used to have.

Calvin Klein boxers and a row of denims went up. Her underwear was plain white but he kind of liked that. She had a sensual, wholesome look to her. All that rural sexuality was something he hadn't considered before, but she had the kind of body a man could trek across for days and still find hidden dips and hollows. Naked, and covered with over-ripe fruit. Such a pity he disliked her so much. On the other hand, hate and desire fuelled an interesting sexual charge when they pulled together.

By the time he'd thought about moving, the bloody car had gone. Not such a blow though, because he found her gold necklace in the grass. The kid must have dropped it. It had her name engraved on a long gold chain. It felt natural to slip it round his neck for safekeeping. In truth, he didn't really want to pack up and bolt down the motorway again. Jesus, he didn't know how Redman lived like this. The logistics of the two locations were a bloody nuisance. He couldn't settle. Maybe Redman was thinking along the same lines because something happened to change some of this. A To-Let sign went up in Patsy's garden. His vigilance stepped up a gear. One morning in July, Redman turned up and collected the kids, then stuffed his car to the rafters with duvets, toys, and suitcases. Then it was a transit van collecting furniture. He followed at a discreet distance, his heart pounding, armpits running with fresh sweat. He couldn't lose them, not now.

When the van pulled into Conwy a couple of hours later, his first incredulous thought was that Redman was moving Patsy into the farmhouse for a threesome but no, the van dipped out of sight and onto the service road along the quay, stopping outside one of the cottages. Very nice.

He gave her a couple of weeks to settle in. Patsy upped the ante for some reason. Her sloppy tracksuits went and she was back to wearing fashionable clothes – not high couture or whatever it was called, that would have looked daft – but smart casual. Man-catching outfits, tight trousers, and low-cut tops, shoulder straps that kept falling down, floaty little dresses that blew about in the sea breeze. Every time Redman called, she came to the door in something different. She was subtle with it; bit of leg one day, cleavage the next, always tossing her hair this way and that. Right little tease she was. Laughing, holding eye contact. Oh, yeah, she wanted him alright.

There was an old sunken bench on the shale beach, nestled in behind the town walls and it was no particular hardship to sit there in the sun and watch all the comings and goings. If he climbed the stone steps onto the walls, he could look down into her backyard all day and no one would think anything of it. He pretended to be bird watching, which was a laugh because wasn't that the truth?

One Sunday morning, an older woman collected the kiddies and headed towards the park, and he knew this was the time. Even so, it took some courage to knock on the door. His hands were shaking and his insides felt like he was on the high seas but the adrenaline was pumping as well, a bit like the night Redman chased him. She snatched open the wooden door, big smile at first, probably thinking Granny had forgotten something, then her expression dropped. 'Yes?'

A beat. 'Don't I get an invite in?'

'I don't think so. Who the hell are you?'

'You know me.'

A sharp intake of breath. In the split second as the penny dropped, Patsy went to shut the door but his foot rammed it open. He was inside the living room in seconds, the door slammed shut behind him with his heel. They could hear the sounds of the quay, voices surprisingly close as they walked by, but he could have robbed and raped her and no one would have known.

The thought of that made his mouth water. She looked like a rabbit caught in the headlights. Never had a single statement summed up that one delicious moment when he was powerful and she was struck dumb. He locked the door and pocketed the key, knowing there was no escape out the back, just towering medieval walls covered in bird shit and moss.

'Get. Out. Get out of my house,' she snarled, her voice hoarse.

'It's not yours though, is it? It's part of Redman's empire.'

He moved across to the sofa, bounced on the cushions, then made himself comfortable. She moved in front of him.

'What do you want?'

He licked his lips. 'My daughter.'

It was the first time he'd said it aloud and the impact was truly magnificent. Patsy looked like she was going to throw up.

'If you mean Chelsey, she's not your daughter.'

'We both know that's not the truth.'

For a moment, the silence was so loud it seemed to pound out the passing seconds with heartbeats. He swung his rucksack down and counted out the cash onto the coffee table. Ten grand. It didn't look much – in fact it only made a little pile next to a fancy fruit bowl and some kids' puzzles, but her eyes were popping. 'What's this?'

'My debt. I'm repaying what it cost for my silence.' He sat back and propped his legs on the table. 'You see, I'm not liking it much any more. I want to shout to the world … see that young woman? She's mine, she's my daughter.'

Patsy wavered, eyes darting to the cash. She hadn't changed much, she was likely already totting up how many pairs of shoes it could buy. 'Where have you got that sort of money from?'

'I'm a man of means these days,' he said, and patted his inside pocket. 'More where that came from.'

She was impressed. There was a greedy look about her she couldn't hide. Redman must be keeping her on a tight leash. Not that he blamed him.

'Jack is Chelsey's father, nothing can change that, not after all these years.'

'I think you'll find it can. There's the small matter of a blood test. I've still got the paper from the clinic. Reckon she'd be interested in that. I wouldn't even need to write a letter explaining it.'

'You were just a lousy sperm donor.'

Sarcastic bitch. He sprang to his feet, breathing heavily. She instinctively moved away, but he grabbed her hair and yanked her head back. 'That's upsetting, you know? I'm trying to do the right thing here. Pay the money back and be a real good daddy.'

'Was it you creeping about in my garden? Following me down the street? Stealing my underwear? It was, wasn't it?'

'I just want to see Chelsey.'

'See her in what capacity? Just barge in and start spewing rubbish? First thing she'll do is call the police.'

'Right, so the three of us are going to sit down and explain it to her. Or maybe I'll send her a copy of the blood test, keep it nice and simple. What do you think?'

'I think the same now as I did then. You're not thinking like a grown-up, are you? What if Jack and I don't go along with your big comeback?'

He let her hair run like sand through his opened fist while he considered this. He hadn't really thought that part through. Fact of the matter was, he knew he was pretty inept when it came to talking about feelings and

104

stuff, but Patsy wasn't. There was plenty of information on the Internet about her and some French fraudster getting the better of Redman, so she must be an expert by now. He shoved her backwards and she almost fell over the hearth. It triggered something hot, like a ball of anger but he had to keep it all together for his little girl. He knew he needed help to approach Chelsey. She was properly educated, he didn't want to mess it up, but it was hard keeping this fact uppermost in his mind when he set eyes on Patsy or Williams. It was easy to get carried away with his other fixations.

He wasn't sure why this should be but women had always been trying to either out-fox him or taunt him. There was no doubt in his mind that they were all-powerful – except during sex, he'd always had the upper hand there. He'd love to capture that somehow. Imagine if he could channel it to do his bidding. The thought of that kind of control was highly arousing.

'I might have to think of something else, something less … pleasant.'

Nothing. No flicker of fear as he'd hoped. Patsy was one cold bitch – either that or she hid it well. She nodded towards the money and folded her arms. 'So, this ten grand is some sort of bribery?'

'You can look at it any way you like, love.'

Her eyes were the colour of jealousy, the colour of banknotes and hard emeralds.

'I'll need time to break it to Jack. Then if you want me to smooth the way to our daughter, I'll need another ten grand. That's a lot of delicate, heart-breaking negotiation on your behalf if you want me to make it good for both of us.'

'We always did talk the same language.'

'In the meantime, stay away from her. No contact.'

'I think I hold all the cards, love.'

'Only in your dirty little mind.'

'If you want a second instalment you'd better be nice to me.'

She laughed, and he came close to grabbing her lying, cheating mouth with his hand, twisting it out of recognition. Somehow, he found enough control to leave her standing there. He fumbled for the key and let himself out of the house, then walked briskly down the quay, fingering a pair of Williams' knickers in his pocket.

CHAPTER SEVEN

Jack

It was the first weekend they'd had alone for several weeks. Mid-July was its usual mix of stormy grey skies and humidity. In sympathy, Anna was preoccupied. Of course, the major underlying reason was obvious – Patsy had moved. On the upside, there was a new art gallery opening in town, and she was determined to approach the owner with a fresh collection. This was slightly unusual for Anna. She was normally happy to take on commissions for family pets and landscapes.

'Half my underwear's missing,' she said, rooting through the drawers. 'I don't understand. It's getting less and less every week.'

'Have the dogs stolen it?'

'Why would they start doing that?'

'I don't know, I'm just trying to think of reasons. Hooper ate all those socks once, do you remember? On the X-ray it looked like he was having puppies.'

She gave a quick smile. It was her birthday. The previous day, Lottie and James had presented their gift: two new ducks in a crate tied up with ribbon. She was genuinely thrilled. As a total departure from presents in the past, Jack'd bought her a ring, an antique sapphire the same cobalt as her eyes, the colour of the lake on a summer's day. The plan was to take her for a five-star lunch at The Lakeside Hotel and present it there, knowing full well she wasn't the marrying sort. Maybe they'd never marry, maybe it would just mean a long-term or forever engagement, but it was a gesture on his part which would hopefully go some way to alleviating the insecurity which seemed to have crept into their relationship. If he was honest, it was a long shot. Anna was not the sort to be bowled over by something sparkly but he felt the need to make some kind of personal, no, some kind of *public* declaration.

His mobile buzzed once on the bedside table, then died. Seconds later, as usual, the landline started ringing in the hall. And ringing and ringing. Anna tutted, pulled on a wrap, and padded downstairs.

There was a curt conversation, then she shouted, '*Jack!* Patsy.'

He swore under his breath. When he got to the hall, Anna was holding the receiver with her hand over the mouthpiece.

'What does she want?' he whispered. 'Did she say?'

'I've no idea. Probably a new tap washer or ... I don't know, maybe she's lost the number for her manicurist.'

He took the receiver and watched her retreating figure go into the kitchen, flip-flops slapping on the tiled floor. Patsy was hysterical. There was no other word for it, she could barely get the words out. Something about Simon Banks.

This threw him. 'Banks ... Simon Banks is in Conwy?'

'He's that peeping Tom, been pinching my bloody washing. He didn't deny any of it. He's followed me here and forced his way in. Jack, he *raped* me once. He wants to see Chelsey, tell her the truth. I'm petrified.'

'*Raped* you? Fucking hell you never told me that.

Where are the kids?'

'With Isabel, I think she said the park. Why? What are you saying?'

The rest of the call was gibberish, with Patsy mostly sobbing. He raked a hand through his hair. A range of scenarios ran through his mind. Kidnap, ransom … missing washing. Yeah, stolen underwear was more his level.

'Calm down. I'll be there in ten.'

The news went down as fully expected with Anna. She gave him the stare, arms folded, but he made to dive back upstairs. 'I need to speak to Patsy face to face.'

'Can this not wait?'

'I'll be an hour, tops.'

There was little point talking over the phone. He needed to see her eyes. His ex-wife was an amazing liar when the mood took her. Although, something about that chase down dark streets at the beginning of the year lent her story the ring of truth. It could have been Banks, it was definitely a man rather than a youth. He hunted round the bedroom for clothes. Why was everything always a bloody stress? No sooner had he dealt with the considerable emotional turmoil which was James when another issue came under scrutiny. It was all Patsy's fault. If he stopped trying to be rational – and any form of rationale was only for the sake of the children involved – he'd get on a plane and go missing.

No he wouldn't. It wasn't in him to run from problems, he had to face this head-on. He took a detour through the park first and sure enough, there was his mother, James on a swing, and Lottie picking daisies. He left his car in the council office car park, deserted on a Sunday morning but for dog walkers, and began to stride across the grass. They didn't see him till the last minute and it struck him how simple it would be to just grab one of his children and run. A rise of nausea had him scanning the park. It was vast, a swathe of well-kept grass and a maze of paths and planted borders running into woods. The mouth of the river sparkled in the rising sun, the noise and bustle of the quay just discernible, mostly gulls and the slap of sail ropes. Closer to hand, he could hear children playing cricket and the thud of a ball hitting willow, an open-top bus roaring past on the main road. The sounds of summer, families on holiday. The innocence made it more alarming.

'Daddy!' Lottie said, and cannoned into his legs.

He lifted her into his arms and wondered what he was going to say. Don't go off with any strangers, will you? No matter what they promise. Would they have a choice? They were so small and vulnerable, a man could snatch them both in broad daylight, knock his mother to the ground. It took Isabel several minutes to operate her mobile phone, switch it on, find her reading glasses.

'Jack, what are you doing here? Isn't it Anna's birthday?'

'Oh, just passing through, popping into Spar. Out of milk. Lottie, take your brother to find some daisies, I want to have a word with Gran.'

Lottie tutted and rolled her eyes but snatched his small hand and dragged him across the grass. He was a quiet child, subservient in the shadow of his sister's personality. When Lottie went to drama school, he was hoping he could take him out and about, just the two of them.

His mother sat on one of the swings. 'Go on, what's this about?'

'There's reports of a sex pest in the area, just wanted you to be aware. Don't leave the children alone or anything.'

She shot him an indignant look. 'I never leave them alone! I didn't hear that on the news.'

'It's on the Internet.'

'Oh, well I daresay there's all sorts on the Internet.'

Like lots of people in their seventies, his mother saw the Internet as something far out in space, although she was shrewd enough to know when he was covering up. Eager to escape her eye, and since there was nothing else he could say, he kissed them all goodbye and went back to his car. They waved as he drove along the single-track road then disappeared from sight when he took a sharp left down onto the quay and parked outside the cottage. Patsy was watching for him and snatched the door open the second he got to it.

'What the hell are we going to do?'

'Stop panicking for a start.'

'He'll be watching. He'll know I've called you. He thinks you know nothing! I have to confess to you first and then we all sit down and tell Chelsey.'

He flopped down onto the sofa and drummed his fingers on the arm, his eyes locked on hers. She perched opposite as if expecting him to come up with all the answers. Too many people knew about it, that was part of the problem. Anna and Philipe, although Philipe was still inside and it was doubtful he'd be interested despite his threats of blackmail at Chelsey's wedding. Anna had told Hilly, and no doubt she'd passed on the gossip to Bryn. Potentially, it was another mess waiting to explode, but there was no way he was letting Banks destroy his daughter's life like this; nor was he going to be manipulated.

'How do I know he's been here?' he said, glancing around.

Her mouth dropped open. 'I would *never* make up

something like that.'

'Is it true that he forced you?'

'He raped me!'

'Why didn't you go to the police? Is that how you got him to clear off all those years ago?'

'No, that was later. Look, I was pregnant and he did a runner. I was seventeen, I panicked.'

'Go on.'

'Jack, you know all of this! We met up again later and that's when it happened. He wanted to have an affair, and I wouldn't. We did the test and he got aggressive.'

'Why *now?* That's what I want to know.'

'I don't know!'

'Well, did he leave an address or a contact number?'

'No, nothing. He looks like he's been living rough. He just seems like a sad, lonely tramp to me.'

'Has he asked for money?'

'No. He's still got a copy of the test though, threatened to just send it to Chelsey.'

He locked his fingers together and gnawed his knuckles, his eyes never leaving hers. 'If he comes back, you've told me. I'm angry. I need some time to cool down. If he wants to take this any further he comes through me and me alone.'

'What if does something stupid, or dangerous?'

'I don't see how that would further his cause, do you?'

'So, if he comes round, I tell him I've told you the truth?' She took a deep breath. 'So, we're not going to tell Chelsey then? I mean, maybe we should –'

'Of course we're not going to fucking tell her!'

She smiled. He made sure he had an angry face and slammed the cottage door on his departure. Actually, he *was* angry, and drove over to the bird sanctuary, where he sat with a cigarette and stared at the herons on the river.

They were half an hour late for lunch. Anna raised her brows as he drank a full glass of champagne without drawing a breath. Their table was on the hotel decking overlooking Lake Crafnant, the perfect spot for a proposal. The ring didn't have a box, it was in a tiny envelope pinned to his leather jacket's inside pocket.

They both ordered local trout. The water was low and a couple of wild ponies browsed amongst the wild garlic, bellies swollen with overdue foals, manes and tails so long that they trailed on the ground and collected bramble. It reminded him of the rift between Hilly and Anna, and the dozens of questions from Lottie about Hilly's ponies. Weirdly, it also reminded him of Patsy and Chelsey.

'So, what was the emergency?' Anna said.

'Do we have to talk about it? I mean, on your birthday?'

'Why not? I'm sure it'll be amusing.'

He played with the stem of his glass. 'I think I know who's pinched your underwear.'

'See? I'm laughing already.'

She listened without interruption as he related the conversation. The trout arrived and the waiter refilled their glasses with a honey-coloured Chardonnay. He wasn't hungry but ate anyway, to save himself from getting too drunk to drive home.

'This is delicious,' Anna said, and clinked her glass against his. She didn't look like a woman in her middle years. She wore a long sleeveless dress with a midnight blue wrap across her shoulders. Most of her hair was piled up, a lot of it falling down.

'What do you remember of Banks? Is he capable of violence?'

113

For a moment, she looked across to the water, hazy in the afternoon heat. 'He certainly had a hint of danger about him. I'm sure that was half the attraction. There was some drug taking, nothing too serious but that was a long time ago.' She took a measured breath and turned to meet his eyes. Another long beat before she spoke. 'Maybe on this occasion, Patsy might actually be right.'

This was not the reaction he'd been expecting. 'Right about what?'

'About telling Chelsey the truth. Otherwise this is going to hang over you forever,' she said quietly, then threw her napkin down. 'Actually, I'm sick and tired of these games Patsy plays with you. How many more paternity issues can she *possibly* come up with?'

'You kept Chelsey a secret as well, if I remember rightly.'

The second he said it, he regretted it. She sighed, closed her eyes. Long eyelashes briefly touched olive skin, then she looked up at him with an odd expression. Disappointment – or something darker?

'Sorry. Sorry, I'm rattled by it,' he said, reaching for her hand.

'You see, that's the trouble. Patsy knows this, likely Banks will as well. Do you really think after all these years this will make any difference to your relationship with Chelsey? She's old enough to handle it, Jack.'

'I'm not backing down, I can't.'

She folded her arms on the table and considered the fish head on her plate. 'Let's go home.'

They walked silently around the perimeter of the farm. The ground was hard and dusty. Even the dogs were subdued and the cloudy humidity had them panting within minutes and flopping down under the trees. He couldn't decide if the verdant growth of the countryside meant seclusion, or ideal cover for a spy. Once upon a time, they might have waded into the lake to swim, maybe made love and lie on the banks to dry, but not this time. All he could see in his mind's eye was Banks, crawling along on his belly like a reptile, with Anna's knickers in his teeth. What he really wanted to do was scour the heather and gorse bushes looking for signs of a camp, thrashing at the undergrowth with a long-bladed scythe.

Not so long ago Llyn Gwyllt held all manner of significant, romantic memories. Now it seemed more representative of an ocean of differences between them, and its translation – wild water – was especially apt.

In the bedroom, the delicious contours of her body enveloped his. Slick with sweat, they neither noticed nor cared. The sweet smell of her hair and the intense rhythm of their lovemaking was practised in its familiarity. Anna was unusually voracious. She fell asleep in his arms, the contented sleep of lunchtime food and drink followed by great sex. The window was open, curtains pulled hastily, and the glow of late afternoon sun was diffused.

A long time later, she said into his chest, 'I love you so much.'

As the Land Rover ate up the empty road early on Monday morning, thoughts of this scene had him distracted enough to almost miss the exit onto the A55. It was stupid to imagine her enthusiasm was some kind of apologetic desperation, but her opinion on the Simon Banks dilemma niggled away at him.

The ring lay next to his heart, still sealed in its packet.

By the time he pulled onto the forecourt at the office, the proposal had all but vanished from his mind as he entered the maelstrom of his other life. The farm was always an antidote to whatever stress was going on with the business, but he'd never considered this analogy the other way about.

During the following few days, he had little time to think about Simon Banks, although it constantly hovered on the periphery of his thoughts. It was at night when he was trying to sleep that his brain decided it wasn't going to cooperate. Anna was completely alone with a mobile phone that didn't work properly. Josh no longer lived there. He wasn't even around for the summer holidays – he was teaching English to children in Cambodia. Her only bodyguard was a partially sighted labrador with arthritis. The other dogs were either too timid, or in the case of Hooper, had a bloody hearing problem. In his mind's eye, he saw her letting the dogs out last thing at night, and Banks barging in. No one would hear her scream for help.

He sat bolt upright, fumbled for the clock. Ten past three in the morning.

Had he got it wrong? Moving Patsy into his personal life was already eroding the edges, but then he'd be reminded why. Open day at the school. He'd not travelled in with Patsy, but she'd been there with James, doing a good job of convincing everyone they were paying parents like everyone else. James was just beginning to accept him as a major part in his life so he couldn't very well ignore them. They'd sat together in the performance room, James on his lap.

His ex-wife had been dressed exactly as one would expect, in a demure summer dress and low-heeled shoes. Her hair was tied back with a velvet ribbon and she looked fresh and friendly, clapped politely when the other children did their bit. Lottie had been dazzling in such a clinical space, like discovering exotic fruit in the desert. She had no fear of an audience, and her childlike innocence coupled with startling moments of mature clarity had everyone fooled. She recited a long poem from memory – Jack didn't even know what it was – and enacted the character parts with facial expressions and body language. If the truth be known, he was slightly in awe of her. Lottie had always been his princess, he was closer to her than his other children. It was disconcerting that she was developing into a miniature version of her mother. Also disconcerting that photographs appeared in the local rag of him and Patsy stood together with James and Lottie. If Anna had seen them, she said nothing but it felt uncomfortable all the same.

He couldn't decide if it was worse to keep quiet about the whole thing or tell her and make fun of it.

'It was torturous,' he'd said in the end. 'The Yummy Mummies were out in force.'

'Then she'll fit right in,' Anna had said.

House sales had slumped but as was usual in these circumstances, the desire for rental property took up the slack. He moved Tony in to this side of the operation and put Oliver on the front desk. Time for a change. Oliver liked being in the back office, so he was fully expecting the glum face but Jack liked staff to know everyone's else's jobs.

'Dad, I hate being on the desk.'

'You mean you have to talk to people?'

'It sucks.'

'Cheer up and put on a happy face. When you've done six months I'll think of something else.'

'I'm not doing six months!'

'Twelve, if you don't get the hang of it to my satisfaction.'

'Fuck's sake.'

Oliver slouched into the sales area and Jack printed off his diary for the day. First was escorting three American businessmen around possible houses to rent for six months. Company lets were always lucrative; there was never any hassle getting paid and quite often the contracts rolled on. He collected them from the Manchester Imperial Hotel and headed out to the rolling green plains of Cheshire. As usual, Jack was expected to know the historical background of every black and white timbered pile, the opening times of Tatton Hall, and where they could buy authentic presents for their wives.

His hands-free mobile rang. Lottie had somehow managed to change the ringtone to something by Britney Spears – Lottie's latest obsession. Not only was he distracted by the conversation with his passengers, he was also in a hurry to silence the music, something about milkshakes in the yard. So much so he failed to look who was ringing before he hit "accept", something he never normally did if he had clients with him.

'Redman.'

Lottie's voice came over the speaker, loud and clear. In the confines of the car, she was overpowering, both in volume and delivery. Perfect, chilling enunciation. 'Redman, I need to have a word with God about this hole.'

A pause. 'What hole?'

'The lady hole.'

Some throat-clearing and sniggering in the back seat. Jack hooked the phone off and pressed it to his ear. 'Sweetheart, Daddy's at work, I'll call you back in a while.'

'It's *disgusting*.'

'Lottie, I think you should talk to Mummy about

118

this and I'll call you later.'

'Mummy's not here. I'm not Lottie anymore, it's babyish. I'm Charley with a Y.'

'What do you mean Mummy's not there? Where is she?'

'Outside, talking to the man with the big thing in his trousers.'

Jesus, what the hell? He negotiated a busy junction with one hand on the wheel. 'What does he look like?'

Some scuffling noises. 'I'm looking now ... he's got his easel out again.'

'Right. So she's just outside on the quay, talking to someone who's painting the boats?'

'She's holding his palette and he keeps all the brushes in his pocket in a long hard thing.'

'I see ... Look, be good and keep an eye on James. I'll call back, alright, Lottie? I mean Charley, with a Y.'

A theatrical sigh. 'Alright, but I'm not discussing this with Mummy because she won't tell me the truth. She says it smells of flowers.'

The guys from Orange County were visibly loosened up by all of this. Even with the phone pressed to his ear, he felt sure the conversation had still been audible. It was difficult to concentrate after Lottie's phone call. Did Banks paint scenes of the harbour? No, that was crazy. His imagination was on unpaid overtime.

They arrived at Alderley House. The sale had fallen through earlier in the year, but the company director of Twilight Times was a prime target. Not only would he be able to move the family in, but he may also see the house as potential for one of his care homes. While they were busy looking at the covered swimming pool and weed-infested tennis courts, he called Patsy's mobile and read her the riot act about leaving the children alone.

'I was five minutes, five yards from the house.'

'That's all it takes. Who were you talking to?'

'Peter. He's opening an art gallery. He's painting the cottage.'

'Oh, yeah, Anna mentioned him. Have you heard from Banks?'

'It's only been a day! You're going to have to be cooler than this.'

'Says you, you were in a right state.'

'I feel better now I've told you.'

'What's Lottie going on about?'

'Oh, she's started menstruating.'

'She's only ten and a half.'

'It's not unusual.'

This was thoroughly depressing. Did that mean she was no longer a child? It seemed cruel, incomprehensible. She was no longer Lottie, she was Charley with a Y. It was one of those life events that reinforced the passage of time, reminding him that change was inevitable, that nothing stayed the same.

On Friday, Jack was organised in good time for the weekend and set off early. He planned on fitting some powerful security lights to the back of the farmhouse and maybe some kind of camera to the front of Quay Cottage. James had been on the phone to him, asking to go to the farm and see the new ducks. This was a breakthrough in their tentative relationship.

Anna called him when he was halfway there. 'I need to cancel.'

'Cancel what?'

'It's good news, in a way. The new gallery? Peter Claymore wants a load of canvases from me.'

'That's fantastic!'

'The only trouble is, and you're going to hate me

for this, but I need to be alone for a few days and get some ideas together. It's a really tight deadline, I'm not sure it's worth you coming over at the moment. Just give me a couple of days?'

'But I'm halfway there!'

'Oh. Oh, this is awkward.'

There was a horrible silence. 'What do you want me to do, Anna, stay in a hotel?'

'I just need to paint. I can't do it next weekend because of the wedding.'

He thumped the steering wheel and indicated to pull over. 'Fuck. I forgot about the wedding.'

'Just give me some space, please? Why are you so wound-up?'

'Why do you think? Banks is roaming free!'

'Oh, for goodness sake. I can't live like this. Look, I'll be locked inside most of the time.'

'With your mobile switched on? We should have a codeword … *marry me.*'

A beat, a laugh. 'That's two words. Alright, if it makes you happy, I'll bolt the doors and keep both phones in my pocket and *if* I get kidnapped, I'll call you and ask you to marry me.'

'Don't make a joke out of it. How do I know Banks isn't holding a knife to your throat right now?'

'Jack, stop it.'

They ended the call and he sat for a moment, watching traffic zip past.

This had never happened before. He'd taken it for granted that they were together over the weekends. He knew she needed creative space to work from time to time, but why should that mean he wasn't welcome? A flame of angry fear leapt around his guts. He drove to his mother's cottage, passing the turning for Gwern Farm and continuing along the mountain road towards the golf course. This meant passing Hilly's place.

Children were turning out ponies at the end of the day and there was another rub.

Isabel had visitors, neighbours from the looks of it, because there were no cars. A group was clustered on the patio with gin and tonics , classical music filtering into the garden. He walked easily down the side of the cottage and made a mental note to suggest fixing a gate across, with barbed wire across the top. Snog, her dog, was preoccupied with a bone under the tree and never lifted his head. Another useless guard dog.

At least his mother was pleased to see him.

'Jack, what a lovely surprise! This is my eldest son, everyone. Will you have a drink, love? Where's Anna?'

An old boy piped up. 'Are you the one who's getting married?'

He tried to smile. 'No, er, that's my younger brother, Danny.'

'Next weekend, it's come round so quickly,' his mother added, and talk of the wedding dominated the conversation.

He followed Isabel into the kitchen and helped himself to a beer from the fridge, flipped the cap off, and took a long draft before he said anything. 'Anna's got some project on, so it seems I'm banned. Can you put me up tonight?'

She moved around the small kitchen, concentrating on fetching ice and lemon. 'Yes, of course.'

Once he'd thrown his overnight bag onto the bed in the spare room, he took his mother's dog for a twilight walk so he could smoke and avoid the small talk. The tail end of Conwy Mountain was a sharp pull up from the circle of bungalows nestled in its embrace, but Snog was up for it and kept looking behind to check Jack was still following. At the top, the collie ran across the heather, stalking and chasing rabbits, while he perched on a boulder of slate and lit another cigarette.

He imagined that it would be easier when his life was consolidated around the farm, but maybe he was being unreasonable, selfish, because he was trying to make it easier only for himself. He tried to imagine concentrating on filling out spreadsheets with someone else's children running about. He got that part, he really did. It was the rest of it that irked, like he wasn't allowed to visit. Across the darkening hills, the same infused sky was setting over the sea, the quay, and the farm. The silence was alive with the odd frantic toots of blackbirds and the singular cry of something predatory overhead, maybe a buzzard.

The dog stood in front of him, panting heavily, tongue lolling.

Maybe it was a creative thing. Or maybe it was a Patsy Redman thing.

CHAPTER EIGHT

Anna

Monday morning, and Anna was reduced to calling Redman Estates to talk to Jack. It had been an odd weekend, but at least she'd been able to finish the piece for Peter Claymore. He'd wanted something to showcase in the window of the new gallery, to attract media attention and pander to the local historians. This told her he knew exactly what he was doing.

Engrossed in her work, all thoughts of Jack and his problems were distanced from her mind. She'd needed this distraction badly. Claymore had opened up a whole new world of possibilities for her. Attempts in the past to be recognised as a serious artist had failed. Pet portraits and landscapes had been her creative world for too long and she needed someone to believe in her. Claymore promised so much more, and it was deeply gratifying that she'd achieved something on her own merit rather than with Jack's help. It not only boosted her flagging spirits, but it restored her professional confidence and on a personal level, had her walking tall again. Who cared that Patsy Redman was in town?

Clare put her through to Jack's office and her heart thumped with a mix of feelings.

'Jack, I'm sorry about this weekend.'

'I missed you.'

'I missed you too. Are you and Ollie coming over on Friday, as planned?'

'If that's alright.'

It was an awkward conversation. He'd spent most of Saturday working in the Conwy branch because Gina had called in sick, then all day Sunday hanging around town with the children in the rain. She asked all the questions, so the information wasn't presented to make her feel guilty, but the upshot meant she felt like the wicked stepmother. The guilt was terrible, but then a small surge of defiance crept in when she looked at all the work she'd achieved.

Jack didn't really understand the creative process. He thought you could turn it on or off like a laptop; start work, stop work. She'd tried to explain the ebb and flow of inspiration, that intense desire to project something onto canvas transcribed from her heart and mind, but she wasn't convinced he totally understood her. Peter Claymore did.

In the past, the foundations of her art had always seemed deeply connected to the farm and the mountains, but Peter had thrown her a challenge. He wanted portrait studies. The characters of Conwy, he'd said, and they'd chatted about possible subjects.

'I'm talking past and present. Can you work from photographs? I'd like to document the character history of the town.'

'I've no idea, but I'd love to try.'

'Let's meet, I'd like to show you the gallery.'

It was no hardship meeting him for lunch at the local bistro. He was an attractive man, open-faced and full of energy. At first, she was unsure if he was flirting with her. She hoped not – she wanted the artistic recognition so much more. He must have read her mind.

'Are you married?' he said. 'You don't mind me asking?'

'No, and no I'm not married, but I do have a

partner. And a grown-up son from a previous. How about you?'

'Divorced. We parted on good terms, I wanted kids and she didn't. I wanted to open a gallery and she didn't. That's about the measure of it. So, here I am, on the other side of a cancer scare. No baggage and looking for some fun.'

'Oh, I can understand your priorities.'

'I'm afraid I may behave rather badly at times. I hope you'll be able to turn a blind eye.'

They laughed, and she was grateful for his honesty. He'd asked a question of her and her response had not altered his original proposal. Sandwiches arrived, and they got back to the subject in hand. He was both passionate and knowledgeable about art, and she enjoyed discussing her craft with someone who understood what she was talking about.

'Do you paint?'

'I dabble,' he said, 'but I'm nowhere near your standard.'

This made her heart surge. 'I've struggled for years to be accepted as a serious artist.'

'Well, I intend to do something about that. I only want to showcase local people, sculpture as well.'

The renovations he'd made to the antique shop were impressive and she was flattered when he asked her opinion on the interior walls. The building was dated 1593 and had stood empty for years, locked in one of those dead-end situations where it was protected by Cadw but no one had the cash to save it. It was a spooky place; low ceilings, thick walls, the wattle and daub visible in huge patches where the plaster had crumbled away. The air was oppressive with dust and thousands of years of history. Rumours of ghosts dominated local gossip from time to time.

'Every single door and window frame is crooked,

it's like some sort of medieval funhouse.'

'Oh, please don't fix it.'

He shot her a grin. 'No intentions of.'

'And I think you should consider leaving some of this exposed,' Anna said, peering at the mildewed lime wash.

'Yes, I'm glad you said that. My problem is getting enough natural daylight in here. As a second stage of the project, I'm going to try and get this back wall replaced entirely by glass. What do you think? A step too far?'

'Wow, no that would be amazing. A total contrast to the rest of it. The old and the new.'

'Exactly! We'd not only capture the evening light, but once the back area is cleared, I'm thinking we may get a river view as well. If I promise to spend a lot of money retaining the rest of it, I'm hoping for some cooperation with the planning authorities.'

'Good luck with that. Lots of people have tried and run out of cash, and patience.'

'Well, my other line of work is very different, the one that earns a crust. I'm hoping to source all the right materials for this project fairly easily. You see, I have a factory on the outskirts of Chester. Supplies to the building trade.'

'Oh, perfect.'

He nodded and met her eyes. 'So, tell me, Anna, are you in on this?'

'I'm very in,' she said and he took her hand with a firm handshake and a cool smile.

'Good. I'm staying at The King Edward most weekends, or whenever I can get away.'

'I know it well.'

'You know where to find me, then.'

The whole experience was uplifting, something which belonged entirely to her, and reaffirmed who she was. On the other seat of this emotional see-saw was Simon Banks. It was intolerable that he could be watching her at home, making her think twice about hanging washing out. Ridiculous. In fact, wasn't it unfair of Jack to expect her to put up with all of it on her doorstep while he was seventy miles away going about his business?

In a fit of pique and desperate for a sounding board, she'd gone over it with Hilly and confessed not only some very dark feelings but opinions which Hilly didn't agree with.

Hilly said she'd overreacted to everything – *was* overreacting. 'I wish you'd not confided half this stuff in me. I hate secrets, especially dangerous ones.'

'Patsy gets away with murder all the time, why can't I? Why are you looking at me like that?'

'Because I think you're playing with fire. I think this Simon Banks could be a loose cannon.'

'Which is why it needs sorting out.'

'But not by you. It's Jack's problem.'

Deep down, there was a logic to Hilly's take on it all, but her own resentment was deep and unforgiving. She expressed some of her fears to Jack. 'What if Simon gatecrashes the wedding?'

'I've thought of that, and it does worry me, but I'm not sure what I can do about it,' he said. He was driving, she could hear the rush of traffic down the phone.

'Well, have you heard anything?'

'Like what?'

'I thought Patsy had some agreement with him?'

'Only to tell me *if* he turns up again, and that he has to come directly to me, that's the deal.'

'I see.'

Her voice came out snappier than she meant it to, and he lost his composure. She could practically feel his stress seeping down the line, spinning through the atmosphere and hitting her in the solar plexus.

'Look, I feel like I'm being blamed and none of this is my fault. Well, is it?'

She wanted to scream, yes! 'No, I guess not.'

Isabel rang on Thursday morning, asking if Anna would like to collect some glasses and linen to help with the arrangements. Danny had given her a generous cheque to cover whatever she imagined they may need to entertain the guests for about three hours while they did photographs and killed time before the reception.

Then it was Ellie, excited about the outdoor photography around the farm. 'Dan tells me the scenery is gorgeous and you have *white* ducks.'

'Yes, Aylesbury.'

'Will they pose?'

'We can ask!'

Then it was Chelsey, confirming that she and Mike would arrive on Friday and if it still alright to stop-over as they couldn't really afford the hotel. Of course she responded in the affirmative and tried not to worry about any possible repercussions. Anna immersed herself in baking and tying hundreds of white ribbons and horseshoes to the apple tree. The only blot on this productive day was Benson, who was dragging a hind leg more often. The vet had warned her about this. His deterioration and the valiant efforts he made to go into the garden to do his business rather than have an accident in the house tore repeatedly at her insides. Sooner, rather than later, the day would come when she would have to make the most awful decision on whether or not to end his life.

When Jack was around, he'd help by slipping a sheet under his front legs like a sling, taking the weight from his joints. When she remembered the animal he used to be, she wondered if this was the end, but when he saw the sheet, his tail would wag and he looked at them with almost human gratitude. Sometimes she wondered if this appreciation was for their benefit. Was it because he knew how to make them smile? Although a few minutes in the garden restored him sufficiently to wander off by himself, to head into the long grass under the trees where he'd stand with four legs splayed at an odd angle. Eyes closed, ears and nose lifted, he looked like the gundog he used to be, remembering the scents of his youth. When he'd had enough, he'd look to the house and even if Anna hadn't seen him, she somehow knew it was time to bring him in again.

At Isabel's house, she wasn't too surprised to see James playing in the soil with a collection of diggers. Snog was tied to a long rope under the tree.

'She's too boisterous with the children, not like Benson.'

Anna nodded and swallowed down the sudden catch in her throat. They went out to the patio with a tray of tea and she wafted her hot face with a brochure about the mobile library.

'Patsy and Lottie have gone into Liverpool. Or did she say Chester?'

'Shopping, I expect.'

'Something about uniform for Lottie's new school.'

It wasn't the heart-to-heart she'd been hoping for. In fact, their conversation failed dismally on all fronts, mostly because James needed a lot of reassurance and kept interrupting, and then it felt awkward, wanting to have a bitch about Patsy when her child was there. She talked about the gallery and although Isabel was thrilled for her, she wanted to talk about her grandchildren more. Clearly, having two of them so close by was something of a novelty, but several times she caught Isabel looking at her watch and making excuses about the traffic. Unable to relax, aware that Patsy could turn up any minute, no doubt with dozens of shiny bags, Anna made to go.

'Anna, is everything alright between you and Jack?' Isabel said, catching her off guard. 'Only, he stayed here last weekend and he seemed terribly down.'

'My fault entirely, a lack of communication.'

'You were busy –'

'Yes, I *was*, actually.'

She regretted snapping but Isabel laid a hand on her knee. 'I do understand, but please don't take it out on Jack.'

'I'm not taking it out on anyone, I just feel under constant pressure to be reasonable about Patsy being here.'

'She hasn't put a foot wrong so far.'

'Oh, she's behaved reasonably for all of what, three weeks? Give her a gold star.'

'All I'm saying is, don't let it come between you and Jack, especially any arrangements with the children, otherwise she really will have something to get her teeth into.'

'Something to get her teeth into? Can we please not talk about Patsy as if there's a separate code of behaviour for her? She uses the children like pawns.'

Isabel looked into her cup, swirled the dregs, and placed it back on the tray. 'Chelsey, Oliver, Charlotte, and James are Jack's children, as well you know, are they not?'

She watched Isabel collect the remains of their afternoon tea before she replied. 'Yes, I know.'

Chelsey and Mike arrived on Friday and helped with

the general preparations. This amounted to dressing the trestle table with Isabel's linen and arranging dozens of white roses in a mismatch of vases. If it was dry and not too windy on the day of the wedding, they could maybe set it up under the apple trees. Chelsey made fortune cookies with cryptic messages, some sweet, some rude. Mike cut the grass, snaking a green path through the long grass, skilfully avoiding the swathes of foxgloves, spent harebells, and dog roses right to the edge of the lake.

Jack and Oliver arrived in the afternoon with recent haircuts, suit bags held aloft, and helped ferry crates of champagne onto the marble shelf in the pantry. Chelsey and Jack hugged and kissed a tad awkwardly; she holding pastry-laden fingers away from his shirt, he with benevolent affection. Anna watched them avidly, convincing herself that any coolness on Chelsey's behalf was in her imagination, but the moral dilemma of the situation swam in her head with confusing direction.

'Sorry we didn't bring Sammy,' Chelsey said to Jack, 'but he'd be into everything, and I wanted to help Anna. Tell the truth, I'm a bit scared of the lake. He's obsessed with water at the moment and I wouldn't be able to take my eyes off him.'

'And you wanted a break, I totally get it. Don't worry, love.'

For a while it was chaotic, and she was grateful for the distractions of guests and wedding preparations, but then at odd moments it felt almost unnatural with Chelsey and Jack in the same room. Knowing the truth of something so monumental coupled with the sting of Jack's remark on her birthday still fresh in her mind struck her as blindly hypocritical. On the flip-side, he was loving and attentive. When they had a few moments alone, he embraced her properly, searching

133

her eyes and kissing her with such sensitivity that she felt her resolve crumble, revealing a dangerous transparency. He wiped her eyes for her and kissed her salted cheeks.

'Don't cry, I'm sorry about last weekend.'

'Me too, not your fault. I just want to forget about it.'

'Thanks for doing this for Dan and Ellie, they'll be surprised when they see everything. They won't be expecting any of it.'

'I've enjoyed it, I like Dan a lot.'

'I know, but I really appreciate all the work you've done.'

She looked around and gesticulated towards the worktops, groaning with homemade nibbles. 'Chelsey and Mike have done lots too.'

He took both her hands in his. 'I, er … *I'm* picking up Lottie tomorrow, so Patsy doesn't need to turn up anywhere.'

'I can handle it, Jack.'

'I just don't want anything to spoil the day.'

'It won't.'

He tightened his grip on her hands. 'And anything you need me to do, anything support-wise, I want you to know I'm genuinely pleased about the gallery and I won't get in your headspace when you need to work, I promise.'

Later, Jack treated them all to dinner at the King Edward. They elected for a bar meal, partly so they didn't have to dress up, but also because the wedding ceremony and main reception was taking place there in less than twenty-four hours. On arrival, they noticed the main function room was closed to the public. Oliver peered through the glass doors. 'Looks busy. Hey, it's all black and white. Bit classy for Uncle Dan, isn't it?'

They laughed and made their way to the public bar. The second she walked in, Anna was aware of her. She'd recognise that laugh anywhere. She was impossible to miss too, perched on a tall stool, drinking cocktails, wearing a sheath-like black dress, the hemline of which had risen up considerably. Her hair dropped like liquid caramel to her shoulders, highlighted with natural chestnut. She looked up and waved, eyes lingering on Jack and taking in every inch of him, long enough to be noticeable. Anna felt his hand in the small of her back, propelling her along, asking what she wanted to drink, but then she was wholly distracted by Patsy's companion. Peter Claymore. He spotted her instantly and slid down from his stool.

'Anna! What great timing. Let me buy you a drink, introduce you to my new friend here.'

Blessed confusion then, as Chelsey, Mike, and Oliver caused a noisy distraction greeting Patsy. Jack ordered four pints of ale and a glass of white wine, shouting across the bar.

'Mum, you look gorgeous. Is that dress new?' Chelsey said.

'I thought I'd treat myself. Harvey Nicks,' Patsy said in a loud whisper, as if no one was meant to hear. Jack frowned at this and asked her where the children were.

'They're with Isabel.'

'*Again?*'

'What do mean, again?'

Peter looked from one to the other throughout this exchange, then raised his brows at Anna and pulled a funny, perplexed expression. 'Oh, um … I feel a bit of twit now. You all know each other?'

Patsy plucked the slice of lemon from the side of

135

her glass and began to suck and nibble the edges. 'Sort of. Jack and I have four beautiful children together,' she said, then shot him a coy smile. 'Haven't we, Jack, darling?'

Jack kept his eyes on the barman and went through his wallet. 'Yes, but we're divorced.'

'Oh, that's right, he's an *ex*-darling,' she said, mostly to Peter, who laughed like only an embarrassed drunken man can in the face of an unwanted shock. '*Four* children. Wow, I had no idea! I knew there was two small ones … Jack, I hope I've got this right, you're *Anna's* partner?'

'That's right.'

Oliver sniggered. 'Shovel job, eh, Dad?'

'Nothing of the sort,' he said, putting pints of beer onto a tray. 'Here, carry these drinks to the table.'

Peter apologised, then introduced himself properly. The men shook hands and Anna was left with nothing to do or say. At their table, the three youngsters had taken the single chairs, leaving Jack and Anna to take the settee facing the bar. Mercifully, Jack was right behind her. He rolled his eyes discreetly in her direction and leant in. 'Where's she got the money to be shopping in Harvey Nicholls?'

'I'm more interested in the current situation with the stalker-rapist on the loose. She doesn't look especially distressed. Still no news?'

Jack just shook his head, eyes downcast and focused on the menu. With Chelsey sat at the table he didn't want to go there. Eventually, food came, with another round of drinks. By their third pint, Jack, Mike, and Oliver were incapable of detecting even the mildest hint of tension. Patsy and Peter Claymore behaved as if they were lifelong friends, laughing loudly in sporadic bursts so everyone turned to look. Both were equally drunk and holding on to each other.

They looked like lovers already, playing with the decorative fruit and twirling the little umbrellas. If Patsy hadn't been there, Peter would likely have joined them. She told herself it was just bad timing, but it felt like something had been stolen from her, whipped from under her nose when she wasn't paying enough attention.

Occasionally, she'd look up and Chelsey would catch her eye. Or she'd catch Chelsey's eye as she studied Jack and this was disturbing. It served to make her feel incredibly stupid, the way Patsy's presence played on her emotions, the way one reaction slid faultlessly into another, depending on whether she looked at Patsy or Peter, Chelsey or Jack. It wasn't healthy, picking over relationships to such a degree, let alone analysing her own gut reaction to everything, but it dominated the evening and bled into the night.

At home, Jack fell into a beer-induced sleep across the bed. Mike and Oliver had stayed out, declaring they'd either crash at Josh's empty flat or at Patsy's cottage. Patsy had disappeared with Peter, no doubt to his suite. It was all so convenient for everyone, this depositing of children with their doting grandma who was grateful for every opportunity, and then the freedom of which bed to choose, which bed to offer other grateful members of the family. She could do no wrong. She was just having fun, like Peter.

She struggled with Benson, lifting him for a final visit to the garden. Chelsey came to help but even between the two of them, they couldn't manage a smooth lift and the dog yelped with pain, then immediately wagged his tail. It's alright, I'm fine, he said, it's not your fault I'm old and crippled.

Chelsey said, 'You should get Dad to put some lights out here, it's pitch black.'

'What, and have every passing fox, cat, and bird

light up the entire garden every thirty seconds?'

'Sorry, I didn't think.'

'No, I'm sorry. I'm tired.'

Back in the kitchen, Chelsey eyed her warily and fiddled with the roses lined up on the dresser. 'It's going to look stunning.'

'Yes, forecast is dry so that's all we need,' Anna said, and went about filling the dogs' water bowls in the Belfast sink.

'Anna, will you and Dad marry one day?'

'Oh, I don't know, why?'

Silence. She looked over her shoulder to see that Chelsey had dropped down into the old armchair by the Aga and was rubbing her eyes and the bridge of her nose. Something told her the marriage question had been a red herring.

She dried her hands quickly. 'What is it? Chelsey, tell me.'

'I've had this letter.'

The air felt clotted with those four words. They came flying at her from every angle and wedged in her throat. She watched the young woman delve into a zipped compartment in her handbag, long, fair hair falling forward. She passed the letter to her and she read every single typewritten line twice then looked at both sides of the envelope. Throughout this, Chelsey kept up a stream of questions.

'Have you any idea who could have sent it? It's not signed, so whoever did this is either a coward or a cruel prankster. But who would suggest that Dad isn't my real dad, and I should go and have a blood test? You used to live with Mum, didn't you, when you were teenagers?'

She faltered at this. 'I did, only for a short time.'

'Is there anything you can tell me, anything at all? I mean, I used to think you and Dad were having an affair, how wrong did I get that? My mother can be … tricky. I'm not immune to her, you know. But I trust you totally, I know you wouldn't lie to me.'

'Chelsey … I'm really sorry but it was such a long time ago, you'll have to ask your mum about this.'

'That means there *is* something. Tell me what you know!'

'No, it doesn't mean anything! It isn't my place to talk to you about this, you really need to talk to your mother.'

Her face was tormented, but she folded the letter and stuffed it back into her bag. Somehow, they managed to claw back to where they were, at least superficially. A tired nod, an apology of sorts.

'Please don't say anything to Dad. *Promise* me, Anna.'

'I won't, I promise. But *you* have to promise me you'll take this up with your mother.'

'I know. I'll talk to her after the wedding.'

It was midnight before she climbed into bed, laid her head on Jack, and cried silently into his chest.

Jack was calling up the stairs to her. At first she thought she was dreaming, the urgency was frightening, the way the voice came closer until he was standing at the bedroom door. 'Are you awake, love?'

'Just about.'

She knew instantly it was something to do with Benson. She sat on the edge of the bed and Jack passed her dressing gown to her. Her limbs felt heavy and slow as she made her way downstairs. Benson had crawled from his bed to the back door, where he lay in a pool of urine. He recognised her through bleary, ashamed eyes. Every shred of strength he had left went into moving his tail. *I'm sorry, I made a mess.*

She knelt on the cold tiles and buried her face in his

coat. It seemed cruel that it was still so vibrant and luxurious other than a light greying around his muzzle, and yet everything inside was breaking down. The top of his head smelt intoxicating, of grass and adventure, of selfless, unconditional love. It smelt of home, faint traces of lavender from his newly washed blanket.

Jack was on the phone in the hall, his voice low, words indistinguishable.

It was a beautiful summer day, full of rolling clouds, light, and shade. It was like the day he'd been born, she said. Jack carried him to the apple trees fluttering with white ribbons, horseshoes, and hearts. As they neared the right spot, hundreds of crows took flight. She sat propped against one of the twisted trunks and Jack struggled to put the dog down on the ground next to her. He kissed her face and went to fetch her some coffee.

They settled together in the long grass and Benson's nose twitched as she talked.

Presently, two vets arrived, one a young trainee who kept staring at her soiled dressing gown and the crazy decorations in the garden. They examined the dog, and the older vet said he'd likely had a stroke and did she want to go ahead with euthanasia? They were gentle without being sentimental. She nodded, Benson's head in her lap, his useless limbs spread on the grass. Jack was silhouetted against the sky, chewing a nail. The trainee vet shaved a neat patch of hair from Benson's foreleg, while the other hunkered down next to her with some paperwork.

'Miss Williams, I need you to understand that once I have administered this injection, your dog will be clinically dead.'

Jack muttered some expletive and turned away. She knew he was wiping his eyes.

'I understand,' she said, and signed somewhere in

the indicated box.

One hand on his beating heart as the lethal drug seeped into his bloodstream, her eyes on his. He licked her hand, almost twice, and even then it seemed apologetic, as if he was trying to comfort her.

I'll see you on another dappled lawn, or a bright sunlit mountain under a thousand cloudless skies.

His silent heart, his soulless eyes. Instantly, the giving and taking of pain. Now all the pain was hers, and there was some comfort in that.

CHAPTER NINE

Jack

Anna was clinging to him in the kitchen, or was it him clinging to her? His rational mind kept saying to get a grip, it was a dog ... just a dog. Anna had lost dogs before of course, but she'd had a special bond with Benson, everyone did. He didn't think he'd ever get that image out of his mind; Anna, in a white nightdress sitting under the apple trees, her long hair flowing, Benson lying dead in her lap. She'd insisted on being left with him like that for half an hour. He'd made the vets some coffee in the kitchen, eyes constantly drawn to the window. After a while, the vets went back out and put the dog in a straw basket with handles, covered him, and took him to the pet cemetery. He helped Anna to her feet. She was so cold by then that he was worried for her but once inside, she'd willingly gone through the motions of having a bath, a warm, sugary drink. Her colour returned and she smiled, simply kissed his hand but rather than soothe his emotions, this action turned his insides turn to mush. She moved fully into his arms, and that's when Chelsey found them.

'It's Benson,' Anna explained quickly.

'I know, I saw,' she said. 'I'm so sorry, Anna. Do you want me to change some of the arrangements? Dan will understand.'

'No! No, don't be silly,' she said, finding another

tissue. 'We'll pull ourselves together in a moment.'

'Are you sure, love?' he said.

'Let's not tell anyone though, not today. Today is about Dan and Ellie, and besides, I couldn't cope with all the well-meaning sympathy. It's a blessing to have the wedding to think about.'

He was grateful for her firm handle on everything but he knew the real sense of loss would come when the weekend was over, and she was alone again. Those odd moments when habit had her turning to see why Benson hadn't followed her down the garden, why she couldn't hear the familiar clack of his claws on the tiles. She seemed to have had her fair share of misery lately. It had been unfortunate that Patsy had been with Peter Claymore the previous evening, and when Chelsey and Oliver were drawn in to this exclusive tableau around the bar, it had been doubly awkward. Of all the single available blokes in the town, Patsy had to flaunt herself with Claymore!

Obviously, it had spoilt the evening for Anna, but Jack had bigger worries to mull over.

On the pretext of walking the other three dogs, he set out to clear his head and check out possible hiding places on the quiet. He failed on both counts. The dogs wouldn't come away from the apple trees and despite his fear of Banks popping up in the undergrowth, what the hell could he do? Even if there was no trace now, there was nothing to stop him walking down from the hills later and perching somewhere to watch, maybe make a move. The thought of him shambling like a hobo into the garden, barging into guests, scoffing food and drink off the tables, and hunting down his daughter was unthinkable.

Inside, Anna and Chelsey were washing and drying glasses. He didn't want to leave them alone and he didn't dare discuss this fragile situation with Anna.

They were carrying the trestle table outside when Oliver and Mike turned up, looking like extras from a horror film.

'Look at the state of you,' he said to Oliver, relieved they were back. 'Where've you been all night?'

'Mum's. I crashed on Lottie's bed and Mike had the sofa.'

'Where was your mother?'

'Dunno.'

Did this come under the heading of predictably tiresome or downright bloody irresponsible? In his befuddled mind, he wasn't sure. A phone call to Isabel revealed that she'd not only had both children overnight, but that Patsy should have collected them an hour ago.

'I don't mind,' she said, in that voice that meant more or less the opposite. 'But I really need to get myself ready for this wedding.'

'I'll come and get them.'

'Would you? James isn't very well, we've had a restless night.'

He drove round to the cottage, not surprised to see his mother looking worn-out. James was full of a cold and running a temperature, and Lottie was as high as a kite. Now she was Charley with a Y, he wondered if it would make it any easier telling her about Benson, but he knew the answer to that. James had fiddled with the television and lost the settings. His mother passed Jack the instruction book and made him a cup of tea. James crawled into his lap, sucking a thumb. For a while he was distracted by the biscuity, baby smell of him and the visit took longer than planned, but this small acceptance by James was immensely gratifying.

An hour later, he pulled up outside the cottage. At least

145

Patsy had the sense to look through the window first before she opened the door. She was still in her full cocktail regalia, looking as fresh as a daisy. He couldn't help looking her up and down. 'Have you just got in?'

'What's it got to do with you? And why the mutinous face?'

'Stop leaving the children with Mum, she's shattered. It's Danny's wedding today, you're not being fair.'

'Oh, stop fussing, Jack! You're like an old man.'

He hung around in the sitting room while she went upstairs with both children, James yelling at being woken from his nap in the car and Lottie complaining about taking a bath and washing her hair. His mobile buzzed and he almost dropped it. Every call now could be Banks.

'Hey, brother.'

'Dan, how's it going?'

'Just got to the hotel. I need some best man duties doing. Can you pop to the chemist? I need some extra-strength Imodium, I can't get off the lav.'

'Are you serious?'

Loud laughter down the phone.

'Oh, very fucking funny.'

Despite the laddish jokes, he knew his brother was nervous, and he should maybe have gone round there but he couldn't split himself in two. The irony was he was actually more strung out than Dan, so what good would that do? As he shoved the phone back in his pocket, Patsy reappeared in white denims, a laundry basket balanced on her hip. He followed her into the kitchen and she began to sort through the clothes. 'I wish you'd stop swearing on the phone. James is already trying to copy you.'

'Yeah? Wait till Lottie starts copying you, staying

out all night with some bloke you've only just met.'

She closed the door of the washing machine and fiddled with the dials. 'Sounds like you're jealous.'

'Of what, exactly?'

He counted to five and looked out of the kitchen window, drawing some comfort from the enclosed back yard bordered by the town walls. King Edward knew a thing or two about enemies. 'Has he been back, Banks?'

'No. It's only been a week.'

'That's long enough, what's he playing at? Look, I don't want anything going off today. If he comes round, tell him he *has* to call me and me alone. Don't let him in.'

'I know. I get it, Jack.'

Somehow, they arrived at the hotel on time for the ceremony. It was a thoroughly modern affair. Not going to a church to witness the vows seemed odd to Jack, but the happy couple were both lawyers and dealt with hard fact, so maybe there was no room for the vagaries of religion. It wouldn't be his personal choice and he suspected it wouldn't be Anna's either. She always gravitated to St Celynin's up in the hills whenever she wanted time out, and then the way she'd dressed the garden suggested something romantically spiritual, even if it was only bonded with nature. He liked the simplicity of that.

They took their seats. Black Queen Anne chairs with white bows and a single vase of assorted purple flowers were about the only decoration he could detect. His brother was in a black suit and the men sported purple buttonholes. Anna said they were anemones and signified anticipation.

'Looks like a bloody funeral,' Aunt Beatrice grumbled loudly.

Oliver, seated on the row behind, tapped Danny's shoulder. He'd already rolled up his Order of Service and was using it as a trumpet. Anna was using hers as a fan.

'I see no hymns or singing,' Oliver said. 'This is quite possibly the best wedding I've ever been to.'

'Me too,' Dan managed to say. He was already choked and studying his shoes. His sister, seated to Anna's left, rolled her eyes. Kate and Dan were polar opposites when it came to emotions.

The music started; 'Bohemian Rhapsody' by Queen, and it was slightly too loud to be classed as background noise. His mother frowned and tutted, as did a few of the other guests. The whistling and squealing meant that Aunt Beatrice had turned off her hearing aid.

'They've done it like this so Dan won't be a blubbery mess,' Kate said. 'He hates Queen.'

She was wearing the same black and white outfit she'd worn to Chelsey's wedding; another reminder of the current faux pas with not only his family, but his love life. At least Anna looked serene in a blue dress, a sprig of natural heather on the lapel of her jacket and caught in her hair. She'd swept it into her usual complicated up-do. In another hour or so it would start to tumble down again. He picked up her hand and she gave him a tired smile.

Ellie arrived halfway through 'You're My Best Friend'. Everyone said the bride wore the trousers, but Jack reckoned this was a good thing being married to someone like Danny. She was tiny, very dark, and definitely not pregnant. He'd only met her a couple of times. Ellie wasn't the sort of girl Dan was usually inclined towards, but then the others had never been wife material. She looked bridal though, in a long – very creased – pale dress and purple shrug. His mother said it was raw silk. Neither bride nor groom smiled, but Danny looked at her with almost stupefied adulation. Some of that might have been down to him holding his breath for too long.

'Gran, will the curtains open? It's a bit like the puppet theatre,' Lottie whispered.

Jack did the business with the ring and the ceremony was all over and done in fifteen minutes. Danny told everyone in a squeaky voice how pleased he was to be married to his very best friend. Everyone laughed, although the two mothers clearly thought they'd been short-changed. Shouting and clapping followed the newlyweds into the bar next door and Jack remembered to say something about arrangements at the farm before the younger crowd took root for a drinking session.

'I Want To Break Free' blasted out from the speakers.

'*Well*, this is a rum do,' Aunt Beatrice said.

The real celebration started when everyone arrived at Gwern Farm, and the rather sombre atmosphere was soon lost. Anna surprised everyone, including himself, when her wedding gift arrived; two arty-looking students carrying a harp and a violin, both in battered cases. Oliver helped them set up, then declared they were both snobs because they'd had the good sense to refuse his offer to accompany them with Josh's electric guitar. Pachelbel's Canon in D Major filled the garden. Three bars in and Danny burst into tears. It *was* moving and totally right for both the occasion and setting.

Lottie was fascinated by the harpist, and tried to copy her hand movements. Oliver sniggered and snapped her on his phone. 'My freaky little sister, playing air harp.'

'Oh, how *completely,* utterly beautiful,' Ellie said, and passed a handkerchief to Danny.

Champagne corks popped and other than the stiff breeze grappling with the swathes of linen, it was pretty close to perfect. Even the sun managed a sustained appearance, blotted only sporadically by white clouds. An intermittently hot August afternoon, the icing on the cake. Anna was pouring champagne, so he went to help. 'The live music's a brilliant touch.'

'Stop looking in the bushes.'

'Is it that obvious?'

'Yes! What makes you think he'll turn up, in front of all these people?'

'I don't know what he'll do, that's the problem.'

Lottie tugged at his shirt sleeve. She wanted to know where the dogs were. 'Where's Benson? Is he dressed up?'

Jack hunkered down to her level. 'No, he's not here, love. Anna thought the crowds would be a bit much for him.'

'Well, where is he?'

'In a safe place having a lovely nap, don't worry.'

Hands on hips, she announced, 'I think you're lying, Redman.'

He was saved from further interrogation by someone shouting for help. His heart leapt into action, but it was only Aunt Beatrice slowly sinking into the lawn on spiked heels. One day he might be able to enjoy a family wedding without some underlying tension. His own? When he looked at Anna he was filled with the sort of longing that ticked every box in his perfect woman portfolio. He heartily wished they could put his past life behind them and move on, but in unguarded moments she looked strained, unhappy. Of course, a lot of this was down to Benson but he had the feeling this was only on the surface. When he looked across to Chelsey, she was pensive too, and only raised a smile if he initiated it.

The photographs went on for ages but it was no hardship sitting by the lake with a champagne flute. Jackets and ties were discarded, high heels thrown in the grass. The ducks waddled out obligingly but despite Lottie showering everywhere with food pellets, it was a full-time job keeping them interested long enough to get them in shot. Within minutes they fluttered away noisily, flying low across the surface of the water but then Ellie discovered the semi-derelict cottage. Hitching her dress above the tussocks of long grass, it was declared *another* perfect backdrop. The photographer had his work cut out, lifting equipment over all the boulders and the prickly gorse bushes. Ellie and Dan looked incredibly photogenic, young and vibrant. Ellie in that delicate, palest lilac against the ancient stones, the sepia reeds, and the heather and Dan looking manly in a white silk dress shirt and managing not to cry. Jack understood the dress now; its natural look was so right amongst the rustic landscape. It had been wasted in that soulless room. Someone said they looked like Cathy and Heathcliff. His mother, probably.

The theme continued into late afternoon, when the garden developed an old film quality in the softer light. That blend of casual elegance supplied by striped deck-chairs, aged oaks, and white tablecloths seemed completely right. The violinist changed to a fiddle and merged classical into rock. Some of the guests danced barefoot on the lawn. Then Lottie recited the poem she'd performed at drama school while the musicians took a break. Everyone was happy and relaxed except for Jack. He felt wired, constantly on watch, an extra on a film set where the murderer was poised to drag another body into the bushes. Eventually, the guests would disappear, murdered and thrown into the lake, and he'd be standing there alone.

Despite the promise he'd made to himself, he expressed these fears to Anna when they were packing everything away. First she looked exasperated, then cross. 'Like I said, until the truth is faced over this, it will plague you, *us,* forever.'

'I can't let Banks do this!'

'Jack, he's already doing it. He can do whatever he likes,' she said, stacking glasses back into a box. 'And for all you know, this could be some elaborate ruse he's concocted with Patsy.'

'I can't let Chelsey discover that her real father is some sort of waster who pinches knickers off washing lines!' Another thought crept into his mind. 'What if she was conceived through rape?'

She stopped what she was doing. 'Jack, whose fault is this? Whose job is it to explain and then deal with the fall-out?'

'I *know* what you're saying, but Patsy is still her mother and Chel won't look at it like that. It'll destroy her. All those memories of her childhood, her identity. All wiped away, like it's been a *farce* and I can't be responsible for —'

'It *is* a farce. My life, and all of this here, is *tainted* because of Patsy. I'm sorry, I don't want anything to do with it. I don't even want to discuss it, not today.'

She walked to the house carrying two ice buckets and the hastily folded table cloth under one arm. The garden was finally empty except for him, standing amid rolling flower heads and hundreds of petals tossed like fragrant confetti. Shadows crept across the lawn. The long-stemmed white roses which managed to survive the breeze were laid beneath the apple trees, fashioned into a letter B.

Dinner and the main reception was back at the hotel. Halfway through the *Boeuf en Croûte*, Jack realised his best man's speech was in the inside pocket of his suit jacket, which was likely still swinging on a branch somewhere down by the lake.

'Can you not remember any of it?' Kate said when he finally confessed during the pudding course.

'Not much, no. Somehow I don't think it's going to matter.'

Danny was already at the stage of hugging everyone like he only had weeks to live. There was duck shit sprayed up the back of his leg, his crumpled shirt was already hanging out of his pants, and smeared lipstick on his chin. Isabel followed him around with paper napkins and a bottle of mineral water trying to clean him up.

The master of ceremonies tapped his glass. Speeches were announced and Jack scrambled to his feet. Barely discernible in the darkened room, he could see Lottie busy with Oliver's mobile, crawling under all the tables and taking random pictures. Like the collective buttonholes, there was an air of expectation.

'I remember when my kid brother first fell in love with a much, *much* older woman and got himself in a right old mess.'

His mother's head came up. 'Who was that?' she said, bewildered.

Complete silence in the room, then polite laughter.

Ellie's parents looked nervous and Kate kept drawing a finger across her throat.

'I guess what I'm trying to say is, love is pretty blind when it's the real thing. And that's a good thing, not to put it under the microscope too often. It's stronger than a family bond, more than a blood tie. It's not simply a shared name, it's years of memories. For Dan and Ellie, it's all about those memories, waiting to

153

be made.'

His mother smiled benevolently, his sister went through the motions of sticking a finger down her throat several times. He was aware of Anna, watching him intently across the table, and lost his train of thought, although maybe that was a good thing too. *Tainted,* she'd said. That was a pretty strong word, as though it was unrecoverable. Across the room, a dozen or so mobiles bleeped, trilled, and buzzed. Unable to resist, he glanced down at his own handset to see several blurred images of legs, swollen thighs encased in drooping knickers. An out of focus vision of the future.

Kate whispered, 'Lighten up, can't you?'

'Remember all those games of Monopoly with Dad? You still owe me, Danny boy,' he said to his brother, then addressed the room. 'Debts going back to the days we used to play for cash, leather jackets, and anything else he wanted that was mine. He was always cheating as well. Moving hotels onto Mayfair from Old Kent Road when he thought I wasn't looking. Actually, sometimes honesty is *not* always the best policy, but I'm an estate agent – I would say that, wouldn't I?'

Laughter and clapping.

'Today though, my brother's the real best man. Today, he's won fair and square. So, raise your glasses please, to Dan and Ellie.'

Toast done, Jack reclaimed his seat.

'Well done. Must be your turn next,' Kate said. 'You and Anna?'

'Somehow I can't see that happening. She's pretty pissed off with me.'

'I know. Fancy a smoke?'

Outside in the car park, the castle turrets were black against an indigo sky and the wind had dropped. His sister lit a cigarette and heaved a sigh. He knew what was coming, and she delivered it without preamble. 'You've made a right hash of it having Patsy live on the quay. And no, don't tell me you've done it for the kids, Jack.'

'But I have!'

'You know your trouble? You always put your children before your relationship.'

'I'm not going to be made to feel bad about that. I can't alter my entire past.'

'It's not the past you should be concerned with, it's the future.'

'My children are part of that.'

Kate shrugged, bored with the same old argument. 'If I was in Anna's shoes right now, I'd be selling up and moving out.'

'There's no way she'd do that.'

'Depends how far you and Patsy back her into a corner.'

'It's not all about Patsy, it's not what you think.'

He asked himself a hundred times a day if he'd made a massive blunder by moving Patsy into town, but still couldn't work it out. If he tried to imagine the worst-case scenario, he had no idea how he'd fix it. Disappointing his children again would be soul-destroying. And it *wasn't* all about Patsy, not this time. If he could tell one more person about Banks he would choose his sister for her forthright honesty, but he just couldn't keep telling everyone. He was on the point of explaining about the dog instead when Oliver snatched open the fire door, fuming and clutching his mobile. 'Dad, can you *tell* her, please? Lottie's sent these fucking pictures to every single one of my contacts!'

Relieved to be rescued from the conversation, he delivered Lottie home. The easy joy of walking the short distance down the main street and along the quay was a small, if not entirely valid, compensation. When he tapped on the door, Claymore opened it. It wasn't as if he'd disturbed anything intimate, the guy was actually apologetic for the previous evening. He stepped aside to let Jack enter, then proffered a hand. 'I hope the wedding went well. You've had a beautiful day for it.'

The handshake was firm enough, honest eye contact too. 'Yeah, good, thanks.'

Maybe he should be pleased, given the current circumstances. This was yet another conundrum though, how Patsy's love life impacted on their children. Did he mention to Anna that Claymore had his feet well and truly under the table? He decided not. At least, if Banks had been planning on a big surprise intro, he'd have done it by now, wouldn't he? So he was either playing by the rules or he'd already bottled out. Or he had a different agenda entirely.

Anna was predictably exhausted by midnight. It had been one hell of a day, bittersweet. They left Oliver, Mike, and Chelsey dancing into the night. Dan was totally plastered by then, wearing a paper lampshade and staggering about to Queen's greatest hits. His bride was remarkably tolerant – or was it just that she knew him rather well?

Danny flung his arms around Jack. 'I *love* you.'

'Love you too. But maybe you should stop drinking now. You won't be consummating anything at this rate.'

He strutted around like a Shakespearian actor, holding his head and shouting to anyone who'd listen. 'But I … I am consumed with *love!* I am on a far loftier plane.' Then it was the lampshade under his arm. 'Alas, poor Yorick.'

They managed to escape. Ellie said she'd make sure he got to their room OK, which made them laugh.

Alone at the farm, it seemed incredibly sane and deadly quiet after the noise of the hotel. Anna shed some tears. He hadn't thought to move the empty dog bed but would it have made much difference? She allowed Jack to run her a lavender bath, light candles, and make herbal tea, all things she liked to do when she felt stressed and upset. He found a fresh nightdress for her and then she allowed him to hold her till she almost fell asleep.

'Do you remember how he used to drool in long strings whenever we got the ice-cream out?' she said.

'Dan?'

A beat, a smile in the dark.

Back at the flat on Sunday evening, he looked up Peter Claymore on the Internet. He seemed very well connected and wasn't on the sex-offender's list. So far so good. He needed every positive vibe he could extract from the situation. Although there was a new feeling of – not jealousy, exactly – something he couldn't quite figure out, but overall he decided it was no bad thing having this guy around his children.

As work took over at the beginning of the week, the tension surrounding Banks slowly dispersed. It was busy in the office. Tony was in Costa del somewhere for a fortnight.

'Is Costa in Spain?' Oliver said to Clare.

'No, it's on every corner.'

'No, that's Costa-*lot*. Three quid for a styrofoam cup full of foam decorated with microscopic traces of actual coffee.'

'So, what was she wearing, the bride?'

'Some sort of weird dress. Got any headache pills, Clare?'

Jack closed his office door and tried to zone out of the Monday chit-chat. His desk was a maelstrom of messages, post, sets of keys, and piles of leaflets waiting for his attention, and he'd only been away since Friday lunch time. He called Anna before he left for his appointments. 'How are you?' he said, shuffling brochures into a file. 'Mike and Chel gone home?'

'No, not yet. What do you want me to do with this suit jacket? It's sopping wet.'

'Dry cleaners? I'll, er, give you a call later, up to my eyes in it today, got to run.'

Actually, he didn't need to run anywhere – he needed a cigarette.

Most of the day he was unfocused and on impulse, turned up at the swimming pool before returning to the office. On the surface of the water, he was like a swan, gliding and cool. Underneath, in the dark rushes, his legs were paddling fast, trying to avoid getting tangled in some dark watery bindweed and dragged down to his death. Drowning must be one of the worst ways to die. He pounded through the chlorinated water, did ten lengths of front crawl, then floated on his back.

He should have known from past experience that all of this was going to come back and chip away at his peace of mind. Chip away? Collectively, it was more like a time bomb. Three years of living with his head in the sand had to be paid for. All he could hope for was the strength of mind to absorb the fallout, to deflect the real damage away from his relationships. The idea that he would have to communicate with Patsy to initiate this was something he'd have to live with.

Ten lengths of breast stroke.

He could hear Britney Spears singing in the locker the minute he stepped into the changing rooms. Water dripping down his face and stinging his eyes, he managed to unlock the door just as it rung off. From Patsy, five missed calls, and one from his oldest friend,

Tim. Under normal circumstances he would have made Patsy wait and called Tim, maybe arranged to go for a beer.

'Seems real urgent,' an old guy said, nodding towards the bank of lockers. 'Been a long time since I looked at any milkshakes in any yard.'

He dragged his clothes over damp skin and roughly towelled his hair. In the car, he hit the number for Quay Cottage and she snatched it up on the first ring.

'Something's happened.'

'What? Has he been back?'

'No. Worse. He's written to her!'

'Saying what?'

'*What do you think?*'

He fumbled to light a cigarette and slid the window down. 'How do you know all this?'

'Chel's been round, giving me the third degree.'

'What the fuck did you say?'

'Nothing, I said I had no idea why anyone would do that.'

'Stop talking in riddles, do what?'

'Send an anonymous letter suggesting she get tested.'

'Why would he say that when he has a copy of the blood test?'

'Jack, I have no idea. I've got the letter if you don't believe me.'

He ended the call, started the engine, and pulled out into the traffic.

CHAPTER TEN

Jack

Only a couple of days ago, he'd stupidly thought how easy it was to have Patsy and the children in Conwy. Now it was a pain in the backside. Traffic was heavy right through the Chester intersections and what normally took just over an hour was almost double that. The town was thronging with tourists and access to the quay was blocked because of a funfair. Patsy called him twice. 'Where the hell are you?'

'Trying to park.'

'Go to the King Edward, I'll meet you there.'

'Where are the children?'

'With Peter. He's taken them for an ice-cream, and before you start, he's a really decent bloke and he loves the kids.'

'Loves the kids? You've only known him five minutes!' He took a couple of seconds to remind himself of Philipe. 'Where are you supposed to be going?'

'Speaking to you about the fees for drama school. I couldn't think of anything else.'

Ten minutes later, he swung into the huge car park and strode to the bar. She was in a side booth, an almost-empty glass of wine in front of her. The smell of food had his stomach rumbling but he had to make do with a packet of nuts and an orange juice.

They didn't speak. She slid the envelope across the

table. It contained a single sheet of white paper, a few typewritten words, undated, unsigned. It told him nothing. 'And you think this is Banks?'

'Who else?'

'How did she take it? What the hell did she say?'

'She was pretty angry, confused.'

'I can expect a phone call, then?'

'I told her not to call you, that you'd be devastated by these lies. I said that whoever had done this will likely contact her again if there's any truth in it. I even hinted it might be Philipe being vindictive. We need to buy some time.'

He locked his eyes onto hers and searched their depths. 'I see.'

She sipped her wine through perfectly outlined lips, her hair and make-up flawless. When her eyes widened and looked over his shoulder, he twisted around to see Peter and his two children, with Anna following behind. She was obviously surprised to see him sitting there but as usual, before he could open his mouth, Lottie had to tell him some story about a boat trip and suddenly everyone was talking at the same time. The first thing that struck him was how happy his children looked. The fact that Claymore was enjoying fatherly pursuits was a tough one to swallow, but he was actually likeable in a buffoonish sort of way. He seemed to float easily above all the angst, although Christ knew what he thought of everyone else – faces full of accusation and deep in miserable thought. Anna said he'd survived cancer, so maybe this general air of detachment was his new way of dealing with life, to mentally skim the cream and bypass everything else.

'Lottie, sorry, *Charley,* insisted we all say hello to Jack,' he said. 'And then we bumped into Anna! Hope I'm not interrupting. What can I get everyone to drink?'

'Not for me, thanks, Peter.'

'I'd have thought those school fees would have had you on the hard stuff by now.'

Patsy laughed. Anna frowned. 'What school fees? I thought the first year was free, hasn't she won some sort of scholarship?'

'Has she?' Peter said brightly, then turned to Lottie. 'Oh, well done, princess.'

Jack folded the letter and slid it into his inside pocket. 'Well, yes, but we need a financial plan in place for after that. And then there's the uniform … and stuff.'

Claymore went to the bar, Anna glared and Patsy beamed with conspiracy. 'Oh, *Anna,* sit down and have a drink. It's like old times, let's have a girly catch-up. You know, you haven't changed? Still wearing those eighties clothes, same hairstyle, even. I can imagine I'm back at school.'

'No thanks,' she said, and walked towards the exit. Jack was pinned down by both children and it took more than a few minutes to extricate himself from the situation without appearing odd or rude to Claymore. Peter returned from the bar with another glass of wine for Patsy and orange juice for the children, then straddled an adjacent stool.

'Oh, has Anna gone?' he said, sipping his pint. 'I wanted to talk to her about the new signage.'

'She has one artistic temperament, doesn't she?' Patsy said. 'How long are you over for, Jack?'

'Only tonight. In fact, I might head back later, got a busy day tomorrow.'

Jack excused himself, both children clinging to his legs and begging him to stay. By the time he got out to the car park, there was no sign of Anna. He walked the full length of both main streets looking for her vehicle.

Shops were closing, families were heading back to their caravans, hotels, tents, and guest houses. He paused at the gallery, recognising her work sealed in a glass case in the new window, and fully alarmed. Somehow, this hefty endorsement by Claymore made him proud of her, humbled in a way he'd not understood, or expressed before.

The big landscape was familiar, but the new painting was of King Richard the Second. A copperplate notice informed him that King Dick was crowned at the age of ten in 1377, lured out of the security of Conwy Castle in 1399, and assassinated by the Duke of Lancaster. Power games – had anything changed? The eyes of the portrait followed him, all-knowing, beguiling.

He drove apprehensively along the mountain road to Gwern Farm. When she saw the letter, she'd understand. They'd have a short discussion about it, then enjoy a meal together and he could maybe stay over.

None of this happened.

First it was Oliver on the phone. 'Your dinner's on the table.'

This would have been funny in any other circumstances. 'Sorry, I'm, er … tied up in a meeting.'

'Well, you could have said! What meeting? There's nothing in the diary. Next time let me know *before* I start cooking?'

'Sorry, love.'

Her Land Rover was outside the farmhouse. Hooper barked when he tapped on the door and walked in. The air was thick with the scents of home, a plate of fresh scones on the table next to a basket of duck eggs and some strawberries.

She was making something. 'Anna …?'

'Why did you tell me this morning you were hellish

busy all day?'

'I was. I got a call from Patsy around five concerning this.'

Since she wasn't going to even look at him, he read it out to her while she continued to butter bread.

'At least the truth is out now,' she said.

'Is that all you can say?'

'Don't tell me you've both denied it.'

'Yes, we have.'

She threw the knife down. 'Priceless.'

'You know why.'

'So touching. And thanks for sticking up for me when she was so rude, by the way.'

'Look, the way you stormed off had Patsy lapping it up, why can't you just ignore her?'

'Oh, I can do better than that.' She placed the sandwiches on a plate, shot him a curious look, and went out through the back door to sit at the wooden bench. He followed her, his stomach snarling. 'How do you mean?'

'I wasn't going to get into this, not yet, but that fiasco just now ...'

'What are you talking about?'

'I'm thinking of selling the farm, moving away.'

If Mars had dropped from the sky and rolled like a ball of fire into the lake, he'd have been less surprised. Everything was sucked out of him as if someone or some*thing* had speared an evil wand into his guts and staked the front to the back.

'Moving away?'

'Fresh start. Downsize. I'll be able to pay you back the money you've spent on this place – which will make me feel a whole lot better – and I'll be able to gift some money to Josh. This way he can buy a flat instead of relying on you or waiting for me to die before he can start to live properly.'

'What the fuck are you talking about?'

'Selling. Know any decent estate agents? Jack, my peace of mind has been destroyed since Patsy moved here. I have to double-think. I can't even speak to Peter without wondering how this will be manipulated or interpreted by her. My stomach is in knots every time I go out into my own garden or into town. I can't see that *ever* changing.' She looked up at him, resolute. 'I've had enough.'

'Can we talk about this?'

'Why? I seem to recall me saying exactly the same thing to you a few months back, when you first got the idea about moving your ex-wife here.'

'It's not like that.'

'It is for me. I won't be your convenience.'

He went back inside the house and slumped at the table, unable to look at her. The scones which had looked so appetising only minutes ago held no powers after all. He didn't think he'd ever be able to swallow anything ever again. Hooper came and pushed at his hands. A million thoughts pierced the fog of his mind, unthinkable and painful, all of which propelled him back outside. She hadn't moved an inch, the plate of sandwiches untouched. Her face was wet though, as if she were silently drowning.

'What about us?' he managed to say.

'Jack, I love you,' she said, then turned to face him, 'but I *hate* what you've done.'

After that, he didn't feel able to speak coherently. This time he went to his car. The shock was quite profound despite the warning signs which had been there for months. His mother had hinted at trouble. His sister had been right, Kate had seen this coming. Even Patsy had been right about one thing – it *was* like being back at school, but minus the excitement, the anticipation. Had he learnt anything at all? He'd imagined that by the time he was in his forties he'd be settled. Instead, he felt like a middle-aged child. It wasn't Banks who was the hobo, it was him. The man with no home. He had two choices. Drive back to Wilmslow to look at his dinner in the bin, or go to his mother's cottage and be interrogated.

Neither choice appealed but he couldn't face a hotel either. In fact, he couldn't make any kind of decision. He started the engine and found himself four miles down the road at his mother's place. There was no reply at the front door so he went round the back. She was in her underwear, listening to a play on full volume and he had to tap on the patio doors to grab her attention. One startled look at his face had her reaching for a dressing gown and switching off the iron and the radio. The doors slid back, unlocked.

'How many times, Mum! You need to keep this locked, anyone could walk round.'

'Jack? I thought you'd gone back to Wilmslow?'

'I did, then I had to come back.'

She followed him across the room. 'What on earth's the matter?'

He sat on the floral sofa like a zombie, close to tears. He couldn't remember feeling this pathetic since Leo had died. His mother started with the questions and he held a hand up. 'I don't want to talk, sorry.'

She squeezed his shoulder. 'I'll get you a cup of tea, then.'

'I'd prefer whisky, if you've got any.'

He heard the tinkle of glass and ice from the drinks cabinet in the sitting room. She placed it in front of him and settled herself opposite, nursing a mug and full of expectation.

'I try to do the decent thing and it blows up in my face,' he said.

'Is this to do with Patsy?'

'I've stuffed up big time with Anna.'

He was forced to tell her the briefest of facts but he laid most of the blame on Patsy and the added complications with Claymore. He touched on the dog, on Anna wanting to gift Josh his inheritance, on her wanting to pay back the money he'd spent over the years. These financial aspects were fairly typical of Anna, they were the symptoms of the problem but the reasons he'd stated so far seemed hefty enough without adding in Chelsey, and Simon Banks.

'Move away? *Anna?* I can't believe it. All her friends are here.'

'What friends? No, I've even made that worse, with Hilly and Bryn.'

'You can't be blamed for everything, Jack! And if poor Benson has just passed, then she's not in the best place to be making big decisions like that.'

He drained the glass then stared at it. Even the ice hadn't melted. 'There's something else. I can't go into the detail.'

'Connected to Patsy?'

He nodded in the affirmative and Isabel sniffed with defiance. '*And* she's got money from somewhere. She was having her toenails painted with a diamanté trim the other day. She's worked a fast one on that Mr Claymore, if you ask me.'

'I don't give a stuff about that. Claymore seems willing to be led by the nose.'

She went to refill his glass. 'Have you eaten?'

'No.'

'I'll make you something, you don't want your ulcer flaring up again.'

Everything *was* flaring up, it was like three or four years previous when he'd been going through the mill the first time. Anna had pulled him out of the mire, but this time he was on his own with absolutely no idea how to fix it.

Two hours' sleep. The alarm on his mobile woke him at six. The last time he'd looked at the clock it had been ten minutes to four and the dawn chorus was well under way. Prior to that he'd lain awake, ruminating. Around midnight, Oliver had texted him, 'If you're staying out all night please have the decency to let me know.'

Then an hour later, 'Where the hell are you? I'm phoning the police.'

Jack called him. 'Ollie, don't be daft. I'm down in Conwy. There was a problem with the Taffy branch last night, that's all.'

'Oh, well, you could have said.'

Somehow he managed to get out of bed and into the shower. In the kitchen, he saw that his mother had ironed his shirt and hung it over the end of the ironing board. She didn't need this aggravation. It was bad enough that she'd had to remake one of the beds in the spare room, having just stripped them both of the children's duvets, then cook him a meal and listen to his cryptic moaning. It was ridiculous at his age. He'd imagined it would be him looking after her – but then he'd imagined all kinds of scenarios and within a few hours, every single one of them had been blown out of the water.

He let Snog out into the garden and forced down a slice of toast. He couldn't remember where he was supposed to be, only that it was busy with Tony on holiday. It was tempting to take the dog and go into the hills for the day but it looked gloomy outside, oppressive, and anyway, he couldn't leave his staff to struggle. Partly in order to substantiate his excuses, he called in at the local branch before they opened and logged on to his diary. It was chock-a-block from 8.30.

He'd never make it across to the other side of Manchester through rush hour. In a moment of medieval clarity, he called Oliver and told him to take over his morning appointments. If King Richard could manage a whole country at the age of ten, maybe he was holding his son back a bit.

'Prince Ollie, saddle your best horse, the most fleet of hoof, and lead the first army across the M56 to Oldham Industrial Estate. I've heard no one comes back alive, but I believe in you.'

A long beat of consideration. 'You what?'

'Marlow Homes. We could do with that contract and I'm not going to make it in time.'

'You want me to go pitch for the River Meadow estate?'

'Sure, why not? All the facts and figures are on file, use my laptop.'

'Are you serious?'

'Go for it. Don't go below one per cent though.'

'I can't believe you trust me with this.'

'Just don't let old man Marlow lay an ambush. Have the sense to walk away if none of it adds up to my base figures.'

A beat. 'Right … I'm going in the bloody car though.'

The morning passed in a gentle blur. The good thing about the Conwy office was that he had no decisions to consider, only whether to make another coffee. His branch manager covered all the viewings and appointments and Gina did everything else, although that was on limited time since she was pregnant. For the time being, though, he could sit on the back desk and pretend to be working, although in reality his eyes were peeled for Anna. When he logged in to his emails there was one from Josh. 'Hi Jack, can you please let Mum know I'm OK? Phones are rubbish here. Should be back in a couple of weeks. Been a blast!'

Outside, the streets were still busy but the pace of business was slower, more colourful. This was how he'd imagined his semi-retirement. Now, he had no sense of direction, let alone the motivation to work towards his end goal. Without Anna, what did his life add up to? On one hand he wanted to beg forgiveness, to try and find a way through the mess he'd made. Maybe if he admitted it was a mistake? But was it? He had a duty to his children and they were thriving, even financially it was so much better. Patsy had actually found a decent fella. In time, this could relieve a lot of the other pressures. She just hadn't given it enough time! He hesitated to go back to the farm before he hit the motorway again, but at the last minute steeled himself to call round … to discover she wasn't in. No vehicle, no dogs. Making herself unavailable felt like another slight. No, it was more than that, it was a kick in the balls. Maybe she was just out.

The rooms were serene and restful, bathed in weak sunlight. A magnificent, complex feat of nature that something so huge in the sky could project a beam under the chair in the bedroom and illuminate a pair of his socks. If he needed proof of the lack of sleep, this was it. Two of her paintings were propped on the landing, covered with a sheet. Through the kitchen window, the long garden was blowsy and overgrown. Some pots of herbs and an old watering can had blown over. Beyond this, the lake trembled. He couldn't bear to look at it. His eyes felt suffused with pain. This couldn't be the end, could it?

He collected some of his things and left a note on the table about Josh then drove away slowly, forcing himself to concentrate. Of course, Anna refused to see any of the situation from his point of view, he understood it was difficult but relationships were a game of give and take, of compromise. His compromise was that he lived part-time in two different places and funded everything. If he went down the pity route – and at that moment it was growing in power – he could feel raw anger clouding his judgement.

Oliver rang him an hour later, when he was sat in Starbucks on the A55.

'Hey, Dad, he signed at one and a half! Talk to you later, I'm on my way to Grosvenor's now.'

'Well done, Ollie. Nice one.'

He almost said something about their trustworthy reputation going before them, but decided that he'd let Oliver take the glory on this occasion. When he walked into the office a couple of hours later, Clare was using the hole punch and stapler like weapons of mass destruction. He could hazard a guess as to why. She wanted the office manager post and here was the king's son leap-frogging his way to the throne through birth right. In the old days, women didn't get involved in fighting battles – and how much simpler that must have been – although Oliver would have been rendered all-powerful now, which was faintly alarming. On the upside, Patsy would have been burned at the stake.

Clare followed him into his office and stood before him. 'Jack, who is in charge of this branch?'

'Me.'

'And when you are not here?'

'You.'

'Then can you please remind Oliver?'

'What's he done?'

'I'm not listing everything, it sounds childish and it would take too long.'

'I'll have a word.'

172

Tackling Oliver's cocky attitude was uppermost in his mind for all of five seconds – he had bigger issues to contemplate.

He was wearing a suit of shining armour and living in Conwy Castle with Queen Patricia the First. Their children were safely ensconced in the tower, smiling and waving long silken scarves out of the window. Banks had been captured and thrown in the dungeon. Danny, the court jester, carried Banks' head through the streets on a stake whenever there was a carnival. Princess Charlotte swept through the Great Hall in a glittering pink gown and Jack had his work cut out saving her from the lecherous old men next door on the trading estate.

Anna appeared like the ghost of Christmas past, a lonely silhouette hovering over the lake. She slipped under the water and before he could dive in and save her, she emerged as a galloping winged horse and flew into the sky.

Something woke him, and then it took a minute to grasp where he was. The sofa in the flat, sunlight streaming in, and a police siren in the street. Britney Spears was singing somewhere under the cushions.

'Yeah?'

'You sound half asleep!' Patsy snapped.

'I am, I was.'

He half-listened to her babbling as he shuffled into the shower and switched the water on.

'And he seems to think I sent it! He *thinks* I've sent this letter to pave the way to him meeting Chelsey. I mean, as if!'

'Banks been round again?'

'Yes! Have you not listened to anything I've just said?'

Once she'd repeated it – bullet-point style – and his

173

mushy brain tried to catch up, he said, 'So it wasn't him who sent it?'

'Phone me back when you've woken up properly! And make it quick because he's on his way over to you.'

He ran over the conversation while he scrubbed himself awake. None of it made sense and he felt strung-out with anticipation, too much caffeine, and not enough sleep. Downstairs, Clare and Oliver were busy with clients.

'If a tramp called Mr Banks comes in asking for me, show him into my office,' he said to Tabitha.

'A … *tramp?*'

'Yeah, yeah it's just … you know, the DSS, looking for cheap rentals.'

She gave him the usual hollow-eyed stare, then bent her head back over a pile of brochures and envelopes. In the privacy of his office, he called Patsy and listened to the re-run of events. This time, she claimed Banks had followed her to the leisure centre. When she was watching the children's' swimming lessons, he'd sidled alongside and asked her what the score was.

Cradling the phone under his chin, he opened the slats on the window blind and looked furtively into the street. 'And *you* said?'

'I gave him grief over the letter. I said you were *fuming*. I told him he'd messed up big style.'

'And *he* said …?'

'He denied sending anything! He's convinced it was me. I've given him your mobile number but he said he'd rather sort it out it face to face.'

'And how do I know any of this even happened?'

'Because he'll walk through the door anytime now, that's why!'

She rang off. He sat and watched the street outside,

tapping a pen on his teeth for an hour and forty minutes until closing time. Nothing happened.

There didn't seem much point driving to North Wales at the weekend for two very good reasons. Banks was the first one. If he was deliberately cranking up the tension by delaying his visit, then it was working. On the other hand, Jack still had to see concrete evidence that any of the aforementioned meetings and conversations had actually taken place.

Anna was his other reason. The thought that she'd maybe put the farm on the market was incomprehensible, and he wasn't sure he could forgive her. The thought that he'd initiated it was also incomprehensible. Both of these problems juggled for supremacy depending on his state of mind.

He'd tried calling Anna, and even managed to speak to her.

'I think we need some space,' she'd said.

'Well, that's easy. We've got seventy miles between us without trying.'

He explained to Patsy that he couldn't see the children because Tony was on holiday for another week, and besides, he was still waiting for Banks to show up.

'Well, what the hell's he playing at?' she said.

'You tell me.'

'He'll be watching, following you.'

'Yeah, well, I'll be waiting for him.'

This also got him neatly out of explaining that he was estranged from Anna. *Estranged*. The word tumbled around his guts and his head like tumbleweed in a vast empty space. Despite its ethereal appearance, it hurt like nothing else.

He remembered to have a conversation with Oliver concerning both his immaturity and the hierarchy in the office, then went out and got pissed and stranded somewhere in the Prestbury countryside.

It was mostly Tim's fault.

They started in the Dirty Duck, which was the first bad idea. It was a popular Friday night after-office, end-of-the-week meeting place. He hadn't missed it, this kind of social networking. It was a hunting ground of sorts for contacts and operated like the golf course, more a case of who you knew or drank with in order to seal a wobbly deal. It was also a hotbed for marital affairs and he wasn't surprised to see Clarissa Harrison-Smith in there, working the tables. She was only tolerated because of her vast fortune. Jack tolerated her because he was still trying to sell her Cheshire pile, but multi-millionaires didn't come along too often so that meant possibly years of keeping her sweet.

Tim ordered a bottle of Sancerre and it arrived in a state-of-the-art ice-bucket with two glasses the size of balloons and a selection of tapas on a piece of polished slate.

'Could have enjoyed a three-course meal for the cost of this little lot.'

'Yeah, well, that's the price of pretension.'

'We earn a living out of pretension, don't knock it.'

It was a sultry August evening, noisy with a hundred different conversations and packed to the rafters to such an extent that extra tables were provided out on the pavement. It amused Jack, the way these people seemed happy to sit by the side of a busy road and pay a premium price for the privilege. After a while, the clash of perfumes and laughter seemed nauseating. Gwern Farm was an oasis in his head. *I won't be your convenience.* Had he treated her like that? Maybe he had taken some things for granted, but it's what happened when you felt secure – before he'd damaged it irretrievably with Patsy.

'It must be your love life, for you to have a face like that,' Tim said, throwing wasabi nuts into his mouth. 'If it was work, you'd be talking about it by now.'

'Yeah.'

He went for his drink, and through the bottom of the up-ended glass, saw the blurry outline of Clarissa Harrison-Smith making her way over. 'Christ, don't look now,' he muttered to Tim, but it was too late.

'Handsome men! All alone, drowning their sorrows on a Friday evening. Jack, you must be the best advert for Levi's I've ever seen. Timothy Chadwick, I haven't seen you for decades!'

'You know how it is, Clarissa, the day job, wife, child.'

'Oh, accountancy is so *boring*, you need some fun. Look at some different figures for a change.'

She leant across the table and speared a smoked mussel, her breasts bumping like airbags between their shoulders. 'Oh, big strapping chaps like you can't exist on a handful of shrivelled olives and fancy nuts. Come for dinner.'

'No thanks, we've committed to something else,' he said, eyeing Tim.

'Oh, don't be shy. I need a couple more men to balance it out. Jack has my address, don't you, darling?'

'What time?' Tim said.

'As soon as you've finished up here, just head over.'

She waddled away and Tim grinned at his hangdog expression. 'I've heard about these parties. Come on, could be a laugh, and I'm starving. She's right about this tapas, I could murder some spotted dick.'

'You might have to.'

They hailed a taxi, or rather Tim did.

Jack gave the address to the driver and fifteen minutes later they arrived at her plush, rented apartment in Prestbury. It overlooked the golf course, not too far from where he used to live with Patsy at The Links. On door duty, there were a couple of seven-foot muscle-men who didn't speak or make eye contact. They were shown into the formal dining room, complete with starched tablecloth, glittering cut glass, a red chandelier, and two female waitresses wearing nothing more than white aprons, red heels, and frilly knickers. The theatrics were mildly distracting, amusing to his sluggish, comatose state of mind. The rich woman hiding behind this ridiculous façade must be desperately lonely to lure semi-drunken people out of wine bars on a Friday night for these sort of antics, and despite filling him in on Oliver's misadventure, Tim was still keen to witness it all for himself.

Chairs were pulled out for them. Opposite, three other diners were already seated, two women in evening dress, and a man. One of the women looked stoned already, eyes glazed and unseeing. The other was loud and articulate with a deep voice and big hands.

In the middle and looking nothing like a tramp, was Simon Banks in a dinner suit.

CHAPTER ELEVEN

Jack

'Simon? Simon Banks?' Tim said, sinking into a chair. 'Well, well. Bloody hell, long time no see. How are you doing?'

'Very well, as it happens. Jack?'

Banks stared across the table, smug and supercilious. Jack stared back, dumbstruck. Tim was only aware of the ancient history between Simon and Patsy. He knew nothing of recent developments, otherwise it may have been more than a raised eyebrow which passed between them. Throughout the rest of the introductions around the table, he zoned out. What the fuck was Banks doing here?

'Simon tells me you all went to school together,' Clarissa said, trying to lighten the atmosphere. Silence.

'Don't fancy yours much,' Tim said, nudging his arm. He tucked his napkin into his open shirt collar with a flourish then lowered his voice. 'I can see some five o'clock shadow under that panstick.'

'Starters, everyone,' Clarissa announced, chins wobbling. 'Oysters on a deep bed of wilted spinach.'

The girls in frilly pants served Krug. It was the genuine stuff, about one and half grand a bottle. Banks had a manicured hand over his tall fluted glass. So much for living like a tramp. What was that all about?

'No thanks, I don't drink,' he said to Clarissa. 'I don't do drugs. I don't even smoke, like to keep myself fit.'

'What on earth do you do to relax, then?'

'Walking, bird watching … sex. I'm a private investigator, see?' He waggled his iPhone for effect then placed it down by his plate. 'I never know when I might be called to action.'

'A *private* dick, waiting to be called to action! How exciting. I bet you could tell us some saucy stories, Simon.'

No, just a plain ordinary dick.

'I could, yes. You'd be amazed the lengths some people go to to hide deceit.'

The main course arrived: steak in a rich sauce with truffles and foie gras. His ulcer pulsed on red alert, warning him not to ingest any of it. Besides, because of Anna's ducks and geese, he had serious animal welfare issues with the pâté. In fact, he ignored all the food, except for the breadsticks, ignored the innuendos and the frilly knickers brushing past every two minutes. The champagne was good though, and he didn't stop them topping up his glass.

'Does the twitching help with your line of work?' Clarissa asked Banks, no doubt drooling with the idea of uncovering some local smut. 'I bet you have to watch a lot of adultery.'

'People getting a leg over where they shouldn't?' Jack said, and Banks leant in.

'My expertise is in observation. You can learn a lot by just watching.'

'Watch this then.' Jack stabbed the tournedos with his steak knife. The blood ran and pooled in the congealed sauce.

'Is that supposed to scare me? You playing with your food?'

'Your powers of observation need working on. That was a demonstration of how sharp this knife is.'

Tim cleared his throat and the stoned woman began

to laugh with hysteria. Clarissa, who'd watched the exchange like a Wimbledon spectator, clapped her hands nervously. 'Er, would anyone like a Manchester Tart?'

'No thanks. And anyway, she's moved to North Wales, so technically she's a Welsh Tart, Isn't that right, Simon?'

Despite the flow of alcohol, the atmosphere plummeted yet again. Jack got to his feet and addressed Tim, who looked mildly panicked. 'Just going outside for some fresh air.'

'Good idea,' Tim hissed. 'Do you, er, mind if I stay for the pudding?'

The apartment was on ground level and he knew the floor plan pretty well, having done numerous viewings before Clarissa moved in. Outside the dining room, he steadied himself for a moment against the wall; he must be drunker than he realised. He found his way out through the garden room and onto the patio. The night air accentuated his inebriated state, although he could only recall half a bottle of Sancerre and maybe half a bottle of Krug, not enough to render him this plastered, surely? He slumped onto a sun lounger and lit a cigarette. As fully expected, Banks materialised behind the glass. He closed the sliding door behind him and walked around the small space, jingling loose change in his pockets. 'I'll get straight to the point. You know why I'm here, Redman. I've had a talk with Patsy about reclaiming what's mine.'

Jack squinted up at him. It was a few moments before Banks came into focus. 'My daughter is *not* some sort of reclamation project, a commodity for you to fight over.'

'Not sure Patsy would agree. According to her, everything has a price on it,' he said, then straddled a chair. 'Just to keep things nice and tidy, I paid back the

181

debt. In return for my generosity, ex-wifey told you the truth, then she wrote to our daughter. She did everything she promised for once. Now I just need you to be reasonable as well, then we can all live happily ever after.'

'Fuck off. What you talking about anyway? What *debt?*'

'The cash. The money she gave me to bugger off all those years ago. I figured it wouldn't be … what's the right word? Ethical? Yeah, it wouldn't be *ethical* to make demands, knowing that was still hanging over me. I have a conscience, you see. Oh, let me guess …' A wide grin split his face. 'You didn't know about any money?'

A tiny beam of light penetrated through the fog of alcohol. 'So, you say *she* sent the letter?'

'Snatched my hand off.'

'How do you mean? You *paid* her for that as well?'

'Slow tonight, Redman. Look, I'm trying to be upfront and reasonable here.'

'You call sending my daughter a letter like that fucking reasonable?'

'Like I said, I didn't actually send it. I'm not very … articulate. I'll be in touch. Or maybe I'll just pop round Chelsey's house with the DNA. What do you think?'

'When I find out who sent that letter … you'll find out what I *think*.'

'Are you saying it was the wrong approach?'

There was no answer to that. He shot Banks a dark look. An odd remark. It was the way he delivered it as well, like a genuine question. Banks just shrugged and stepped back inside. The patio door slid shut.

He either had no understanding or comprehension of human feelings or he was spending too much time on Planet Stupid. Maybe his brain was mashed from all the cocaine he used to do at university. Either way, it left him with a nasty taste in his mouth. He ground out his cigarette. Patsy and Banks. Still a match made in heaven. Why couldn't they just leave things alone? He staggered to the bottom of the garden where it petered out to a small copse and relieved his bladder. Throughout this, he held on to a sapling but then it swayed so violently, he felt the damp ground tilting towards him.

A long time later, he opened his eyes and knew instantly that movement was going to hurt. His face was crushed up against someone else. The someone else groaned. It was dark, and a vicious breeze played over his legs. He managed to roll onto his back. Under his hands he could feel damp sand. Nothing made much sense but the chill in the air was incredibly sobering, and after forcing himself to slowly reach a sitting position, he realised that the other body was Tim. They were in a deep hollow, outside. For some reason, this reminded him of *The Wind in the Willows*, Lottie's favourite book, but that's where the romance ended. They were in fact, both in a bunker on the golf course. The next, probably bigger revelation was the discovery that neither of them was wearing any trousers.

When Tim eventually came around, his face was so white it was like a beacon in the gloom.

'How did we get here? Where are we?'

'You're the golfer, you tell me.'

Some time passed in miserable silence as Tim came to terms with their location and lack of trousers. It could have been so much worse – at least they had shoes and socks. In fact, Tim was still wearing his shirt and tie from the office. Everything was present and correct – except for one pair of Levis and a pair of grey, pin-striped trousers. Tim crawled to the edge of the bunker, shivering and holding his balls. Shirt tails flapping in the breeze and pink boxers somehow made him look more vulnerable and comical than it should, but an overweight bald accountant missing the lower half of his Saville Row suit was never going to be taken seriously.

'Right, this is the ninth hole, so I think the clubhouse is over there.'

'Brilliant. The clubhouse? You're not serious?'

'No, but we can, uh … walk in the general direction, find the road.'

'Then what?'

'I don't know. What on *earth* will I tell Margaret? There must have been something in that booze for us both to pass out like that, when you think about it.'

'I don't want to think about it.'

They started walking. His mobile told him it was ten to two in the morning. The eighteen-hole championship course was massive, like a green desert but with huge lakes and so many undulations it did little to ease the nausea or the general feeling of helplessness. A thick belt of trees preceded the clubhouse and a sweep of manicured grass encircled the building. The car park was packed. 'Must be a function on,' Tim said. As they drew closer to the building, they could make out crowds of glitterati, the cream of Cheshire at play. They were less than a metre away from the action when a bank of security lights, powerful enough to light up the whole of Prestbury suddenly illuminated their position.

A hundred well-bred eyes swivelled in their direction. A second of shock, then guffaws of laughter.

Too tired to run, it took them a good few minutes to backtrack beyond the circle of light.

'Fuck! Do you think anyone recognised us?' Tim

asked. 'I'm sure that was the director of Goldseal Investments in there.'

'I've had enough of this. I'm phoning Ollie, get him to pick us up.'

When he finally answered the call, Oliver grumbled sleepily and asked a lot of questions. 'Where are you? Can't you get a taxi?'

'Prestbury Golf Club.'

'Are you at Maxwell-Brown's bash?'

'No, and don't go to the main entrance asking for us. Me and Tim are stranded in the bushes.'

A long beat while he considered this. 'So ... your *exact* location is like, in the *bushes* at Prestbury Golf Club?'

'Got it. Bring two pairs of trousers. As soon as you like.'

They had a protracted conversation then about exactly where he was to stop the car on the three-mile driveway, which was punctuated with antique street-lights and rhododendrons. He dutifully turned up in the Fiat some twenty minutes later and passed some trousers through the window. Tim, hopping about through the undergrowth, could only get them up as far as his thighs and had to waddle to the car.

'You snake-hipped devil, Redman, I can't get these anywhere near me.'

Throughout all of this, Ollie sat with his forehead on the steering wheel, snorting with tears streaming down his face, barely able to breathe let alone talk or drive. When he did try to communicate, his voice came out as a high-pitched squeak.

'What happened?'

'Just drive, drop Tim off first.'

The motion of the car rendered them both into a sickly silence. Back at the flat, his son wanted names and details, he even stabbed his finger on the chair arm and said something about their reputation, but all Jack wanted was a bath, a pint of water, some painkillers, and a very long sleep.

Towards the middle of the week, he began to feel something approaching normal, at least physically, and snippets of conversation returned to memory. There remained a black hole, a missing two or three hours from being in Clarissa's garden to finding himself stranded at the opposite side of the golf course. He worried that Banks may have engineered something sinister, and a selection of large black and white photographs would perhaps appear in the post. The headlines could be juicy, but Banks had nothing further to gain by blackmail, did he? Overall, he was more angry than anything else, a feeling of being coerced along a route he had little control over. He didn't even have a contact number for Banks, let alone know where he was staying. And then, along with the feeling of being watched, waiting for him to pop up in whatever disguise he fancied was slowly but surely driving him to distraction.

Tim was curious about his hostile reaction to Banks. 'I don't see why you bothered getting him mad, it's all water under the bridge, it was years ago.'

'I know, I just don't like the guy.'

'Margaret thinks we were date-raped.'

'Don't be so bloody stupid.'

'We'll laugh about this in a few weeks.'

'You might have to remind me.'

Oliver laughed all the time, determined to get to the bottom of it. Jack thought he'd deflected his questions and assumptions brilliantly, but then on Thursday morning Clarissa strode in and deposited a dry cleaning bag on the reception desk in front of his bemused staff. He heard her conspiratorial whisper, a pathetic pretence at discretion which was actually loud enough for the whole office to hear.

'I had to have Mr Chadwick's trousers dry cleaned. They were grass stains I think, do apologise to him for me. Ciao!'

His son brought them through to his office and hooked them onto the back of the door.

'I'll speak to you about this later,' he said sagely.

In truth, he was beginning to feel suffocated, and it was torturous not being able to discuss any of it with Anna, but she'd made it perfectly clear she'd washed her hands of the whole debacle. Visions of her flitted into his mind so often that he was forced to admit defeat on more than one level. She'd been right about Patsy. How to proceed with any of it was beyond him, but not having any clear direction had never stopped him in the past.

Tony came back from his holidays and time was less restricted again. He made two phone calls: arrangements with Patsy to see the children and in as reasonable tone as he could muster, arrangements for a private talk.

'Have you seen Banks?' she said, warily – or was that his imagination?

'I have, but let's talk in person later.'

The second call to Anna was less reserved, more borderline begging. When he arrived at Gwern Farm early on Saturday morning, the dogs rushed to greet him, but when he saw Anna he felt like a stranger, almost as if he had to ask permission to be there. To his relief, she came into his arms and the physical connection was so intense it blew apart the awkwardness, real or imagined.

'I've missed you,' he said.

The words were inadequate. There was nothing

which better explained that hollow feeling, that nagging, helpless ache. Did people with a terminal illness feel like this? Like there was something rotten in their insides that needed replacing? Her arms went around him and the very essence of her was healing to his soul but knowing it was possibly on limited time almost reversed the effect. How could he contemplate losing her again? He *couldn't* let history repeat itself. He took hold of her hand and they went through the garden, heavy now with the promise of golden apples and ripening berries, and up onto the open hillside.

It was sad without Benson bumbling along behind them. No need to keep stopping, turning, and looking. They used to become exasperated, waiting while he sniffed the same patch of ground. At some point, he'd struggle to endorse it with a pee, then forgot where he was up to and went back to the beginning, nose down.

Lottie always said he was reading Dog News.

The second half of August was warm, grey, and dull, with a strong breeze ripping through the heather. It was flowering, and other than a flash of yellow gorse, the vast purple domes seemed to be the only vibrancy in the landscape. At the top of Pensychnant the wind was cold. Small trees seemed to be crouched, bent double with their backs to the sea, arms flung to the ground. There was a makeshift bench overlooking the valley with names and initials carved into the smooth wood and they sat, arms wrapped around each other, contemplating the view but not really seeing it.

'I don't know how to fix it,' he said eventually.

She hooked her hands into the ends of her sleeves. 'Fix what, exactly?'

'Any of it. Chelsey. Banks. Patsy living here and interfering in your life. To think that all these problems are serious enough to have you even think of selling the farm, it's just …'

'A mess. All caused by one person.'

He sighed, he couldn't disagree. 'Can you not ignore her? Patsy, I mean.'

'Jack, I don't want to *have* to. And now every time I arrange something with Peter, she's there as well!'

'I'm sorry about that, I really am.'

'I used to think I was rooted here.'

'You are. *We* are.'

She scanned the horizon. 'It doesn't feel like that anymore.'

'Can you give me some time to work it out? If you can't, then I don't know where that leaves us.'

'I know how to fix some of it,' she said, meeting his eyes. 'If you'd just tell Chelsey the truth, at least you won't be held to this ... this emotional ransom. It will force Patsy to take responsibility.'

She maybe took his silence as an agreement of sorts, but no matter how many times he tried to envisage a conversation like this with his eldest daughter, he couldn't get his head round it. Banks would want a piece of her! *Unthinkable.* He imagined the same scenario with himself in pole position, with his mother admitting that Leo wasn't actually his father. Betrayed, that's how he'd feel.

He felt betrayed by Anna. What was that saying, caught between a rock and a hard place? That's how it felt. He used to admire her independent spirit, her principles, her fight. Now it was his actions which were under scrutiny, it seemed she was just stubborn and unbending. He hugged her goodbye and she had tears in her eyes.

'*Please,* Anna, meet me halfway,' he said. 'That's all I'm asking.'

'I was already doing that, when she lived seventy miles away!'

'I love you, and if you love me then we can work it

out, can't we? We're bigger than any of this!'

'That's what Hilly said.'

'You've spoken to her?'

'A little. Maybe I'll pluck up courage to go and talk to her again.'

In contrast, the children were happy, eager to see him and it did help distract from his considerable on-going heartache. If he needed further proof of how tough it was to be in love with someone who had no real vested interest in your children and hated their mother, this was it.

Patsy was polite, friendly, the model ex-wife. And like a model weekend father, he took Lottie and James swimming. His daughter was confident in the water, but James clung to him. The boy was coming out of his shell though, and after twenty minutes, allowed Jack to let go of him as he splashed across the shallow end in his armbands.

'Da!' he said, reaching the rail at the other side. James had never called him Daddy and if he was honest, he wasn't too sure how to let this struggling bond develop. They hadn't had the best start, but if he needed further proof of how much his parental role meant to him, then this was it.

'Why are you crying, Daddy?' Lottie said.

'I'm not, it's the water stinging my eyes.'

They went to the cinema, and then to his mother's for tea. Lottie wanted to know why she couldn't ride Hilly's ponies and why they no longer spent any time at Gwern Farm. She struck a pose, hands on hips, her bottom lip out.

'I want to see my friend, Benson. There's something I need to tell him, it's important.'

Isabel raised her brows. 'I'll take James in the garden for a minute while you two have a chat.'

He had no idea how to approach the farm or the

pony problem. He supposed they had to go on the back burner with a load of other stuff, but he had to tell her the truth about the dog. There was no point sugar-coating anything with Lottie; she was far too astute. Although to say Benson died naturally was a hundred times better than the awful reality, and side-stepped the possibility of any probing questions.

'Have you noticed that God spelt backwards is dog?' he began, cringing at his own cheesiness. She knew he was bullshitting, she could read his soft face like front-page headlines. It was harder than anything he'd had to do, including his divorce and the death of his father, and her little body was racked with shuddering, heaving sobs in no time. He tried to paint the image of a peaceful passing under the apple trees, the birds singing and God reaching down to lift him up on a white cloud. His mother overheard this part and he could tell she was touched, although a look of faint disbelief crossed her face towards the end. Maybe he'd overdone the God bit. He pulled Lottie onto his lap.

'Come here, love. Don't cry anymore.'

'I'm *not* crying, the water's stinging my eyes,' she wailed, then pummelled him thoroughly with both fists.

He couldn't win. Even Snog got the cold shoulder.

'You go,' Isabel said to him quietly, 'she'll get over it. I'll look after her. Go take Anna out for dinner. It's time you two got yourselves sorted out.'

If only. It was a beautiful evening, the clouds had cleared and the wind had dropped, leaving a mellow late afternoon sun hovering over the town. Danny rang him just as he pulled up outside Quay Cottage.

'Dan. Good honeymoon?' he said absently. Patsy opened the cottage door, arms folded, feet apart. Ready for battle.

'There's stuff you never told me,' his brother said.

'Not what it's cracked up to be, is it?'

'What, married sex or the Dominican Republic?'

'No, the resort was really nice. This marriage lark. Now that we're back, she won't even keep my sock drawer in order. Listen to this, she refuses to take responsibility for pairing them. Is that grounds for divorce?'

'Dan, I'm a bit busy, can I call you back?'

'Oh, I get it. I'm one of the smarmy smug married set now, am I? Look, I just wanted to thank Anna for everything she did. What can I send her?'

'No idea. I'll call you back.'

Patsy stood aside to let him in. New perfume. She'd put some background music on and poured two glasses of wine. Laughable. He fiddled with the new CD player and managed to silence it. She picked up a glass of wine but they remained standing, Jack with one hand on the chimney breast. There was a new watercolour on the opposite wall, and a sculpture in the corner. Claymore?

'I've spoken to Banks. First, he's clearly not a tramp unless he's some sort of hybrid type, one that keeps a dinner suit in his tent just in case. Oh, and he has an iPhone and a manicurist. Go on, look all surprised.'

'You're angry.'

'He paid you.'

'He's lying.'

'I don't think so. He paid you to send the letter as well.'

'I *didn't* send the letter! How can you think such a thing?'

'Then who did? The more I think about it, the more it doesn't add up to be Banks.'

'Jack, I swear on my life I didn't send that letter.'

'But you took money from him? Come on, Patsy, I

know you too well. Look at all this new stuff, you can't help yourself, can you?'

She clenched her teeth and looked at the ceiling. 'Alright, yes!'

He moved across to the sofa, sat down, rested his head back against the velvet cushions and matching throw from Harrods, and closed his eyes. When he opened them she was perched opposite on the chair, leaning forwards earnestly. 'Jack, listen to me, I admit I took the money, but I *didn't* send the letter. I just told him I did.'

He dragged a hand over his eyes. 'Why the fuck would you do that?'

'I'm scared of him. I just admitted it was me to get rid of him.'

'Tell the truth. You told him it was you to get money.'

'But I *am* scared of him, Jack. He's got an evil look in his eye.'

'Like mine?'

He couldn't get out of there fast enough. The whole conversation had lasted less than ten minutes but his head was reeling with the implications. He didn't get back in his car, he didn't trust himself to drive. Instead, he walked along the harbour front towards the castle. By the time he'd paced back again, Patsy was leaning on his car. 'Can we talk about this?'

'Everyone told me it was a mistake moving you here and they were right.'

'Jack, please.'

'You're only here because of the children. One more attempt to dupe me or cause any distress to Anna or any of my family and I'll move you out of here within twenty-four hours. Understood?'

'None of this is my fault!'

She looked about to turn on the waterworks so he

blipped the central locking and got in, started the engine, and reversed too quickly out of the parking spot. No, it wasn't Banks who'd sent that letter and he was pretty sure it wasn't Patsy.

That left Philipe, a highly unlikely suspect and … *Hilly.*

Fired up by the events of the day, he decided to pay her a visit. He felt compelled now to flush out whatever else was lurking in the background. It perhaps wasn't the best frame of mind but he figured he hadn't much to lose. As he drew up, Hilly was turning the horses out in the fields, but waved a handful of halters when she recognised his car. He took a deep breath and clambered out. It looked like Heather was a permanent fixture, sat on the steps of a caravan and rolling tobacco. He wondered at the sensibility of that in a yard stuffed with hay and wooden buildings. The place looked a mess, not the sort of place he'd want to bring Lottie even if it was on offer. There was another caravan parked up round the back, a nasty-looking dog on a chain, and dozens of horses he'd not seen before corralled in a small paddock. He was no expert but they certainly didn't look like children's trekking ponies. Big-boned, rough-looking. They trotted one way then back again, restless and taking lumps out of each other.

'Admiring the youngsters?' Heather drawled.

'Where are they from?'

'Ireland. Got all their papers. That woman of yours, the artist. Still looking for one, is she?'

'Not at the moment.'

Hilly closed the field gate behind her and gave him a cautious look, but he smiled and indicated they go inside.

'This is all very mysterious, Jack. Is everything alright? Want a coffee, or something stronger?'

'Nothing, thanks.'

'I see. Not a social visit, then?'

'No.'

He followed her into the kitchen and sat at the table, wondering where to start, his foot tapping with tension. The sink drainer was piled high with washing-up and Hilly began putting pots and pans away in various cupboards, wincing when she hunkered down. She looked tired. What was she, sixty something?

He started with the letter. 'There's only a handful of people who know about this and I've struck out the two main suspects,' he said, not convinced she was listening. 'He really doesn't like me and Anna, does he, your intended?'

'Bryn? He's just old-school Welsh, it's nothing personal.' She faced him then, waving a potato peeler. 'I know what you're thinking but even if I'd told him about your daughter, why on earth would Bryn do that? We've got enough to do here without meddling in other people's affairs.'

'Yeah, I'm clutching at straws. I admit I'm baffled, and I'm sorry, it's just that we had that awkward conversation earlier in the year, and Anna –'

'Plenty of locals don't like the way Bryn is running the business, but we're making more money, just buying and selling. I know they'd rather see it all pretty with hanging baskets and a little white picket fence but when you're my age and on the verge of bankruptcy you get past caring about that.'

'*Bankruptcy? Christ*, I'm sorry, Hilly. I didn't realise. I don't think Anna does either.'

She turned back to the sink and begin to peel potatoes. 'I'll be straight with you, his sister calls all the shots and we're both getting a bit tired of that, but trying to make an honest living is getting harder, and we're not getting any younger. I want – no, I need – a

195

bloody pension!'

'If you need some advice I can point you in the right direction.'

'No. Bryn's got his own way of dealing with things, you know? That's if he can keep a lid on the stress.'

There was a ring of truth about all of this, although it hadn't gone unnoticed that she'd neatly changed the subject. He raked a hand through his fluffy, chlorinated hair. 'What's going on with you and Anna? She feels so alienated, she's thinking of selling the farm.'

She kept her back to him, scraping vegetables with a lot more force than probably needed. 'What's she got to worry about? She'll be a millionaire. Things change, don't they?'

'Change, yeah, I get that with the business but not with friends. What's with the animosity?'

There was a loud, audible sigh and the sound of a bag dropping to the floor. He turned, to see Anna silhouetted in the doorway, arms folded.

'Don't shout at Hilly, she's on your side. It was me. I sent the blasted letter.'

CHAPTER TWELVE

Jack

He couldn't believe his ears. He made her repeat it. So she did, this time with a slight jut to the chin.

'I sent the letter.'

'So Patsy is actually due *another* apology from me?' he said, more comfortable with shouting than thinking. 'I've just been round there, reading the riot act! Twenty-four hours' notice if she upsets you.'

'Well thank you, that makes it sound as if I've been whinging.'

'I can't win. Why, Anna? *Why?*'

Her eyes blazed like a smoking blue fire, although she was close to tears as well. 'If you had more faith –'

'*Faith?* Are you including you and me in that?'

'If you had more faith in your relationships, Patsy would become powerless.'

'What are you talking about?'

'Chelsey!'

'What about her?'

'Do you honestly think she'd suddenly start calling Simon Banks "Daddy"? Jack, you'll be run ragged by Simon and Patsy until Chelsey will demand the truth. You're fighting the inevitable, but you'll do this the hard way until you fall over and drag everyone else down with you, won't you? Because that's what you do!'

There was a long minute of silence while he tried to digest her words.

'Well, this is awkward,' Hilly said with a sigh, then turned to Anna. 'I'm glad you came clean. I don't know how much longer I could have kept quiet. The whole idea was a ticking timebomb.'

'Go on, say it. I told you so.'

'I told you so!'

Somewhere in the middle of this, he picked up his car keys and apologised to Hilly. Quite a lot of things fell into place – in fact *everything*, more or less fell into place. What he was unable to comprehend was Anna's behaviour, the whole sneaky, underhand aspect of sending an anonymous letter to his daughter and professing to know nothing about it! Lying by omission used to be Patsy's forte. Anna was poised to say something else but he made a throwaway gesture with his hand, the sort of thing Oliver did, the sort of thing he hated, and she was forced to flatten herself against the wall as he shoved past her. There was a beseeching moment when their eyes met but there was defiance on her part too, and he had to look away.

He must have taken a couple of years off the Range Rover the way he reversed it, leaving Heather engulfed in a cloud of dust and exhaust fumes. He didn't apologise to Patsy. For one thing, he felt too sick to the stomach to go round there again. Instead, he drove all the way home, lulled into a trance on the motorway. It was fortunately as empty as his mind. He even forgot about the children, and found himself apologising to his mother instead.

'I thought you were coming back!'

'I'm sorry, Mum, I lost track of time.'

'Oh, well, they've gone to bed here now. I thought I'd best let Patsy know as well.'

'Right, I'm sorry, I thought Patsy was collecting them,' he said lamely.

'No … and she said you'd been round there earlier.

I thought you were taking Anna out?'

Christ! It was lie after lie. 'Yeah, yeah the bath's got a leak. Look, I'm going to lose the signal in a minute ...'

It wasn't the only thing he was losing. He felt blasted to smithereens, peppered with emotional gunshot.

Oliver was surprised to see him turn up back at the flat around ten. He mumbled something about Anna being busy, him not feeling great.

'Why didn't you stay at the farm then?' Oliver said on his way out. 'Seems brainless, driving all the way back.'

Jack coughed. 'I'll just sleep it off here, don't want to pass anything on.'

'So you thought you'd pass it on over here instead?'

'For Chrissakes, just go out, will you?'

'Chill, Dad. So obvious you've had a domestic.'

His feet thundered down the stairs. The bottom door slammed shut and silence descended. A domestic; it sounded like a friendly difference of opinion. The flat looked a mess, littered with wet towels and takeaway cartons. Clearly he hadn't been expected back. He left everything festering and lay across the bed. So, this was it. His future was resigned to being an old cuckoo in the nest, staring at the ceiling and wondering where it had all gone wrong for the second, no, the third time with Anna. *Anna.* What the fuck have you done?

It was only a matter of time before Patsy worked out who had actually sent the letter. She knew the shortlist as well as he did, it didn't take a huge leap of imagination to put a few facts together and fill in the grey areas. It'd be simple once she got wind that he and Anna were no longer an item. Because they weren't an item, were they? How could they possibly come back from this? To add insult to injury, Patsy had come up smelling of roses. Not only did she have an unblemished relationship with Claymore, but she was sitting pretty on a wad of cash without even getting her hands dirty. Well, not much. Who cared if she'd fleeced Banks?

Anna had played into those hands blindly, stupidly.

For the hundredth time he considered confiding in Tim or his sister, Kate. Would it make matters even more complicated, having someone else's opinion thrown into the mix? What actual options were there, other than waiting for Banks to show up? He knew word for word what Anna thought, and he could hazard a guess that his sister would maybe side with her, even go one step further and get the cash back off Patsy as well, with interest. He could foresee what would happen with Tim. They'd go for a few beers, drink too much, and discuss getting Banks hunted down and beaten up. Tempting as this was, he already had a police record for beating up Philipe. So other than feed the offending letter through the office shredder, he had no option but to wait for Banks. The problem with that was the actual waiting, especially when he had no idea what he was waiting for.

The working week was punishing. His concentration span was zero. He delegated everything he could, aware that he was spending a lot of time staring shiftily through the blinds, sometimes flicking them shut so they were in semi-darkness. Tabitha opened them when she thought he wasn't looking, and he closed again them when she went to lunch. Banks was out there somewhere. What the fuck was he doing, watching and waiting? He was beginning to feel hunted, under surveillance. Was this how Anna felt, living with Patsy down the road? A tiny pin-prick of guilt pierced through the fog. He searched the Internet for private eye Banks, using every different combination he could think of, but drew a blank. Maybe it was all a lie, a smokescreen.

With nothing better to do, he rearranged the rota and opted to work on Saturday, allowing Oliver an unexpected day off. Claymore was taking Patsy and the children to his parents' place in the Lake District for the weekend. Under normal circumstances this would have given him and Anna an opportunity to be alone or go away somewhere themselves, but that wasn't going to happen now, and anyway, he was far too angry and strung-out to enjoy any leisure time.

If Banks didn't turn up soon with his tail between his legs, the only option left *would* be to hunt him down and get him beaten up. When Friday came around, he wandered over to the Dirty Duck, eyes peeled for a repeat performance. He ordered a beer and opened his laptop so he appeared busy, not like some sad middle-aged waster looking for trouble.

Clarissa homed in on him. He saw the nipples first, like a couple of baby feeding teats on full-alert, wobbling beneath a tight sheen. She perched one bum cheek on the stool opposite. 'I'm sorry if the boys were a little boisterous last week.'

'Is that what you call it? Tell the truth, I didn't appreciate been drugged and dumped on the golf course.'

She had the grace to look cowed and played with the drink mats. 'I'm sorry, you won't say anything, will you? I mean, if there's anything I can do to make it up to you?'

'You er, didn't happen to get a business card from Simon, did you?'

'No, why?'

'I need to find someone. A bit of debt collecting, off the record stuff, you know.'

'If it's just a bit of pressure you're after, I can lend you the boys. I'll get them to pop round the office.'

'The boys? You mean the men on the door?'

'Twins. Lovely, aren't they? Dum and Dee. Stayed with me after my old man did a bunk.'

This was better, a feeling of empowerment. It lasted about thirty seconds, until he opened his email to see that Josh had sent him a link to the gallery and a polite enquiry about the flat. The boy answered his phone on two rings.

'Hi, love, have a good trip? What's this about the flat?' he said, one finger in his ear. Another loud burst of laughter from the bar. Clarissa pinching someone's backside.

'Yeah, it was amazing. I, er, just wondered if it was still OK to stay here?'

'Of *course* it is! Why do you ask?'

'You and Mum? She's a right mess. You're not splitting up, are you?'

'I don't know. I wish we weren't, hope we don't ... sorry, not much help am I?'

'Right, well, she's got this gallery opening coming up on the twentieth of September. Jack, she's worked all her life to get this kind of buzz.'

'I know and I'm not going to stuff it up for her, if that's what you're thinking.'

'Well, will you – *can* you – be there for her?'

'I'll do my best,' he said, knowing full well he would be there for him as much as for Anna. A surge of respect for Josh had him adding the date to his diary, cross that he hadn't asked Anna about it himself. 'Listen, before you go, tell me something ... if your real dad came back on the scene now, how would you feel about him?'

'Ashamed of him. Why?'

'Just wondered. I mean, would you want to get to know him?'

'Not especially. Is this what all the hassle's about with you and Mum? Has he been in touch?'

'No! Nothing like that.' Actually, it was a lot like that. 'Just thinking out loud, how complicated these things are.'

'Yeah, but he'd be like a total stranger to me. And I don't need him. You've been more than a step-dad to me these past four years.'

He looked at the ceiling. Christ, this was hard. 'I'm still here for you, so is the rest of the family. That won't ever change. Just, look after your mum and ... good on you for being a bloody decent guy.'

'You too.'

It was touching but it took the wind out of his sails, left him looking round the wine bar to see if anyone had overheard him or noticed his eyes filling up. What was he doing, watching strangers go by when his own life was happening somewhere else?

He drained his glass and looked at the gallery website. Conwy Art Centre; opening on September 20th and introducing Anna Williams. There was a beautiful colourful photograph of her, in intense blues and greens. It was one he'd not seen before, with an out of focus background and set into a wide, white border, and the entire image was superimposed onto an easel. She looked tentative, as if she were wondering if the photographer had actually taken the picture or not; hair just lifting from her face, the suggestion of a smile. Looking into those eyes was like free-falling into deep water. Like watching his life flash before him. All the mistakes he'd made, all the desires he'd ever felt and as many hopes and dreams for the future he could possibly need in one lifetime. He loved her like nothing else. And yet he couldn't bring himself to speak to her. He closed the lid of the laptop and the image was gone.

On Saturday morning, Britney Spears woke him from the first deep sleep he'd managed in a week. He'd been dreaming about love, when it sometimes delved into a sixth sense and produced magic. When it became the taste of sunlight, the sound of distant snowfall, the perfume of water.

If he carried on like this he'd be writing poetry soon.

Oliver kicked the bedroom door open and slung his mobile onto the bed. Milkshakes in the Yard was on at full volume, and combined with Oliver, it was enough to wake the dead.

'It's Chel,' he said, tearing at a piece of toast. 'For you.'

It took him several seconds to come round and free his arms from the duvet. He was trapped in it, wrapped like a chrysalis. He'd been dreaming of winter, and trying to find enough wood to burn to keep warm on the farm. Other than a powder-blue sky, everything was white or grey and cold. His footsteps crunched across the sugary ground and the air hit the back of his throat with the sharp, clean smell of snow. Down by the lake, the water was frozen at the edge, dead grass and reeds petrified in ice. He scuffed it with his shoe and it splintered like shards of glass. Benson barked, his breath like smoke. He saw her, lying face-up in the middle of the lake, her hair tangled with the weeds, just floating, staring. Blue lips, cerulean eyes.

Britney again.

Heart hammering, he hit "accept". This was it. Banks had been to see his daughter, verified the letter with a copy of the blood-test, and introduced himself as her long-lost father.

'Hello, love,' he said blearily.

'Hi, Jack, it's Mike. We've had the email.' It was her husband, using her phone. Could Chelsey not speak to him now?

'What?' he said, urgently. 'What email?'

'About the art gallery? And the answer is yes, we'll be there, more than happy to show some support.'

Jack propped himself on one arm and rubbed his eyes. 'How did you know about the gallery?'

'Her son, Josh, I think? He's sent invites to everyone he can think of. Talk about a PR job! Anyway, we just thought you could pass the acceptance on to Anna? Kate, Dan, and Ellie will be there as well. I think it's brilliant, don't you?'

'Yeah, she's worked really hard.'

Another reprieve. He staggered into the kitchen and filled the coffee machine. Oliver was pulling on trainers. He always seemed to be going somewhere, this time with a piece of toast dangling from his mouth. 'Are you going to Conwy later?'

'Not this weekend, no,' he said, gulping coffee. 'Anna's busy and your mum's away with Lottie and James.'

'Might go over and see Josh, we can crash at the farm, can't we?'

'No, you can't. Look, stop using the place like a bloody convenience, it's Anna's home.'

'Alright, keep your hair on, *Britney.*'

'Oh, and before you disappear, change that bloody ringtone for me, will you?'

Oliver fiddled with the phone for thirty seconds and was gone. The bottom door slammed and the entire flat shuddered. It made him feel like a teenager, sharing rooms with Ollie and splitting up with his girlfriend, partner ... lover. The thought of his future stretching out for years in front of him, without her, without the farm, was beyond comprehension. But so was her betrayal of trust. He knew he wasn't blameless, he'd stuffed up with Patsy, he'd turned a blind eye to Anna's feelings, he'd allowed outside forces to take control. If he was honest, the cracks in their relationship had started six months ago, and he'd subconsciously registered the signs but done nothing about it.

He gave up forcing cereal down his throat and slung the bowl in the sink.

Anna ... fucking hell, this is purgatory.

She didn't want to be his girlfriend, his partner or his lover, let alone his wife, did she? He needed to get real, face facts. Even if he fixed the Banks-Chelsey problem, he had no idea how to fix the Patsy-Anna problem, let alone the Jack-Anna problem or the-rest-of-his-life problem. Work.

Downstairs in the office, he opened up, flicked computer terminals on and filled the coffee machine. He opened the blinds, fully. Dusty sunlight streamed in but did little to lift his mood, reminding him how much he missed the farm through the summer. Long evenings drinking wine at dusk, the air heavy with the scent of old-fashioned roses and cottage garden flowers. Her hand in his. His body on hers. Her mouth on his.

Anna ... fucking hell, love, this is purgatory.

Tabitha arrived, obviously dismayed that she had to work all day with her cuckoo boss, but at least his relaxation with the blinds meant she could see what she was doing. She printed off a long list of appointments, wall-to-wall viewings, market appraisals, and measure-ups, removing any necessary keys from the system before locking the cupboard again.

'Here you go,' she said, desperate to get rid of him.

'If two big guys come in called Dum and Dee, tell them to wait for me, will you? Debt collectors.'

'Am I still looking out for a tramp as well?'

'A tramp in a suit. Anyone who asks for me, call me on my mobile and tell them to wait.'

A beat of consideration, arms folded. 'Right.'

The first property on his list was a shabby three-bed semi on the outskirts of town. He punched in the alarm code and the musty smell had him opening the ground-floor windows. Seconds later, a smart rap on the open front door had him looking around, expecting to see a couple of first time buyers. It was Banks.

Back in his casual gear with a rucksack over one shoulder, it took a few seconds to recognise him from the previous week. In sober daylight, he was far leaner than he could recall from their schooldays. A cropped haircut, big boots, and combat trousers made him look mean, but Jack wasn't convinced this hard exterior went all the way through. It was the look teenage lads went for. Coupled with pinching washing and trying to get Patsy onside with letters only cemented in his mind that he was essentially pretty pathetic. Banks sauntered round the room, eyes everywhere. 'Very nice. Apart from the swirly carpet, that's a bit naff. Take an offer, will they?'

'Oh, very clever.'

'More amusing, I thought. Your staff are a pushover, they don't ask nearly enough questions.'

'I'll ask them all now, if you like. Full address, phone number? Occupation?'

'Questions, questions … if you watch and wait long enough, you get the answers anyway, you know?'

'I've a feeling I'd reach the same conclusion.'

'Don't make assumptions. I could still buy this

place, cash, if you like.'

'You like the fact you've got some money in your pocket, don't you? Makes you feel powerful, does it?'

'Has its advantages.'

'As in bribery? Not worked though, has it? Even my ex-wife saw you coming. My daughter has seen the letter and disregarded it as utter tosh, she's not interested. And I personally saw to it that it's been shredded.'

'So, where do we go from here?'

'Nowhere. It's a dead-end, got that?'

'I'm her father, I've got rights.'

'You gave them up when she was an embryo, remember that?'

He ignored this, one finger tapping the side of his nose then jabbing it in his direction. 'I've been thinking, thinking it all through. I know it wasn't me sent that letter and you seemed to imply, or at least you've been told with some conviction, that it wasn't that scheming bitch of an ex-wife, was it? So I reckon whoever sent that letter, whoever wrote and posted it, is on my side. They want the truth to come out the same as me. Now all I have to do is find out who that special someone is and we can sort this out together.'

His mobile sprang to life. "Your sex is on fire!" screamed out of the tinny speaker at full volume. He kept his eyes on Banks as he wandered round the room, picking up china ornaments and putting them down again. His conversational logic, if you could call it that, was skewed beyond normal intelligence. He answered his phone.

'Dumb and Dumber are here,' Tabitha said. 'It looks like there's two gorillas in reception.'

'Give me twenty minutes. If I'm not there then, give them Mrs Barnaby's address.'

He flipped his phone off and Banks laughed. 'What

do you think I'm going to do?'

'It wasn't you I was concerned about. It was more what *I* might do.'

Banks lifted both hands in a patronising gesture. His phone rang again and Lottie's tinkly voice filled the room. 'Redman! I've got something to tell you.'

'It's *Daddy* to you, not Redman.'

By the time he'd persuaded her to postpone the conversation, Banks had already sidled towards the door with a mutinous expression. He had to cut Lottie off in order to take a bad photo through the lounge window – Banks, disappearing down the path, garden gate swinging. He had no compulsion to chase after him, that was best left to someone else to deal with. In fact, a lot of tension had dissipated. He doubted very much that Banks was dangerous, or even posed a threat. He was like a cardboard cutout, pretending to be a private investigator and copying every cliché he'd ever seen. If everyone took their bloody washing lines in, what would he do all day? Twat.

He drove back to the office with a sense of, not victory exactly, but no anti-climax either. He had no more time to spend on this, he needed to get his life back on track just as soon as he'd followed up with the physical confirmation.

In his office, Clarissa's boys filled both sofas in reception. Red, bullish necks spilling over collars and fingers like sausages. They wanted photographs, information. All he had was a few sketchy details of where Banks had been seen, a school picture in black and white, and the blurry one on his mobile.

'That it?'

'I know it's not much, but he was at Clarissa's last Friday.'

'The private investigator?' They both laughed. 'What's he done? Owe money, does he? Tried to touch up the missus?'

'No, nothing like that. He's bothering my family with weird rumours, upsetting the children.'

'We can't have him upsetting the kiddies.'

'I don't want him beaten to a pulp, just frighten him off.'

'You mean like, bend his little bones instead of snapping them?'

'Not even that. More like knocking an irritating fly away.'

Dum grunted, then Dee. Handshakes ensued and both men had to turn sideways to pass back through the doors.

Tabitha raised her brows. 'Any feedback on the viewing for Mrs Barnaby?'

'No, it was a no-show.'

As late summer broke into a wet September, Lottie's excitement grew as the start date for drama school grew closer. A new television series based in Chester was rumoured to be holding auditions across the country to find child actors. Lottie had already looked into it and set her heart on the part of Lucy Jo, a precocious nine-year-old. When she received an enormous amount of money for this she was going to buy a black labrador puppy and call it Sonny B. Jack reckoned it was only a matter of time before this became reality and she was Charley Redman for real.

Despite the potential attraction of being a yummy mummy to a gifted child, Patsy seemed increasingly exasperated with Lottie's rapid development. Over the summer she seemed to have morphed into a young teen, argumentative and rude.

'For the hundredth time we are not having a dog!' Patsy said, tipping swimming gear out of bags and onto the kitchen floor. 'It's too small in here. Anyway, you can keep one at the farm.'

'We don't go there anymore!' she yelled, then turned to Jack. 'It means son-of-Benson. I know it won't really be Benson's son but that won't matter, will it?'

'No, not if you love it.'

Patsy held his eye contact, itching to say something, and followed him out to the car when he made to go. It was high tide and the water slopped over the edge of the quay, grey and choppy. The wind rendered the gulls silent as they hovered and watched, their heads down. Feeling chilled, he grabbed his jacket off the rear seats.

'So, what's happening with Simon?' Patsy hissed. 'Surely you've spoken to him by now?'

'I've dealt with it. It's sorted.'

'How?'

'Banks has been warned off and I've shredded the letter.'

'Shredding it won't make the problem go away.'

'All we have to do is stick to what you said originally. It's Philipe, or someone being vindictive.'

'She won't swallow that.'

'Well, has she said anything else?'

'No, but ... well, who *did* send it? That's what I want to know.'

'Look, the subject's closed. Just keep your mouth shut. Can you manage that?'

She folded her arms. 'Why don't you go to the farm anymore? *Jack!*'

He slammed the car door as if he hadn't heard her.

The town was quiet. The tail-off of school holidays and a change in the weather meant a lull before the adult holiday season kicked in, couples with no children and the elderly. Even the one-way system was clear of boats and coaches and he was on the mountain road in minutes. A couple of weekends had passed. He still hadn't seen or spoken to Anna, but he intended to do something about that. With the gallery opening coming up he needed to talk to her, see what they could salvage of their relationship. A huge, yawning ache roamed around his insides, intensifying as he drew closer to the farm.

The familiarity was like coming home after a long absence. The hurt of what she'd done was eclipsed with love, finally. But then he saw a Jones-Parry For Sale board at the end of the drive, and another, albeit smaller, irritation; Peter Claymore's Mercedes parked in his spot beneath the wisteria.

CHAPTER THIRTEEN

Anna

Peter was bowled over when she finally allowed him to see it. In fact he didn't speak for several minutes, just looked from several different angles and rubbed his chin. She was nervous of his critical eye. She'd wanted to break away from classical correctness, and paint freestyle. The result was a personal interpretation of Llewellyn the Great. The six-foot canvas filled the room with his haunting presence. The intensity of Llewellyn's gaze was likely a manifestation of her own unhappiness, but didn't truly great creation begin with unrest and despair?

Her inspiration had always grown out of landscapes, or so she'd thought. Llewellyn's history, full of epic battles with King John of England – first a friend, then a foe – echoed centuries of disquiet along the Welsh and English borders. She'd immersed herself in his life, walked the Roman roads across the hills where he'd likely travelled, climbed the castle walls and stood where he'd stood, looked across the mouth of the river Conwy and down at the crumbling walls of his town. There was so much of his heritage remaining it was easy to find the right vibe.

For the first time in her life, she'd painted what she'd felt, and not what she'd seen.

Eventually, Peter spoke. 'I'm going to hang this at the top of the apex and have it angled slightly forwards so he's looking down. He'll come alive in that space.'

'I can't wait to see it. He should be in a beautifully preserved building.'

'I agree,' he said and moved closer. 'Those eyes … *astonishing*.'

'It's the thought of being invaded by the English.'

He turned and laughed, his expression finally relaxed. 'You're not joking, are you?'

They moved into the kitchen and she poured drinks, last year's elderflower champagne, as promised. Peter passed it under his nose then held it to the light. 'A woman of many talents.'

'You haven't tasted it yet.'

He took a careful sip, eyes closed. 'Oh, it's like drinking summer.'

'It's pretty heady, so don't be fooled by its innocent perfume.'

'Ah, must be female,' he said, and returned her quick smile. She busied herself with the pot-roasted chicken and he hovered around the table with cutlery. 'Jack not joining us?'

'Oh, he's busy with the children.'

'Great kids.'

'Uh-huh.'

'I, er, I know you don't get along with Patsy.'

'You've noticed?'

'I've noticed the sign at the end of the road as well. Seems a terrible shame, I can't help wondering …'

'I'm downsizing, moving slightly out of town, that's all.'

'But where will you work, paint? The loft space here is perfect.'

Yes, the loft space was perfect – it was just the rest of her life that wasn't. She had no idea what was happening with Jack; she'd hurt and betrayed him, and it seemed to have all backfired dismally. Sending that letter to Chelsey had been an impulsive, stupid thing to do. Her reasoning was skewed, she knew this. Showing up Patsy as the lying cheat she really was had been the driving force, but she'd also felt strongly motivated by her own, and Jack's, future sanity.

Patsy had been insufferable lately. An invasion of the English army couldn't have made a better job of making her feel uncomfortable in her own skin, in her own space. Putting the farm on the market was perhaps another badly thought-out idea but it seemed the only way to have Jack realise how serious she was, how much of what he'd done disturbed her peace of mind. Whether she'd actually have the bottle to go through with it was another matter entirely. And if she and Jack didn't actually have a relationship after all, what would be the point of moving? Patsy was only so nasty because she and Jack were together under her nose.

Peter helped himself to roasted vegetables, and although she did her best to hide her true feelings, it was difficult not to give away her trembling insides. She was about to grasp the ladle when he covered her hand with his, unusually serious. 'Anna. I'm sorry if my relationship with Jack's ex makes anything awkward, but *please*, please don't let her get in the way of what you want to do, who you want to *be*.'

'I can't lie. I hate her living here. But that's not your fault, it was a misguided move on Jack's part.'

He nodded sagely and removed his hand. There was a deeper layer to Peter but it was usually concealed by his natural bonhomie. She suspected his marriage break-up and the cancer had damaged him far more than he let on, but she was more or less certain that his 'fun' with Patsy was nothing more than that. He never talked about his relationships beyond the basic, superficial facts. He helped himself to more elderflower champagne while she cut wedges of warm summer pudding and spooned clotted cream on the side. Before long, they were back talking about the launch.

'Here's an idea,' he said, back in his comfort zone. 'If you do move, downsize or whatever and find no suitable area to convert to a studio, would you consider working in the gallery? I've had the go-ahead on the final phase.'

'The wall of glass?'

'Yes, and I was thinking mezzanine floor? And I was thinking studio space? And if you might like to be my gallery manager?'

'What are your plans for the gallery?'

'We'd only open to the public Friday through to Sunday to start with, but you could use the premises any time.'

It was a lifeline of sorts, a flattering, incredibly attractive option. Her own beautiful white space, uninterrupted by the comings and goings of day-to-day life. She'd be untouchable behind a wall of one-way glass. 'You've been doing a lot of thinking.'

He laughed. 'I have. To be honest, I've been a sleeping partner in the family business for too long, what with being in remission and now this project, but I do need to get back into the swing of things over there. On top of this I've had an offer accepted on a building in Cornwall which I'd like to develop in the same way as Conwy. And then my house has been terribly neglected. It's been tenanted for a while but they've not renewed the contract.'

'If you're looking for a tenant, I know one.'

He shot her a rueful smile. 'I did think of Patsy and the children, but to be honest I'm not sure Jack would go for that. He's only just moved them here, hasn't he?'

216

'Yes. No, I'm sure you're right. I'm clutching at straws.'

'Well, for one thing it's a pretty big house for one adult and two children. And the children do seem to have had a lot of upheavals.'

She couldn't dispute this, but she was aware of his empathy, the way his eyes followed hers. Of course his investment in her peace of mind was very much linked to future projects, not that that was a slur on his part.

They'd just finished coffee when she heard Jack's car outside. Her insides turned to electrified mush. When the knock on the door came, Peter let him into the hall, glass still in his hand. It was odd that Jack had knocked at all but Peter didn't notice. The dogs leapt around Jack's legs and he hunkered down to fuss them. He must have been swimming because his hair was slightly damp.

'Jack! Perfect timing,' Peter said, loudly and expansively. 'Would you believe we've been discussing the launch? Patsy's sick of hearing about it but Anna and I can talk for hours. Have you tried this elderflower champagne of hers? I think it's superb, I'm trying to persuade her to serve it on the night.'

'Yeah, I have,' he said. His eyes held hers then scanned the remains of dinner.

'Have you eaten? There's plenty left,' she said, turning to the Aga.

'No, but no thanks. I don't want to intrude if you've got things to plan.'

'Not at all, we're just about done,' Peter said, looking for his jacket. 'I'm on my way while I can still legally drive.'

She followed him down the hall and he bent to kiss both sides of her face and clasped her hands. 'Thank you for a wonderful meal.'

'Thank you for being such good company. I

promise I'll consider everything we talked about.'

'Good,' he said, holding her eyes.

He folded himself into his Mercedes then as a last thought, pushed his head out of the window. 'And think again about the champagne; we could have enormous rustic vases everywhere, bursting with elder.'

'It's not really champagne, we would have to call it Hedgerow Cava or something.'

'I love it!' He made a bon appétit gesture and began to reverse as the window slid back. She waved him off, then took a deep breath and went back inside the house.

Jack was like a loose part, car keys still in his hand. 'We need to talk.'

'Let's go through to the sitting room.'

The dogs wouldn't leave him alone. Hooper commanded prime position on the sofa, front paws on Jack's lap, licking his face every time he began to speak, so she used the opportunity to tell him about Peter's proposition.

'I see,' Jack said eventually, clamping Hooper's muzzle. 'He's got it all worked out, hasn't he? He's virtually encouraging you to sell up and move. Or was that Patsy's idea? Have you considered that?'

'I don't think for one minute that Peter would be coerced by Patsy, he's far too astute. And I'd like to think that he's offered me this opportunity based on my skills and trust.'

He sighed and rubbed his face. 'No, you're right, I'm sorry. Josh has invited everyone he can think of to the launch.'

She dropped down onto the sofa next to him. 'You are going to be there, aren't you? I *want* you to be there.'

'Yeah, course.'

They had a round-the-houses conversation again about the same problems which had beset them at the beginning of the year. Although he forgave her for sending the letter and understood her reasoning, he seemed determined to cling to the misguided belief that Chelsey needed protecting at all cost.

He said, 'I admit I made a mistake moving Patsy here, although I couldn't foresee she'd begin a relationship with Claymore, could I? You say you made a mistake sending that letter, so can we not call it quits and try to move on? Can we not face these issues together?'

'But that's just words. They're gone in seconds. *Nothing* has actually changed.'

'*You* have. That's not just words. And to even *think* about selling this place, I don't understand it.'

'If I stay here there's the problem of a certain someone forever in my face.'

'What can I do about that?'

'Move her out again.'

'Both children are about to start school, you're not being fair.'

'*Fair?*'

She couldn't help exhaling dramatically but it stopped her from crying or losing her temper. She crossed to the window and looked at the garden. It felt like autumn was waiting in the wings but it was still technically summer, though the horse-chestnut tree glowed with a handful of topaz leaves. The new white dove-cote – courtesy of Dan and Ellie – was like a beacon in the gathering dusk.

'There just seems to be too much baggage to keep hauling over my shoulder, and my cheek is tired of being turned. I don't know, it feels like everything is in the wrong place at the moment,' she said.

'Including me.'

She heard him shuffle to his feet, heard Hooper jump down and pad into the kitchen to his water bowl and she expected Jack to come to her, to fold his arms around her. Her skin, every fibre of her body was poised to be reunited with him. When he didn't touch her, when she was forced to turn around, he'd gone from the room and the dogs were stood in the hall, dejected and uncertain, the front door slightly ajar.

He was in his car, head on the steering wheel. He was so upset he could barely look at her. She opened the passenger door and scrambled in. Hooper tried to follow, his hind legs missing the steps by miles. It almost made her smile but it was too desperate.

'No, not including you,' she said, her voice breaking with emotion.

He came into her arms, but it was awkward, like there was an invisible pane of glass between them.

She'd always been commitment-phobic. Some would call it independent, but having someone invest all of their hopes and dreams in her was just plain scary. She'd let Alex do this, and he'd got carried away and left her behind. With Jack, their situation hadn't put any pressure on her until now. She knew he wanted more, to live full-time with her and have his children within reach, marriage, even. She couldn't blame him, but the current state of play was not based on a solid foundation. She could place one foot on the scaffold, but not two. And instead of looking up at the stars, she tended to look down into the deep water. It didn't help that since she'd researched all that history, there were certain behaviours that were repeated over and over throughout the centuries as if it were inevitable.

Hilly thought she was cutting off her nose to spite her face by putting the farm on the market. They were in the old tea shop on Castle Street, since Hilly refused to set foot inside the new coffee shop on High Street. At least it was next door to the doctor's surgery, so Anna could pop in for her blood test results in person.

'I think you're totally nuts, but I know you won't listen to me,' Hilly said, pouring tea out of a chipped pot. 'How much more can you put that poor man through?'

'Poor man? You mean Jack?'

'Of course I mean Jack!'

She pushed her cake plate to one side. 'I think something has happened to my common sense, it seems to desert me these days when I'm under pressure.'

'Oh, I'm no stranger to that. It's been an awful year,' she said sheepishly. 'I'm sorry we fell out, I'm as much to blame.'

'I couldn't help wonder if there was some truth in you saying I was menopausal, I've had a test. Oh, maybe I should just throw my clothes into St Celynin's well.'

'What good would that do?'

'To see if they float? It used to mean you'd be cured of whatever ills you were suffering from.'

'There's no cure for you, take it from me. Everything would sink to the bottom, especially those gumboots.'

'Thanks! Anyway, now you've cheered me up and solved my problems, tell me what's happening with you?'

'I'm calling it a day, the trekking, that is. I'm officially closed to the public; I've no insurance for one thing.'

'Oh, *Hilly*. End of an era!'

'I know but, well I just can't do it any more. Not only am I too bloody old, I'm having to declare myself bankrupt and Bryn's taking over in his name, running it as a livery yard. And then there's the buying and selling.'

'With Heather?'

'Bryn doesn't like it either but we're only keeping our heads above water through shifting Heather's stock on Facebook.'

'You're selling horses on *Facebook?*'

'Big and Irish, it's called,' she said, slurping tea. 'She brings them over and we do the rest then split the profits.'

This sounded thoroughly depressing, as if the poor animals were crates of handbags. She wouldn't be surprised if some of them were stolen, brought over on the boats with fake passports then dispersed through the UK with cash changing hands. Hilly shot her a look. 'I know what you're thinking and I don't like it either, but what can we do?'

'Ask no questions?'

'Something like that. And if you go looking for that website don't go on Big, *hot,* and Irish. That's something totally different.'

Her blood test results confirmed that she was indeed on the periphery of the menopause. She was standing on the abyss of something she didn't want.

'Mid-forties. You're on the young side,' the nurse said, pumping the blood pressure cuff. 'But it's not that unusual. Cheer up, there's worse things, believe me. You're otherwise pretty fit and healthy. It's not like it's the end of your active life or anything.'

It felt like the end of something, though. She was officially a woman of a certain age, the butt of jokes. When men thought, 'She looks really *hot*,' they would mean it in the literal sense. Curious that she thought of something as shallow as that when all her life she could never recall thinking it mattered what men thought of her. Could she lay the blame for her recent behaviours wholly on menopausal tendencies? The way she'd gone about decisions lately had certainly been less than sensitive. She'd always been blunt, maybe this would become more pronounced, like the instinct for survival, females who could no longer reproduce were useless in nature's cruel cycle.

Suitably admonished by the nurse, she came out with a handful of leaflets, thinking that at least they'd make a decent fan if she didn't get around to reading them. Jack's mother was at the reception desk making an appointment, and they looked at each other awkwardly.

'Oh, Anna. Are you alright? We've not had a chat in ages. Are you free for a drink?'

'Not for tea or coffee. I've just done that with Hilly.'

'We could go to the Fisherman's on the quay and sit outside?'

They walked past the harbour master's offices, the lifeboat shop, and the mussel unit. Anna found a picnic table and shooed away the seagulls. She was grateful when Isabel came out with the drinks, a pint of ale and a sweet sherry, both in the same size plastic tumblers. The leaflets were on the table. Isabel was quick to understand the implication and gave her a rueful smile.

'Lottie is at the beginning, and you're at the end,' she said. 'Both of you early starters. Forty years of The Curse followed by The Change of Life, that's what my mother used to call it.'

'More changes,' she sighed, stuffing the offending leaflets into her bag. 'Oh, poor Lottie.'

'Of course it's been left to Jack to explain it all,' she said. 'My mother would have been horrified and deeply ashamed by that – a *man* explaining menstruation to his daughter? Unheard of! I doubt my father even knew what actually happened, it was never spoken of. It was all a closely guarded secret, as if they'd be damaged if they knew the truth. Leo wasn't much better, you know, he used to whisper if Kate had a period. I'm quite proud of my sons in that respect, I broke the chain. I made them read *The Female Eunuch* and I sent them into chemists for female products from a young age. Neither would flinch now. You see, some things change for the better, don't they?'

Anna smiled and studied Isabel's profile. No make-up, good skin, and well-cut hair, uncoloured. She and Jack shared those chameleon eyes which shifted easily between the grey of storms to the soft, dove grey of kindness. There was something essentially good, dignified, and intelligent inside Isabel, a lot of qualities which reminded her of Jack.

Oh, Jack. What have we done? I feel like my life is slipping away without you.

His mother took her tightly closed eyes to mean something else, and took hold of her cold hand. 'Just embrace it as the next stage in your life, no point trying to fight against the inevitable. You're still *you*. A beautiful, talented woman in her prime.'

'Thank you,' she said, pulling herself together. 'I know what you're saying … I just don't feel it.'

They finished their drinks and walked back the way they'd come, linking arms, heads down against the wind from the incoming tide. Isabel said, 'Are you looking forward to your launch? I've peered through the windows. Peter's transformed that old building.'

'I think so. I'm nervous, though. He seems to have coerced not only the local press but one of the nationals as well, and a couple of those arty critique types.'

'You'll be a runaway success,' Isabel said confidently, then as they approached the car park by the surgery, found herself held more firmly. 'Oh, Anna. What's wrong between you and Jack? I hope you feel you can talk to me, I won't betray your confidence. I'm just as much on your side, I don't always agree with Jack.'

'No, I know.'

'I'm *your* mum too. I think of you like a daughter and it upsets me when you and Jack are at loggerheads. You can tell me to keep my nose out, if you like.'

'I could never do that,' she said, then shrugged and looked to the castle to the Welsh and English flags united in the wind. 'I don't know. We just keep hurting each other, arguing and going round in circles.'

'There's always a compromise.'

She was right of course, they just needed to find it.

In the meantime, the agent sent people round to view Gwern Farm. She felt detached, watching them wander through her home. Jack's belongings were more or less as he'd left them. To remove them or tidy them away held a significance she didn't want to think about, so she continued to fall over his shoes and stub her toe on his toolbox. By way of compromise, she began to fill bags, some for the charity shop and some for Josh. It was cathartic in a lot of ways; after all, there were only so many sets of old fire tongs one needed, worn-out shoes and trousers which no longer fitted. The leaflets from the surgery said she could look forward to getting even fatter, more sweaty, and irritable, so why was she holding on to these useless, uncomfortable items? Her clothes resigned to outside jobs, dog walking, and gardening were over-subscribed as it was. Feeling ruthless, she threw her riding gear onto the pile as well.

It seemed in no time the back of the Land Rover

was overflowing, but it felt good to be proactive and take some control back into her life, however small.

A couple of days later, she took the dogs for an early morning run on the beach. They weren't impressed at being squashed onto the front seats of the Land Rover for the journey, but on realising they hadn't arrived at the vets after all, ran joyously across the rippled sand. It was a serene September morning, still summery with only a subtle shift of temperature, a discreet undercurrent of cooler air. Low tide, and the mussel banks were prominent, covered with oyster catchers and gulls.

Beyond the car park, there were hoof prints across the dunes, deep disturbances of the sand where horses had plunged and slid on their haunches before cantering across the beach towards Penmaen Head. Even scouring the horizon, there was no sign of them, but the tracks went on forever across the unblemished surface. It made her feel unutterably alone. As if something had come and gone without her. As if she'd not been quick enough to catch it and hold on to it, or it had simply run away. She automatically looked round for Benson, and Hooper pushed his cold sandy nose into her hand.

Had she done the right thing, pushing Jack away then rubbing his nose in it?

She looked at all the second- and third-hand paraphernalia pushed up against the windows of her car and decided that no, she was almost pushing her own nose in it for being too stubborn, too ashamed and not looking hard enough for a compromise. Yes, she'd admitted it, she *was* ashamed. The weekend she'd sent Jack away was the turning point, the turning of the screw. The weekend she'd sent the letter. Although, didn't she do this on a regular basis? If she really,

really loved him, wouldn't she want to be with him on a more permanent, equal footing?

The dogs jumped back in the footwell, tongues lolling, faces expectant.

It was still early, before opening time, when she bumped up onto the pavement next to the Oxfam shop. To her irritation, Patsy was in the square helping Lottie onto the school bus. She was impossible to miss with that long, loose, chestnut hair, blow-dried to perfection. A short, white woollen coat, designer denims, and an oversized shiny handbag completed the urban look. Bad timing. She hesitated, then sighed and began to haul the considerable pile of dustbin liners and boxes out of the Land Rover. After a short while, she could feel the evil eyes seeking her out, watching her every move.

The bus roared away and she looked up in time to see Lottie waving rather forlornly from the back window. She lifted a hand and smiled, then turned back to the bags, throwing them unceremoniously onto the pavement. One of them gave way, spilling clothes into the road as Patsy headed over. Green eyes flashing, she nudged a pair of horrible old shorts with her foot, then folded her arms and laughed.

'Good grief, Williams, how old are they?'

'Excuse me, you're in my way.'

'I've heard you're moving. I'm not surprised. I'm already bored beyond comprehension here,' Patsy said, shooting a cursory look into the shop window. 'I've lived in some dumps but this takes the prize for country bumpkins and a dead night life.'

'Well, then, there's an easy answer to that. Move.'

A sneer from Patsy while she watched her pick up sundry items that had rolled into the gutter; her grandmother's brass trinkets, pottery cats, and a butter dish. She piled everything neatly against the shop door then began to rearrange the toolkit, shopping bags, and old towels for the dogs in the back of her car, her eyes resting momentarily on the dog poop she'd been obliged to pick up off the beach earlier. Patsy moved in, close and personal, shadowing her movements.

'It *was* you, wasn't it? You sent the letter. Tell the truth.'

'The truth? What would you know about that?'

'The truth is, even Jack's had enough. You really are a fat, bitter old maid, aren't you?'

She was about to close the tailgate and thought about it for no more than a second before flicking the poop at her. It happened in the blink of an eye, almost a reflex. Patsy didn't even move aside. The overfull bag split on impact, and the glutinous mess splattered across her white coat like chocolate mousse poured over vanilla ice-cream. A lot of it went in her hair. At first it looked and behaved like wet sand, but then the smell must have hit her like a toxic cloud. Her face contorted slowly.

Her expression reminded her of those funny facial gymnastics opera singers go through before they break into a dramatic performance. The glorious, overriding difference was that Patsy was too shocked to open her mouth.

CHAPTER FOURTEEN

Jack

Patsy was incandescent, barely able to breathe. It was virtually impossible to understand what she was saying. It didn't help that he was on the reception desk and it was busy; two couples waiting to see him and his mother on hold on another line. Once he'd established there was no emergency with either of the children, he tried again to get a word in, but Patsy could only communicate on full volume.

'THAT WITCH FLUNG *DOG* SHIT AT ME!'

Several people browsing the For Sale display looked across. 'I'll call back when you've calmed down.'

'I'll *never* calm down! My Chanel coat is ruined.'

'What are you doing about a job now the children are in school?'

'A job? There's nothing here! All the beautician jobs are in Chester.'

'There must be something you can do.'

'I CAN COMMIT A MURDER!'

This was audible to everyone in the immediate vicinity. Tabitha looked especially haunted, shooting a sickly smile at the hovering customers. He cut her off. A vision of Patsy and Anna throwing dog shit at each other in the street was not something he wanted to think about. It wouldn't be the full story of course, but he was worn out with thinking. He simply wanted

Anna's arms around him, to be able to lay his head next to hers at night. It would be nice to enjoy a reasonable work-life balance as well. Nothing more, nothing less. He wanted to be with the woman he loved, was that unreasonable? He worked hard and looked after his family to the best of his ability, but nothing seemed good enough, there was always another goal, another fight, another bloody battle to be won. He had no idea where he stood with Anna, and mixed with the despair and the insecurity, rapidly germinating seeds of anger were taking root.

He loosened his tie. His mother was next in the queue.

'Anna was in the doctor's, I didn't tell you, OK? She's started the menopause. I told her, I breezed through it.'

'You might have done, but me and Danny didn't. If I remember rightly, you tried to push us both down the bloody stairs. Dad moved out, didn't he?'

'Oh, you're mixing it up with something else. And blowing it out of proportion.'

'I seem to remember hanging around A&E quite a bit.'

'What I'm trying to say is, be sensitive. I think she's finding it hard, and she's nervous about the launch. You will be there for her, won't you?'

'Yes!' He threw his pen across the desk.

He didn't return Patsy's call, he tried to speak to Anna instead. She was frosty about the whole incident and they had a horrible, stilted conversation about some people who'd viewed the farm. Why should he give her any advice? The very thought of it gave him angry palpitations. He changed the subject to the gallery. Did she want him to pick her up so they could arrive together?

'To be honest, I'm not totally sure what's

happening yet. Can I meet you there?'

'Fine.'

'We can talk afterwards, yes?'

'Fine.'

The weekend before the launch was miserable. Anna hadn't told him to stay away exactly, but she hadn't offered her time either, and given the current status quo he didn't even want to ask, let alone beg. He wanted to feel sorry for himself for a change, and so stayed in the flat although it was impossible to relax as he was clearly in Oliver's space. Evidence of this manifested itself with a vengeance when he came face to face with a virtually naked Amy in the bathroom on Saturday morning. Thank Christ he was wearing boxers, although Amy had no shame whatsoever and looked to be wearing only false eyelashes and a furry black and white animal tail, held firmly in place by a thong. What was the deal with that? What was she meant to be, a racoon?

'Hi, Jack!' she said breathily, her huge, expectant eyes on his. When he didn't respond, at least not verbally, she squeezed past him while he stood flattened against the wall with his eyes closed. He heard Oliver's bedroom door slam shut, then muffled giggles. He couldn't even go and see the children because Patsy and Peter were away with them, something he hadn't factored in to the general scheme of things and caught him out yet again with another set of feelings he was unprepared for. To be fair to Claymore, he was difficult to dislike. The guy had even called him midweek first.

'Did you have anything planned for the weekend? I don't want to muscle in, Jack, it's just that my parents have offered and I think that Lottie and James might enjoy it, they live very close to Alton Towers …'

'No, no go for it. Thanks for asking me.'

He couldn't help wondering how Claymore handled the now obvious problems between Patsy and Anna. And if Claymore insisted on taking Patsy to the launch, was he going to be responsible for her behaviour? Maybe he should say something about that and start being a bit more proactive.

'Actually, I could do with a private word, maybe before everyone gets too busy?'

'Oh, OK. I'll be around all day Friday. If I'm not in the gallery I'll be grabbing a sandwich in the hotel bar.'

Not knowing what else to do, he booked himself into the hotel as well, then worried whether he'd tightened defences effectively around Chelsey. Would the battlements be overrun? Although he'd promised himself not to overthink anything, he called Dum, or was it Dee? It had only been a couple of weeks but he couldn't keep Banks under surveillance forever, and he'd rather get it all out of the way before the gallery opening and before he had to interact with Chelsey. Surely this one problem could be dealt with and out of his hair?

On Thursday morning, Dum and Dee manoeuvred themselves into his office. Jack closed the door and looked at them both expectantly. 'Not much to tell,' Dee said, throwing a file onto the desk. 'Bit of a sad geezer.'

'Tell me something I don't know.'

'He's of no fixed abode. Looks like he had a flat, gave it up. Shunts between five-star hotels and camping. No living relatives, no previous, no loans. Clean as a whistle, pays for everything in cash.'

'What does he do all day? Is he still watching my family?'

'Yeah, that's the weird thing,' Dum said, glancing at his notes. 'Your daughter's address, Chelsey, is it?

He's been following her, just watching. So we had a word.'

'And?'

'He won't be feeling too good for a while, crawled into his hidey hole.'

'Where?'

'Conwy. We waited till he'd got his camp set up, we're considerate like that. Middle of fucking nowhere, but that kind of made the job easy for us, you know?'

All they could give him was a vague area near the druid's circle, and the registration number of a second-hand Ford which was stationed in a secluded parking spot off the mountain road. From there, it was an easy enough climb onto the open hillside, although Dum and Dee must have been cursing at the incline.

'Did he speak to her?'

'Not that we could tell, and not that he's admitting.'

A certain measure of relief came with this information, but the fact that Banks was in Conwy was vaguely unsettling, although if he hadn't approached Chelsey by now he was unlikely to find the balls to do it with her family around. Clarissa's boys were anxious to be off the case, clearly bored now that they'd completed the duffing-up stage, and since their employment was based mostly on a favour, he felt obliged to shake hands on it.

The day of the launch was a mellow autumn day. Hoping this was good sign, he called Anna and she seemed in high spirits.

'Thanks for the roses and the lilies, they came just now.'

'Good. I'll, er, see you later, then? Good luck. Anna, I ...'

'Yes ... I'll see you later.'

It was an odd conversation, as if they'd gone backwards in their relationship. The second he disconnected, Chelsey's name came up on the screen, call waiting. His pulse quickened.

'Hi, love.'

'Mike and I have booked in to the hotel and I'm meeting Mum in the bar at five. Please will you be there as well? I've something I need to say to you both.'

'What do you mean?'

A beat. 'I'd rather do this face-to-face.'

'Oh? Sounds serious.'

'It is, yes.'

'OK ... I'll, er, see you later.'

He couldn't tell anything from her voice. What the hell was that about? Fully distracted, he pulled an overnight bag from the wardrobe and started to place various items inside, not really paying attention. Something had happened, something he had no knowledge of, but then it wasn't necessarily anything to do with Banks, was it? It could be anything. A new baby? No, she sounded too down for that. Marital problems? Well, she and Mike had booked a room together, so maybe not.

Calm down. Banks was out of action, the launch would be a success, and he'd get everything sorted with Anna.

He went thoughtfully down the stairs and threw the holdall into the back of his vehicle. At this rate, he could look forward to a queue of people waiting to argue with him, give him bad news, or scare the living daylights out of him. Great way to spend the weekend.

In the office, his staff were at the helm. Tony was busy dealing with maintenance issues on the rental properties and redesigning the website. Clare was out on appointments, mostly his. Tabitha and Oliver were covering reception. Oliver had shown no interest in the gallery, choosing to stay in Wilmslow instead. No doubt he'd be having a party in the flat the second his back was turned. He appeared at his office door, throwing an apple from palm to palm.

'Dad, can Amy move in?'

'No.'

'Why not?'

He sighed and began to close down his computer and put the stapler away in the drawer, along with the box of paperclips, before slamming it shut. It was no good, he couldn't remain calm.

'I have a problem with this on so many levels. A lack of respect? If you like Amy enough to sleep with her, go and start a life together somewhere else. I don't *want* naked racoons in my bathroom. This is *my* place and I'm not paying for you two to live like bloody students at my expense.'

'So it's a no, then?'

'It's a no to her even staying over if I'm in residence. Got that?'

'If you're in *residence?*'

'Got it,' he said, then slid his mobile across the desk. 'And while we're on the subject, can you please delete that stupid ringtone? My sex is *not* on fire.'

He took a big bite of the apple. 'What do you want instead?'

'I just want it to ring!'

The ring. It was still in the inside pocket of his leather jacket. If everything had been right between him and Anna, the post-launch party would be a great opportunity to ask her. At this rate he'd be lucky to get two words in private, let alone set her sex on fire. He said a grumpy goodbye to everyone and they all wished him a nice weekend and best of luck to Anna, blah blah.

On arrival at Conwy a couple of hours later, the town looked deceptively calm. The tide was in, leaping at the foot of the bridge and slopping against the quay. He couldn't help thinking that Banks was only a couple of miles away, or at least his car was. What on earth had he done, getting him beaten up like that? He hoped they hadn't gone too far. Maybe they should have gone to the police, but then it would all come out, and Chelsey hadn't exactly reported him. It was tempting to go looking, but what would that achieve? Anyway, the whole point of Dum and Dee was for his own protection.

The hotel was full. He checked in, showered, and changed into denims and a black jacket before walking to the gallery. Claymore first, get that out of the way before he bumped into anyone else. He tapped on the door with his keys. Peter's face appeared through the small circle of glass, then the door opened wide.

'Jack! Come in, come in. What do you think?'

He walked silently across the wooden floor and took in the vaulted ceiling, the partially exposed walls, and the beginnings of a mezzanine floor mostly covered by huge swathes of muslin. Everything he'd been going to say dropped out of his mind like rocks plummeting through water. He stayed silent because God knows what ignorant, unartistic crap would come out of his mouth otherwise. Everything he'd rehearsed to say about Patsy was suddenly irrelevant when faced with not only the transformation of the building but the way he'd positioned and lit Anna's paintings. Her landscapes he'd seen before, but now it looked like real sunlight glinting on wet slate. There were life-sized sculptures too, tortured-looking statues and bronzes of historic characters.

Here and there, huge rustic vases held masses of delicate, foaming bunches of elderflower.

'Not real, I'm afraid,' Peter said. 'They've stopped flowering, but these look OK, don't they? I'm serving the hedgerow champagne, you see.'

'Nice touch.'

Further along were portraits. Claymore seemed excited by these and drew his attention to a full-size canvas suspended from the rafters. 'Llewellyn, like you've never seen him before!'

'Did Anna paint that?'

'She did. I'm going to throw a muslin over it, then we can unveil him later.'

He was thrown by the power of the canvas and the sense of occasion, the sheer professional grandeur of it all. For some inexplicable reason he felt enormously proud, humbled, and emotional. His own petty problems shrunk into a dirty corner somewhere in the back of his mind and he felt compelled to ensure that the evening ran smoothly for her, whatever their personal difficulties.

'About Patsy –'

'All over,' Claymore cut in. 'I let her down as gently as I could.'

'Right … Well, I wasn't expecting that.'

'I was never totally comfortable with the whole package, Jack. I think it would be unfair to your children for me to have a frivolous relationship with their mother; and it was beginning to interfere with my professional projects.'

'You mean the dog shit incident?'

A wry, knowing smile at this. He unstacked a couple of chairs and they sat facing each other. 'I can't have the star of my show embroiled in street fights, but I've known them both long enough to guess at the backstory. I've offered Anna a manager's role. I think your ex-wife living here is, how shall I say, cramping her style?'

'I stuffed up there.'

Claymore nodded in agreement then leant forward, suddenly serious. 'Look, Jack. I have a six-bedroomed house in Chester. I need some tenants. I can't sell because I'm in the middle of a complicated divorce and the property is tied in with my business and my ex-wife.'

'Been there.'

'My older sister and her lady partner would like it very much, but they can't afford the full deal. Teachers' salaries aren't what they used to be, so here's the proposition: would Patsy and the children consider sharing?'

'Oh. Right, I wasn't expecting that either.'

'No, neither was I. I know it's a long shot but things change, don't they? And I know it's a little unorthodox, but I'd like to be able to come and go from time to time as well. I'd just take one of the smaller rooms. You see, I couldn't get this sort of deal if I was doing it through an agent. I mean, there's no way this would happen with a bunch of strangers.'

He agreed. The afternoon was already on fast-forward, his head full of scenarios he hadn't considered in his wildest dreams. Claymore didn't hang about with plans, but then he'd had a couple of years fighting cancer, so who could blame him? He talked about other potential premises in Cornwall and how he wanted to spend six months of the year working in Chester at his building company and then the six summer months between Conwy and Tintagel. Jack partially zoned out, trying to imagine Patsy sharing a house with two middle-aged teachers in a same-sex relationship.

'I know you have the children's interests to consider,' Claymore went on. 'And I know it's not ideal from an access point of view, but will you give it some thought and let me know by the end of next week, say?'

'Sure.'

Despite the obvious solution for Anna and the farm, his immediate thought was for James. Lottie's drama school was midway between Chester and Conwy and a move was unlikely to cause a problem there, but his small son would have to face yet another change in his life. Patsy would have no trouble finding work, but that in itself was another negative for James and he wasn't sure if he could bring himself to initiate it. At least Claymore had dumped Patsy, another plus for Anna. A warm glow of retribution flooded his senses, coupled with the assurance that it was very unlikely she'd turn up later.

On the face of it, things were mildly positive on that front and he hadn't even lifted a finger.

Back at the hotel, Dan and Ellie were in the bar, still wrapped round each other in loved-up bliss.

'Where's Anna?' they said. He was saved by Josh, scanning the bar for them.

'Mum's in a right flap, I wouldn't go anywhere near the farm,' he said with unusual vehemence. 'I've just dropped off the champers for Peter.'

'Does she need a lift down?'

'Nope. Got a taxi ordered. I think she's planning on drinking most of that stuff herself.'

They all laughed and the atmosphere eased, until Mike materialised and took Jack to one side.

'Change of plan. I know Chel arranged to meet you in the bar later but can you pop round to the cottage now? Patsy's in a bit of a state.'

'Oh, alright. What's it about, do you know?'

'Yeah, but I'm in danger of getting my balls chopped off if I say anything.'

'Right.'

He made the short walk to the quay and steeled himself to tap on the door. Chelsey opened it immediately, a world-weary expression playing around her young eyes, but they exchanged the usual platitudes about the drive down and the weather. Patsy was in a state alright, surrounded by wet tissues. The children had been dumped on Isabel again, although that was probably a good thing under the circumstances. His eldest daughter was her usual calm, sensible self and handed him a glass of whisky. In the past, she'd sided with Patsy when their marriage had started to fall apart, but over the years, the scales had fallen from her eyes. Despite this, he had an uncomfortable, racing pulse where the waterfall of tears were concerned. That, and Chelsey's forthright demeanour. She was very much in charge.

'I suppose you've heard Peter's finished with me?' Patsy said.

'I couldn't care less. I certainly haven't come round to listen to that.'

More tears, snivelling, and nose blowing. Chelsey, perched on the sofa arm, gave her mother a firm look. 'No, it's *not* about Peter Claymore. Dad, sit down, will you?'

At least she was still calling him Dad. Of course she was, why wouldn't she? He swirled the whisky round then drank most of it. She took a deep breath. 'I received a letter a few weeks ago saying I ought to get a DNA test done because you're not my real father. I've asked Mum twice and she's fobbed me off with rubbish. It's played on my mind for weeks, so now I'm asking *you*. Is there any truth is this allegation? Are you even aware of it?'

The world seemed to tilt, the blood pounded through his ears, loud and booming. He couldn't think straight. The remainder of the whisky slipped down his throat as he looked into her eyes. All the time he'd been worried about Banks, he'd taken his eye off the obvious ball. Of course she was eventually going to question it, there was never smoke without fire. Could he lie to her, face to face? If he flicked his eyes over to Patsy she'd know instantly there was some sort of collusion. The very moment he'd been fighting to avoid for months, maybe for years, had caught up with him. If Anna had never sent that letter ... He exhaled and looked at the carpet.

Chelsey said, 'I'm taking your silence to mean yes.'

'Chel, listen ...'

'All I want is for you both to tell me the truth.'

A horrible, stilted beat of silence. Patsy broke it. 'Oh, this is stupid. Your real father is a horrible man called Simon Banks and he's been pestering me for months.' She spat the words out, full of bitter self-pity. 'There, now you know. I've carried this burden for too long.'

'Well, thank you for your honesty at last,' Chelsey said. 'how long has Dad known about this?'

'Since your wedding day.'

'*My* wedding day? So you duped Dad all those years?'

'I didn't dupe anyone, it was for the best!'

They argued and argued. Chelsey took it out on her mother. He felt like a spare part, sat there not speaking or thinking. He wasn't even the sperm donor though, was he? Did he have a right to say anything? Patsy ran upstairs and the slam of a door somewhere disturbed him from inertia. He remembered getting to his feet to go and look for the whisky, but Chelsey stood in front of him and tried to catch hold of his hands. He had difficulty meeting her eyes so he studied the ceiling. He rubbed his temples. His voice was already becoming strangled with emotion. 'Chel …'

'You don't need to say anything. It's over and done with, *nothing's changed.*'

She hugged him, and his lips grazed her scented hair. 'Thank you for being so amazingly grown-up.'

'I'd like to say I inherited my maturity from you, but I'd be lying.'

He half-laughed, relief beginning to flood through him. 'I've been *dreading* this.'

'You're my dad and I love you. As far as I'm concerned, that's the end of this stupid mess.'

They stood in Patsy's kitchen drying their eyes on paper towel, or at least he did. In the end, they had nothing else to say and just laughed. He'd expected a long, drawn-out difficult conversation, Chelsey wanting every detail and then picking over who was to blame for it all and who'd sent the letter. But she didn't ask a single question about Banks. Presently, she said something about getting back to the hotel, but he needed to make arrangements about the children. He crossed to the window and watched Chelsey walk back down the quay, and it was the best feeling in the world when she turned and waved.

'She hates me, doesn't she?' Patsy said. He let the curtain fall back into place and turned to see her descending the stairs.

'Hate? You seem to have a knack for bringing that out in people.'

'It wasn't me who started this!'

'No, but you were more than happy to take the cash. Actually, Anna did us all a favour. I should never have doubted her.'

'That fat cow gets away with everything: throwing dog shit at me, breaking up my relationship with Peter, sending secret letters! No wonder you're not together.'

'She's been busy with the gallery, that's all.'

'Oh, that *fucking* gallery! I'm sick to death of it.'

'You know what I'm sick to death of? You!'

She shrank back against the wall, more tears springing to her eyes. 'Don't, Jack.'

'Don't what?'

'Talk as if you hate me too. I couldn't bear that. I thought ...'

'Go on, what?' he prompted, and moved in closer, fascinated by her doe-eyes. 'What did you think?'

'That we might have had a second chance.'

He must have looked dumbfounded. He certainly felt it. He searched in his mind to try and recall if he'd said or done anything to give her this idea before he stepped away from her. 'I'll collect the children tomorrow lunchtime.'

She looked down, slinky hair hiding her face, and he let himself out of the door. The fact she'd been harbouring such a fantasy should have taken centre stage in his head, but Chelsey's simple, heartfelt words ran through his mind over and over. Banks never had the slightest chance in hurting his family. He'd underestimated his thoroughly smart, grown-up daughter.

Nothing's changed. You need to have more faith in your relationships.

Dinner was a lively affair with eight of them. Josh, Mike and Chelsey, Dan and Ellie, and then his sister turned up at the last minute with a new man in tow. He tried calling Anna but only got the answerphone. Josh said, 'Oh, she's got some guy round there doing an interview and pictures I think.'

'That's a shame, she could have joined us.'

'Doubt she would have eaten anything, she was proper wound-up this morning.'

'Price of fame, huh?'

Isabel declined as well. She sounded worn-out but promised to be there for the main event.

'I've just dropped the children home and not only was Patsy sobbing, but she was *unforgivably* rude.'

He laughed. 'That's because Claymore's finally seen the light and dumped her.'

'Don't gloat, Jack.'

'Why not? She's not getting her own way for once. She's blown it, big time.'

Isabel tutted and disconnected, and he allowed another considerable swell of gloating to warm his insides. It was good to be on the other side of the fence for a change. Let the miserable, conniving bitch stay home alone with the children, out of everyone's way. He'd drop the house-share bombshell tomorrow, after he'd gloated a bit more with Anna. He had so much to tell her and he needed to apologise. She'd been right about the Banks conundrum. Maybe he could get a dog for Lottie and James. Claymore's house was bound to have a sizeable garden, wasn't it? Yeah, a black labrador called Sonny B.

The early evening passed in a happy, alcoholic blur with his grandson sat on his knee, pinching chips from his plate. When it crept towards seven, they moved en-masse to the gallery. Claymore had pulled out all the stops. There was a real buzz in the street. He'd simply thrown back the double doors and allowed people to wander in. Some of them had catalogues and special invitations. There was a huddle of press and a photographer, smoking and laughing in the street, waiting for Anna to arrive.

The atmosphere was great and he began to relax and enjoy himself. The harpist and fiddler Anna had commissioned for Dan's wedding were in situ somewhere towards the rear of the building. He could hear them tuning up, and then as the first strains of

Pachelbel's Canon in D Major filled the space, Danny's face began to crumple.

'Come on, Dan, it's a reminder of a happy occasion.'

'I know,' he managed to squeak out from behind a tissue. 'I'll be alright in a minute. I just need to find my wife.'

Hilly waved a rolled-up programme through a sea of faces to grab his attention. Bryn ambled behind her, looking uncomfortable in a suit.

'Hilly!' he shouted, 'have you seen Anna today?'

'Yes, this morning.'

'Was she alright?'

'Oh, in fine form. We went through lots of outfits together.'

'I'm glad you're friends again.'

'I think we were both to blame, stress can wreak havoc with common sense,' she said and pulled Bryn into the conversation with a nod. 'He's got something to say as well.'

Bryn's apology about his capitalist remark months ago came in the form of a string of daft excuses, but it was an apology nevertheless. The evening just got better and better. Now all he needed was Anna, in more ways than one. He wanted a new Mrs Redman very much. He wanted a romantic wedding in that old church in the hills Anna loved so much, with friends and family filling the ancient pews. He could see the old stones decorated with bunches of heather, sunlight streaming through the stained glass, and Lottie carrying a basket of wild flowers. They'd have to tranquillise Dan.

'Have you fixed a date yet?' he said to Hilly and Bryn.

'Can't even afford the banns at this rate, so no.'

The music ramped up a gear and the hedgerow

champagne went round.

Claymore was fussing with the drape over the painting of Llewellyn, then he began to push through the milling crowds, looking distinctly flustered.

'Where is she? She should be here by now!' he hissed, still smiling at passing guests.

'She'll be here.'

'Cutting it fine. I've tried ringing and texting, but no response. I can only hold off the press for another twenty minutes.'

When he glanced at his watch he was staggered to see it was close on eight. An hour late?

'I'll try calling her. Actually, I might go over there.'

'Would you? Josh is going to stand in and do her speech, he knows it word for word, apparently.'

Outside, he wandered down the street looking for a full signal. When he reached the old fountain in the square, he sat on the edge and lit a cigarette. The statue of Llewelyn looked resolute and ready for battle. There was a rare text from his mother. 'Sorry, darling, please give my apologies to Anna, but I'm exhausted.'

Of course she was. Another damn good reason to move Patsy away from her convenient child-minder. There was no reply from Anna's mobile or the landline. The dark turrets of Conwy Castle against the starless sky made him shiver and he pulled up his collar. Instantly sober, he walked briskly to the car park at the hotel, and slid into his car.

He concentrated on the mountain roads in the dark and pulled up outside the farmhouse. Her Land Rover was there, no lights on inside but the dogs were leaping in a frenzy at the sitting room window, barking and yelping. He used his key to let himself through the front door. Other than the dogs, it was silent. The kitchen tap dripped into a bowl of water. His eye went straight to the money on the table, a considerable stack of fifty-pound notes. What the hell? Had someone given her a cash deposit for the farm? Pretty stupid place to leave it.

'Anna!'

Another cacophony of barking from the dogs, who were shut in the sitting room. He made for the stairs, worried that she'd maybe fallen or passed out, but the bathroom door creaked open to reveal nothing but evidence of a recent bath. The bedrooms were empty. In the master, clothes were flung all over the bed.

'Anna, where the hell are you, love?'

He went back downstairs and let the dogs out. They knocked him flat. Full of trepidation, he followed them back through the kitchen where they skidded with excitement across the tiled floor and nosed open the back door, which wasn't fully closed. Picking up the torch off the log basket, he followed them across the dark garden.

CHAPTER FIFTEEN

Simon

It was difficult to pinpoint the moment his feelings changed. Everything got mixed up with his angry voice because no one was listening to him. Then Redman's muppets turned up out of nowhere and beat the living daylights out of him. Not nice at all. He had plenty of time to think, lying in his tent listening to the birds. He didn't have a mirror, but he knew how black and purple his face must have looked and that kind of scuppered his plans a bit. Well, a lot. He couldn't face his daughter looking like this.

Who was he kidding? He couldn't face her at all, not after that incident a few weeks ago. He couldn't stop thinking about it, that was the trouble. She lived in the posh leafy suburbs of Wilmslow, a two-up, two-down on a family estate. That surprised him a bit, he'd have thought Redman would have got them a better place. Married to a teacher, she ran some kind of mobile catering business from home, although when he looked through the kitchen window once, it was the size of a shoe box, piled high with cake tins, rolling pins, and pans. That's when he started to draw the money out. She'd listen then, if she could see what a difference he could make to her life with a couple of hundred thousand. She'd understand that he wasn't some kind of waster then. Money changed everything.

A hot afternoon in August. He'd followed Chelsey and the little boy to the park on the corner of Prestbury

Road. There were other young mothers and children having a picnic. It was weird how all this brought back memories of his own childhood. Identical park, same scene, different mother.

He'd wanted to kill himself.

Aged eight and stumbling across that sort of action in the bushes wasn't something he liked to dwell on. His own mother, her summer dress round her waist, with two men. One of them was watching, waiting for his turn. What sort of mother did that? His guts had twisted with shame and revulsion for months, years. Soft drugs and drink had blurred it to some degree through his adolescence, but it left a dirty scar.

If there was one tiny thing he could thank Redman for, it was how he'd brought his girl up.

Redman needed to step aside now. Of course, the problem lay in his own failing; it was a daily struggle to trust what was right and was maybe wrong. He knew his perception of love was broken. What he couldn't tolerate was being ignored and kicked aside. So on the day she went to the park, he decided to just walk up to her and start talking. How difficult could it be? They were flesh and blood, after all. He'd hung around for an hour or more, watching them all spread out on the grass in their shorts and skimpy tops, waiting for the right opportunity. Every time she moved or looked over, his palms grew sticky and his whole body shook with anticipation. Maybe she'd recognise him! Would she? Would there be an instant bond?

His vigilance was rewarded when his daughter eventually walked away from the others and towards the ice-cream van. She walked right past, so close he could almost touch her. He even caught the scent of her perfume as she wafted by. Golden hair swept up and a blue dress. Christ, her eyes ... they were his.

They were his mother's as well, and that caught him out a bit. Not everything was passed down though, was it? Physical was different to character, wasn't it? Next thing he knew, one of her friends was pointing him out to some guy in the crazy golf hut with a Walkie-talkie. A big bloke came and grabbed hold of his arm and escorted him out through the gates like he was some kind of stalker or a child molester!

'Dirty old perv,' someone shouted.

It sent him back, sent him plummeting into a dark place, the idea that she and her friends saw him like that, like she wouldn't be proud of him. He needed some kind of lure, a prop. No, it wasn't that, it was a gift to make up for all the years he'd never been a dad. It needed careful explaining, though. She was a class woman, a good mother who baked and cooked.

So he continued to withdraw the money. The bank continued to wind him up.

'Have you thought about investing this sum in an ISA? It won't earn any interest in a deposit account, you know.'

'I don't want any interest on my money, got that?'

The stupid comments carried on every time he called in. What did it have to do with them what he wanted the cash for? They were desperate to know, like they were taking bets on a list under the counter. Imagine if he told them what it was really for! What the fuck did it have to do with them though? Questions, questions …

'Going somewhere nice?' the fat female cashier said.

'Buying a new car?' the geeky male cashier said.

It was a comfort, being able to smell it and feel it when he wanted to. Stashed in a big rucksack, it didn't take up that much room. Eventually, over a matter of weeks he'd removed the lot and kept it with him at all times. He liked to walk round town with it strapped on his back. Recovering from his wounds, he rested his battered head on it and wondered what to do, how to get it to Chelsey.

Patsy Redman would spend the lot before his daughter knew of its existence, so he'd ruled her out early on. It was the sender of the letter he needed to connect with. The more he thought about it, the more certain he became. It was that interfering bitch who'd split up him and Patsy all those years ago. Miss nose-in-the-air Williams with her fancy art gallery. He'd watched her and Patsy in the street, still at each other's throats. And then Redman ... well, he'd backed off, spent more time in Wilmslow now than with Williams. Why had she done it? Why had she sent that letter? Revenge for Redman dumping her, or just because she wanted to expose Patsy? Or maybe she really did think that the truth deserved a chance after all these years, she'd heard about his quest and felt his pain. Didn't she have some sort of rough childhood, parents killed in a car crash, fostered out, then sent to live with Granny? Yeah, they had some stuff in common. The fact that she was so good at telling the truth convinced him the cash would get to his daughter somehow. And then Chelsey would want to meet him and thank him. She might have his mother's eyes but she had manners, didn't she?

The day of Williams' fancy bash in town – there were posters everywhere – he started to feel better, like it was a sign. He looked worse though, because the bruises were developing into dark, angry weals across his ribs and jawline. Dark glasses to conceal his black eyes and letting his beard grow was simple enough camouflage. Moving around was easier after he'd smoked something from his emergency stock. Smack did more than one trick, though, so he had to be careful not to treat it as his friend again, but he was pretty desperate for help and the time was right. Chelsey was here, just a couple of miles separated them. The pain relief and the euphoria would get him through the next few hours, then he'd find the strength to ditch it again because this time he'd have his daughter. The best reason.

Sheer determination and the desire to see what was going on had him pack up camp and stash everything in his car, then walk into Conwy with the cash in his backpack. He needed to touch base with Patsy. If there was anything he needed to know, she'd tell him. Early evening, and everywhere was busy. As he'd imagined, the Redman clan were in residence. No heavies. The bastards had beaten him up with no warning. It was tempting to go after Redman but then he'd just be shooting himself in the foot in front of Chelsey, and after all, there was more than one way to skin a cat. It had been a long time since he'd had a woman. He reckoned Williams could fulfil several dreams and desires in that department. What better way to piss off Redman and quench another, more urgent, need?

At first, he had no real idea of how he might execute all of this and come up smelling of roses, but he watched and waited in the entrance to the churchyard where there was a good view of the gallery. He was mostly invisible in the trees and treated himself to another smoke before scrambling up the stone steps onto the town walls. It was tricky in the dusk, easy to fall, but on the plus side it heightened his senses and he was back on the case, back to his special investigation with a vengeance. It'd take more than a couple of bouncers to stand in his way. He was a professional after all.

He took the exit at the top of town, meandered onto

the quay, and banged on Patsy's door.

She snatched the curtain to one side and glared through the window. Her face looked puffy, as if she'd been crying. The bony bitch mouthed something through the glass, then opened the tiny aperture at the top and yelled through that.

'Fuck off!'

'Charming. You owe me.'

'I don't owe you anything. I'm sick of this place and I'm sick of you. Chelsey's not interested, got it?'

'How do you know that?'

'She's been here just now with Jack and I've had hell over this!'

'The deal was that we all talked together.'

'I did what you asked and it's a no-go, she's *not* interested. Now fuck off or I'll call the police.'

'You didn't send that letter, did you? Was it Williams? Answer me!'

'What do you think?'

This made sense. This added up very nicely. His imagination went into overdrive as the rest of the evening fell into place. Not only would Redman's family be there to watch, but the local press too. He imagined the pictures when he spilled the cash. Maybe they'd have him throw it up in the air, Chelsey running through it with her hands outstretched. He'd be some kind of hero! The headlines would be "Father returns from the past with two hundred thousand pounds for his daughter."

'I've been saving this money for my entire life, for this one special moment,' he'd say to the reporters.

He saw himself and Williams, walking into the gallery arm in arm. She'd do a speech and introduce him. His daughter would be left in no doubt as to his sincerity, and then he'd produce the money. The perfection of it took his breath away. Williams was his nemesis, after all. The whole beautiful package.

He caught a bus with some other hikers as they travelled up to the youth hostel on the mountain road. He even alighted at the same stop, but then carried on walking. The driveway up to Gwern Farm was a long walk but his reward was within reach. He felt sure she was still there, and judging by the crowd down at the venue, was alone. Around half six, dusk was closing in. As he approached the farmhouse he was pleased to see no security lights, nothing illuminating the place other than a fly-encrusted light by the front door. The dogs let rip, although after a short while it was pretty obvious they were shut in one room. He made his way round the back, quietly unlatched the back door, and stepped inside. There was a single lamp on the Welsh dresser, lending a soft glow to the kitchen. Nice, very tasteful. He helped himself to a chunk of fruit cake and lowered the rucksack onto a chair.

'Oh dear, Miss Williams, you really should be more careful; anyone could walk in,' he said. The dogs continued to bark and whine but he could hear running water and a hairdryer, all of which disguised his tread on the creaking stairs. When he reached the landing, his mouth still bulging with cake, he saw her. She was facing the dressing table in white lace underwear, long, dark hair to her waist. Although she had her back to him, her reflection triggered a rush of blood to his groin.

She saw him through the mirror and dropped the hairdryer. Eyes flashing, she spun round to face him and there was a tangible moment of suspension before she spoke.

'Who the *hell* are you?'

It was one of the best moments of his life, that feeling of control in her bedroom, heightened by the presence of the cash and knowing the pleasure to come. He moved slowly and sat on the bed, bounced, then carefully lay flat. His ribs were protesting so a lie down wouldn't hurt. It was one of those old-fashioned brass affairs with expensive covers, clothing thrown all across it. She was pulling on clothes, shoes, anything and everything. His juices started to flow, thinking of the many layers he could peel from her at his leisure.

'Williams. Long time no see. Nice cake by the way, plenty of juicy cherries,' he said and sucked his fingers. 'I'd kind of like another bite of the cherry, know what I mean?'

'Get out!'

'Not yet. I know you're not supposed to mix business and pleasure, but I never did do convention.'

A horn pipped and the approach of a vehicle had the dogs barking again. Before he could think what to do, she made a dash for the door and almost reached the bottom of the stairs. But he was right behind her and grabbed a fistful of her long hair. She jerked backwards, slipping off the last two steps and falling onto her side, and it was easy then to place a hand across her mouth and hold her still with his weight, spooning her like a lover. She felt like no other woman he'd ever had. The pleasure of restraining and his desire throbbed against the small of her back.

Someone banged on the door and shouted, 'Taxi for Williams!'

There was some shuffling outside, but it was only a matter of seconds before the guy got back in his cab and leant on the horn again. When he heard it rumble away, the hint of a tear glistened in the corner of her eye. The titillation of her cleavage was right under his nose, and he slid a finger between her damp breasts.

'Williams,' he whispered. 'I don't know whether I want to fuck you first or tell you what we're going to do later.'

She swallowed, a drop of sweat on her upper lip. 'I'm meant to be at the gallery. People will come looking for me.'

She was panting, scared. This wasn't necessarily a bad thing.

'Redman? Nah. He's quaffing champers with the rest of them. It's just you and me.'

'There's no you and me, you're deranged.'

'You're not listening!'

He twisted her hair round one hand like a tourniquet and dragged her forcibly towards the table. Keeping a tight hold of her with one hand, he pulled the bag closer, loosened the toggle on the drawstring, and began to stack the wads of cash on the table. The phone rang and her eyes leapt to it. It stopped after five rings. The pile of money looked impressive but she was more interested in looking around the kitchen. There was a knife on the worktop, its serrated edge sticky with cake. He yanked her head back and pushed his face close to hers.

'This cash. I want it to go to my daughter and you're going to help me like you did with the letter.'

'I didn't send it to help you.'

'But you're going to help me now, aren't you? Answer me, bitch!'

He made her nod forcibly, his fingers grinding into her scalp but she gritted her teeth, eyes everywhere except on his. This wasn't good. He needed her full attention, needed her to be more compliant. Putting the empty rucksack over her head was a stroke of genius – he didn't have to look at her face. The inner sleeve was fashioned like a duffel bag. The neck of the pouch could be closed with two strong toggles on a cord, so he could pull it tight around her neck. When she realised what he was going to do, her foot connected with his shin and her nails caught his jaw.

'Not a good idea. Unless you want to play rough?'

He shoved her backwards and she fell against the edge of the table, china and cutlery falling to the floor. The dogs started up again, barking and growling. For a moment it was like putting a wildcat into a sack, but he only had to smack the side of her head and she was instantly subdued. Even the sobbing was muffled. She was stronger than he'd imagined though, and once the bag was in place he pulled her up and held her in front of him in a tight clamp. Christ, she felt good, but he couldn't risk her getting away from him before he'd had chance to explain. His eyes fell on a dog lead. Yanking her arms back, he wound it quickly round her wrists before she had a chance to lash out. All the time this was happening, a mobile phone was buzzing somewhere, then the dogs were whining, scratching, and sniffing under the door. For fuck's sake, he couldn't think straight.

Then it came to him. Outside, there would be no distractions. Phones, dogs, knives, other sodding people … all beyond reach. Nature was his domain, he functioned better outside. He snatched open the door and pushed her out, grabbing a fancy walking stick with a bone handle. At first, she fell over a lot, then lay curled in an embryonic position on the ground and refused to move. In the end, he whacked the back of her legs with the cane and dragged her up by her arm and she began to stagger and stumble across the garden. It was pretty dark but he was trained to deal with this sort of thing.

He kept her moving, up onto open ground away from the shadows of the trees and the huddles of sheep. Where to? The sluggish moonlight illuminated several mountain summits, defined against a lighter sky in the west. In fact, the closer they moved towards the coast, the better the vision would be. There was a disused quarry on Conwy Mountain, no more than twenty minutes marching across country. The tracks there were wide and well defined, he'd camped there several times. It was a weird place, an abandoned mining settlement defined by towering piles of slate and a reservoir. Like the backdrop for one of those off-the-wall films, everything in monochrome and running with water.

The bitch started to cry and retch big, painful gulps.

'Hey, Williams, you're not impressing me much for a first date.'

He tightened the bag to muffle her bleating and propelled her along. After a short while she stopped snivelling and he managed to light another smoke without too much trouble. After all, where could she run to with a bag on her head? Not only had it given him a good laugh but he started to enjoy himself in a way he'd not thought possible. This is what Private Investigator Banks was born to do. His vocation to be a daddy was about to be fulfilled in the most ingenious way. Not only would he get the girl – that would come later – but he'd got the hot woman as well!

He watched her backside traverse the incline and licked his dry lips.

Conwy Mountain was barely a mountain, more of a hill with a manmade path off the road where years of erosion and footfall had necessitated in a strip of white stone and bleached tarmac. It gleamed white like the stairway to heaven. He could shin up there in a matter of minutes but Williams slowed him down, panting and snivelling.

'Where are we going?'

'Heaven.'

He dragged her across the rough ground, across the heather and the boulders, across the gorse, and through a tumbledown gap in a drystone wall. There it was, his personal film set. The bare foundations of several miners' cottages and one remaining wall of a chapel, complete with arched windows, were silhouetted on the skyline.

The derelict quarry had a silence about it.

It was death.

Beneath a long straggle of bilberry bushes, he got Williams down on the ground. She fought like a wild animal, kicking out and screaming, twisting into every conceivable position except the one he wanted. It was easy to fix but it took all his wits to keep hold of her, so it was easier to lie on top of her while he ripped away some of her clothing and pulled her bra down to her waist. He even took the bag off and she made a heroic effort to bite and spit, but a hand across her throat soon stopped that. When he lowered his mouth to her breasts the adrenaline rush was mind-blowing. A surge of complicated erotic emotion hit him first in the genitals, then dug painfully around his subconscious.

A sudden vision of his mother in the bushes at the park. Two men, one of them suckling at her breast like a baby taking milk, and the other watching with his pants round his ankles.

His fucking mother had him screwed up.

He wanted to kill himself.

CHAPTER SIXTEEN

Anna

Was he going to rape her? Please, *please* let it be quick.

She knew her knees and her fingernails must be running with blood, and her scalp was pulsing with pain. She was so cold her teeth were beyond chattering. When he began to tug at her clothing she heard herself scream but it didn't really sound like her voice. Any struggling only served to excite him. When he removed the bag from her head she almost begged him to put it back on. At first, she could only distinguish a hundred shades of black, conical piles of slate beneath a shrouded moon and the whites of his eyes.

Far below, sounds of the sea splashed over rocks at Penmaen Head. They were at the old quarry.

She couldn't move an inch. Stale breath and smoke invaded her face, then his mouth on her breasts. Why couldn't she do something? Knee him? Any shred of strength she had left seemed exhausted by raw fear. She prepared herself for the inevitable and tried to zone out, but even this seemed impossible with every nerve tuned in to Banks. Tears started to trickle into her ears.

This should have been the best evening of her life. She should be drinking champagne at her presentation with Jack. She missed him so much, unthinkable what she'd put him through, what she'd put herself through!

If he'd been with her properly, she'd not be in this situation. If she'd never sent that letter, she'd not be in this situation. If she hadn't been such a stubborn idiot, *she'd not be in this situation.* She'd not only taken him for granted, it felt she'd taken her whole life for granted. Faced with something truly horrific only served to show how blessed her existence had been, how insignificant her worries and irritations were when she was forced to look from a truly dangerous angle.

Please, God, I'll honour any pact you place on me.

Banks looked into her face and her heart almost stopped. God only knows what he saw there – but he hesitated and his weight shifted. Something changed, something which later cemented her belief in love, karma, and prayer. There was a noise, a distinctive rattle of someone or something running across loose slate. A dog's nose investigated her hair then licked her face. Two hands grabbed Banks and propelled him forcibly across the ground, and he was gone from her. Her dogs clustered round, full of excitement and adventure, we found you, we found you!

She recognised Jack's legs, the pale gleam of denim, and then his voice, guttural, murderous.

'I'm going to fucking kill you, Banks.'

'That right, Redman? You tried once, a right couple of mummy's dummies they were.'

'No, that was just a warning. This time it's for real,' he said, and dragged him up by his jacket, only to hit him so hard he was lifted momentarily off his feet. Seconds later, Banks staggered upright holding what looked like an old pickaxe. Jack used it to push him backwards, then wrenched it from him when he overbalanced. Inches away, she knew there was a terraced embankment down to the reservoir. It was a natural lake of sorts, contained by steep concrete sides to stem the loss of water gushing down to the sea. There was even a leaning sign warning of the drop. It was well protected by an iron rail and coiled barbed wire but on the ground and in the dark, it was perfectly possible to skim underneath the safety barrier or miss it entirely.

She shouted out but Jack was so intent on his quarry he simply didn't hear her. He'd either commit murder – and she was convinced that where his loved ones were concerned, he wouldn't hesitate to fight to the death – or both men would fall, grappling hopelessly, into the deep water. She saw Banks crawling along on all fours, spitting out teeth. Legs shaking, she finally got to her feet.

'Jack! Stop, *stop it.* Think what you're doing. Stop, *please ...*'

He looked around, and studied her as if he were uncertain who she was. Finally, he came to her. Those same hands touched her gently, pulled her carefully into safe arms. The tears came then, an inexhaustible stream as she tried to answer his disjointed questions, but when it came down to the facts, he was rendered as incapable of coherent conversation as she was.

'Don't let go of me,' she said, hoarsely. Was it was that simple? Could it be that simple? 'Just ... don't let go of me.'

'Never.'

She could see Banks moving around over Jack's shoulder, slowly, painfully. No longer a threat, surely? He'd found the rucksack and was filling it with broken slate, crawling along on all fours like Gollum. Her dogs were torn between staying with her and going to look what he was doing in case it was a game. If Benson were here he'd have homed in on the object of her distress and gone in for the kill. When the bag was full, he struggled to get it up on his back, heaving himself along like some lopsided creature. Then he began to crawl towards the escarpment.

'Jack!'

Sounds of shale and broken slate rushing as one, then plopping slowly into deep water.

'Jack, he's …'

He spun round. '*Banks!*'

His voice bounced off the mossed walls, echoing and unanswered. She knew full well what Banks was doing. They both did. Morbid curiosity had them peer over the edge. Well, mostly Jack. She hovered behind his shoulder, holding onto his arm. Banks disappeared for a moment, hidden by the natural overhang, then they saw him, floundering unsteadily down the terrace of steps and old iron stairways, his balance hampered by the weight on his back. Miraculously, he didn't fall. He even stood for a moment, looking up at them, his upper torso visible above the contained swell of water. Then he fell backwards, his arms across his chest like a baptism. The surface of the water erupted into a bubbling cauldron.

'*Jesus!* He's …'

Gone. She searched the dark water, already rapidly descending into tranquillity, and then she searched the sky as if answers would form elsewhere. Jack wanted to wait, to make sure Banks hadn't performed some kind of evil trick, but there was no way a man in his condition could have stayed submerged like that then swim to safety and manage to haul himself out. Surely not? She made Jack look at her.

'Should we call the police, Jack? Jack!'

'Need to think.'

They hobbled the mile back to the house, hard to believe it was still early. In the garden, Jack's mobile rang like Big Ben and he whipped it out of his back pocket, read the text quickly, then showed it to her.

Josh, wondering where the hell they were.

'What the *fuck* do I say?'

'Tell him I'm ill.'

She watched his bloodied knuckles, his fingers fumbling as he tapped in the reply, telling her son not to worry, she just had a tummy upset. It was laughable. A couple of hours ago she'd have been pissed off if she'd had a tummy upset. Now here she was, wishing that was the simple truth.

They did a double take at the ridiculous pile of cash on the kitchen table.

In complete silence, he ran her a bath, bathed her knees, and made her drink sweet tea and take two painkillers. In bed, he curled around her and they lay sleepless, cocooned in a suspension of horror, relief, and shock.

The following day was strange and surreal. They'd both witnessed a suicide and done nothing about it, but the words wouldn't form between themselves, let alone a third party. Maybe there just wasn't anything to say. As daylight came, it began to rain. Heavy, grey sheets of rain that looked as if they were set forever, as if the sun would never shine again. Jack rose at dawn and went back to the quarry with the dogs. He returned soaked through, his face haunted.

'Nothing. It's like he never existed. The rain's washed everything away, every footprint.'

She was unsure how it made her feel. Apart from the cash, every trace of the event had gone except in her mind, where it would remain forever. The vision of him falling backwards into the water replayed over and over every time she closed her eyes. She felt sure Jack suffered the same nightmare. Several times in the night she'd woken from a semi-slumber to find him wide awake, staring at the ceiling.

She dealt with it by thanking God she was alive.

He dealt with it by being proactive. By fitting powerful security lights around the entire perimeter of the house, CCTV cameras and alarms, extra bolts on the doors. He burnt her clothes and everything Banks had touched, except for the money. He stuffed that into a holdall and slung it on top of the wardrobe. She heard him on his mobile, talking to someone in a low voice about Banks' car on the pass and how to get rid of it. Clearly they weren't calling the police, but then it was likely too late to report it from the moment she'd lied to Josh.

'Jack, I'm not coping.'

He was on a small step-ladder, fixing window locks. 'We've done nothing wrong.'

'Yes we have! We're carrying on like nothing's happened. A man has died. His life savings are on top of my wardrobe!'

'Anna, you saw what happened. Did he jump or was he pushed?'

'But we didn't try to stop him.'

'My life would have been in danger, you know that! Even *if* I'd managed to drag him out, what would we have done then? Patched him up and sent him on his way? How do you prove intended rape, exactly? How would I have explained his injuries? The police have already got something on me for Philipe, I'd not get another chance. Do you want the police digging around, blowing the whole can of worms open again for Patsy to pick over? For your career to go down the pan with the scandal and God knows what else?'

He threw a screwdriver into the toolbox, making her jump.

'So, we're just going to forget all about it? It feels wrong.'

'So it felt right when he was on top of you, did it?'

he snapped. 'He's in the best fucking place, believe me.'

He apologised. They both cried.

It didn't help rational thought in that neither of them had slept more than a couple of hours. Instead, they spent hours wrapped round each other, lying on the bed, lying on the sofa. There was an unspoken pact between them now to protect not only themselves but their family. It was too late to change anything, although as they fielded concerned phone calls from Peter, Josh, and Isabel, they discovered it was far more difficult in theory. Friends and family seemed to swallow their pathetic story, although in private they probably imagined she'd bottled out, consumed by nerves. She didn't care what they thought, although there was a horrible underlying shame at all the trouble Peter had gone to. Sooner or later, she'd have to face everyone and outright lie.

Sunday came round too quickly and she dreaded the thought of Jack driving back to Wilmslow. The thought of being in the house alone had her nerves jangling, but he called Clare well before she voiced any concerns.

'I won't be in next week, Anna's really not well,' she heard him say. 'Cover my appointments, will you?'

She could hear the incredulous response at the other end of the phone too, like an explosion of babble, but Jack seemed to be of the same mind set as herself. None of it really mattered.

By Sunday afternoon they'd run out of milk and Jack said they needed to face the music before other assumptions were made, and they should go and do normal things. He waited in his car with the window rolled down, smoking while she went into Spar, where she bought a random selection of stuff she didn't want and smiled at people she didn't know. On her return she slung a plastic shopping bag onto the passenger seat. 'I think I should go and see Peter. I can't leave it any longer.'

'Shall I wait here?'

She shrugged but he didn't move so she went down the street to the gallery alone. Everything was cleared away, the posters and banners gone. Her heels were loud across the wooden floor and she thought her heart might explode with tension when Peter looked up inquiringly from the desk. Could he see the deceit in her face?

Hi, sorry I wasn't at my launch but I was almost raped. It's OK though, he's drowned. Dead. Keep it to yourself, will you?

'Anna ...' He came round to her, took both hands in his, full of concern. 'How are you?'

'Miserable. Humiliated and ashamed. Peter, I'm so sorry, but I've been so sick.'

'You do look awfully white.' Maybe it was his good breeding or just plain old-fashioned manners, but he didn't grill her. 'Talking to the press, selling paintings ... it's not life and death, believe me.'

'No, I guess not. Not when you put it like that.'

'Actually, it went off pretty well. Josh did your speech and we managed to field the press with a concoction of imaginative stories. We even sold Llewellyn.'

'Really? That's ... fantastic.'

'Look, we can do another launch with some new stock, maybe around Christmas?'

'Right, yes,' she said, wondering if she'd ever be able to smile again, let alone paint, with any genuine feeling.

Peter hitched himself onto the corner of the desk and tapped a pen against his teeth. 'I, er ... Anna, have you thought about the manager position? It's just if you don't want to do it, that's absolutely fine, but I'll need to start advertising for someone soon. I'd like to get on with other things.'

'Oh, yes. Can I let you know tomorrow?'

'Sure.'

He looked at her curiously, as if he wasn't quite sure whether to say something else. 'And I don't know whether Jack has mentioned it, but Patsy and I are no longer an item. He's considering moving her out to my property in Chester. I'd appreciate it if you could nudge him along with that?'

'Of course.'

Her mind was racing. Was she in any sort of position to make a decision about any of this? When had Jack decided to move Patsy and the children to Peter's house? Not so long ago, this had been a major deal breaker. Since her ordeal it had contracted somewhat in importance, but she couldn't deny how much this changed everything. She made to go, got as far as the door, then slowly retraced her steps. 'Actually, Peter, take that as a yes from both of us. If it's any different, I'll let you know tomorrow at the latest.'

He shot her a quiet smile, as if he'd known all along that her answer was predestined.

'We must have dinner together, the three of us. I'll prepare some contracts, nothing too complicated.'

Her insides contracted at the thought of food, but she managed to arrange her features into something approaching friendly and grateful. When she told Jack, she watched his face avidly, trying to determine what she saw there when he talked about moving his children again. Not only did he seem to have made this decision already, but he thought it was a good idea to be seen out celebrating with Peter, and immediately made arrangements with him for the following Friday.

'Are you sure about this?' she said.

'Positive. It's a gift horse, isn't it? I'm glad you're going to accept the job. I'd hate to think Banks has taken everything from you.'

'He did, he has. He's got my peace of mind.'

'Not forever, I *promise*. We'll find a way through this, I know we will. It's just a case of finding the right compromise.'

She knew full well that for him, it was far more than a simple compromise to move his children again.

It was a huge, complicated sacrifice.

Somehow they lived through the week. Jack was secretly obsessed with the quarry, then the campsite around the druid's circle and the space where Banks' car had stood. She didn't ask what he'd done about it or where it had gone but she grew increasingly concerned about the stash of money. What on earth were they going to do with it? she asked tentatively.

'I don't know,' he said.

'I don't want it in the house.'

'I'll take it back with me, put it in the office safe if it makes you feel uncomfortable.'

'Everything about this makes me feel uncomfortable.'

He caught her hands across the table and told her about his meeting with Chelsey, how she'd virtually dismissed the letter, dismissed the whole idea of meeting Banks. He was more or less saying she'd been right to tell the truth from the very beginning. But that was before Banks had killed himself. This was her cue, a way of re-balancing the guilt.

'Jack, he wanted Chelsey to have it. The money, I mean.'

A beat. 'No. She'd ask far too many questions, even if she accepted it.'

She sighed with irritation. 'Charity, then?'

'Same. I don't want a single fiver traced back to us.'

'What then?'

'I don't know yet.'

Peter was as good as his word and proffered two contracts, one for her employment at the gallery and one for Jack's half of the rental at the house in Chester. If it hadn't been such a long, protracted journey to arrive at this point she'd have been not deliriously happy exactly, but maybe something approaching contentment.

Everything seemed weighted in her favour. Jack was knocking himself out making everything right. She really, really wanted to contribute something to their relationship but after recent events, would any kind of gesture from her come across as inherently selfish? If she asked him to move in with her full-time, would he just see this as her way of feeling physically secure again? The truth was, subconsciously, she'd already come to this conclusion before she'd lain beneath Banks and feared for her life. The actual horror of the previous weekend and the events leading up to it had forced her to not only take stock, but to motivate her wary, sluggish heart.

In her bedroom, Jack had moved the furniture round so her mirror no longer reflected the landing. He'd listened to her account of what had happened with tears in his eyes and a nerve pulsing along his jaw. His love was fierce and sometimes misguided, but he was her soulmate, in more than the conventional sense. She looked across the table as he pored over the contracts, and she knew for certain that not only did she owe him all the love in the world but she owed herself the same, fully-committed grown-up

271

relationship. A contract of love. He passed a sheet of paper to her and she signed it without a second thought, her eyes on his.

'Are you alright?' he said when Peter went to the bar.

Her plate of food lay mostly untouched, a well of emotion building in her chest. 'Can we go?'

They managed to extract themselves from Peter's well-meaning generosity and walked to the car park under a battering of rain. The nights were drawing in and a handful of leaves were stuck to the windscreen in autumnal hues, trapped helplessly under the wipers, scraping to and fro.

'I'll tell the children what's happening tomorrow,' Jack said. 'I think October half-term is a sensible timescale to move them, what do you think?'

'I'm sorry that you have to do this, and I'm sorry for Lottie and James.'

He touched her hand briefly. 'No, I should have done it this way in the beginning. You were right about that, and about Chelsey. If I'd listened to you from the start, everything wouldn't have got in such a mess, would it?'

'I don't know. Maybe it's fate. Maybe some lessons need ramming home over and over.'

'And I never learn, is that what you mean?'

She turned to look at his profile, horrified. 'No, no, I was thinking of myself.'

As they approached the house, the new security beams lit up the entire area like noon on a summer's day. The bare wisteria looked especially incongruous in the artificial light, but at least there were no shadows. Once inside, Jack turned off the bleeping alarm and she dropped the bolts across the door. Taking his hand, she led him upstairs and began to kiss him with an almost manic conviction, as if it were somehow life or death.

He caressed her as if she were a fragile, priceless porcelain doll and it irritated her.

'I don't want you to treat me differently. Whatever you do,' she said, unbuttoning his shirt, 'do *not* ask me if I am sure. Do not ask me if I'm sure about making love, do you understand?'

'No ...' he said, a tad uncertainly, 'but what the hell, I can lie still and be quiet.'

She half-smiled at his nonplussed face, not entirely sure if she understood her own logic, but it was a relief to discover that he felt the same beneath her hands and mouth: warm, safe, sensual. It made no difference whether her eyes were open or closed, and when he moved into her, it was Jack, her Jack. And he smelt of summer and love and life; her life, her love. And she had no doubt he could be, *was* ... her endless summer.

Was it merely fanciful or delusional to think that they simply needed to get through a winter before they could enjoy the sun? The passage of time worked for everything else in the universe, so she had to trust it.

'Am I allowed to speak?' he said after a long while.

She twisted round to face him. 'Live with me. I mean, properly, full-time.'

A long, slightly incredulous beat of contemplation. 'You mean live here with you?'

'Of course here with me!'

'Why? I mean why now?'

This was the question she'd prayed he would never ask. How did she explain that a lifetime of cowardly non-commitment had been blown away? It would take forever. 'I love you?'

'You've answered my question with another question, but I understand the answer, and the answer is yes.'

'I know it's not that straightforward, the commute's a nightmare.'

'Anna, I'll move fucking mountains! With everything that's happened, I wasn't sure you'd want to even stay here.'

'Wherever I go, what happened will come with me in my head. Staying here, I've got chance to work through it.'

He pulled on denims and an old sweater with a triumphant smile, then jogged outside and felled the For Sale sign.

They walked to Llangelynin church. It was the end of summer, although the hillsides were still green they were mostly obscured by light mist and low cloud. Here and there, a solitary tree stood inflamed with colour and the hawthorn hedges were heavy with berries, hanging like jewels in clusters of scarlet. Blackberry and sloe were less easy to find but she collected anything which represented a harvest.

Inside the tiny church it was musty and dim, like a tomb. She laid her fruits and branches of colour on the altar, petals already falling from the wild rose. Jack sat next to her on the ancient pew, both of them in deep thought although he held her hand securely in his.

'I hate what we've done,' she whispered.

After a moment she turned to him and rested her head on his shoulder. The only sounds were bleating sheep and water running over rocks outside. They sat till they were cold and the dogs began to whine, then they began the trek home. She was achingly aware that he'd have to leave soon to see Lottie and James then drive back to Wilmslow to sort out his business, his life.

'I think I know what to do about the money,' he said as they began the descent. 'Well, I've had an *idea* what to do about the money.'

She didn't ask. She imagined he'd take it back with him to the office and lose it somehow in his vast, complicated array of business accounts. She wasn't happy about it, but at the farm he pulled the holdall down from the wardrobe with a serious face. 'Come on, I want you to come with me.'

'Where? What are you thinking?'

He marched outside, stashed the holdall in the car and motioned she get in. They drove two miles down the mountain road and turned in to Hilly's place. She looked at him in abject horror. 'Jack, we can't!'

'I know someone who can make it dissolve, no questions asked, and at the same time we can do an amazingly good deed. It came to me while we were sat in the church.'

'That doesn't mean it's a message from St Celynin!'

'I never said it was.'

She rolled her eyes. Resolute, he went to knock on the door, the holdall bulging with cash at his side. When did they turn into Bonnie and Clyde? She clambered out, taking in the dismal state of the pastures and the row of untidy caravans. It was heartbreaking to see it so run-down, but could they redress the balance in such an unorthodox way?

Hilly answered the door and they went inside, smiles fixed and unnatural like they'd been to the dentist.

'Well, this *is* a surprise. How are you?' Hilly said, 'The bloody jungle drums are rumbling in town.'

'I'm sure I'm already yesterday's boring news. Having a stomach bug is hardly scandal of the year.'

'It is round here. You don't look well.'

'She's still not fully recovered,' Jack said, his eyes boring into hers. 'Where's Bryn?'

275

'Having a nap.'

'Give him a shout, will you?'

Hilly shot them a curious look, but yelled up the stairs. She set about making coffee and they made small talk until Bryn materialised. He pulled a chair out and they sat around the kitchen table looking at each other.

'What's this about, then?' Bryn said, slurping coffee.

If Anna'd not had a gastric problem the previous week she was pretty sure the threat of one was about to attack her intestines with a vengeance. She hid behind her mug, grateful that Jack would have to do all the talking since she didn't have a clue how he'd approach such a suggestion.

'I'm after a favour,' Jack said. 'I've got some cash I need to get rid of.'

'Tax dodge?'

'Something like that.'

'How much?'

'Couple of hundred grand.'

'You can buy a nice horse for that!' Hilly said, slicing open a packet of biscuits.

'No, we don't want to buy anything.'

Bryn placed his mug down and scratched his chin. 'You mean you want an investment?'

'Kind of. But I don't want any receipts or a contract. Just a gentlemen's agreement.'

'And this money, where is it?'

'In that bag there.'

They all stared at each other, then looked at the holdall as if it might leap up and bite them. Bryn pulled back the zipper and let out a low whistle when he saw the bundles of used banknotes.

'I'm sure Heather can filter it through the horse business,' Jack said, watching Bryn's face. 'Maybe even set up a bank account for you in Ireland.'

'Where's it come from?'

'It's not stolen or anything. That's all you need to know.'

'And you ... just want us to get *rid* of it? Why would you do that?'

'I'm helping some friends out.'

'What's in it for you?'

'You can bring back that bloody Arab horse for Anna. The blue one.'

'And all this is no questions asked?' Hilly said, casting around for confirmation and meeting blank faces. 'I don't know what to *say*. It will get us out of such a hole.'

'Hold on,' Bryn said. 'I haven't agreed to anything yet. I never had you down as a tax fiddler,' he said to Jack. 'Or whatever it is you want to call it.'

'Tax fiddling is still pretty respectable where I come from.'

There was a peculiar signing off to the conversation when their eyes did the talking. Hilly removed the coffees and brought out a bottle of Scotch and four tumblers. She was overcome with nerves and kept spilling things. They drank a measure, then Bryn spat in his palm, and Jack did the same. The men shook hands, and that was that.

CHAPTER SEVENTEEN

Jack

He was unsure if Anna was cross with him over the money or simply shocked at his nerve. All he knew was that he had to find solutions quickly. He felt as if he'd been trapped inside a computer game for days, not knowing what was going to pop up out of the woodwork or what form of evil it might take. If Anna hadn't stopped him, he would have torn Banks limb from limb, he knew that for certain. Thank Christ she'd stopped him.

She hadn't wanted him to leave. He wasn't keen on the idea either; after the ordeal she'd gone through, leaving her alone with her thoughts and unable to confide in anyone was soul-destroying. What terror she'd endured with Banks was bad enough for him to deal with, so God only knew what was in her head but they had to behave normally, whatever that was.

The other certainty was that Patsy had run out of chances.

He parked on the quay and his children came to the cottage door, throwing it wide open. James was clingy and held out his arms. Lottie was in character, presumably a cast member from the soap she'd been auditioning for. She was wearing a pink headscarf over some old-fashioned hair curlers, and across her chest were two plastic kitchen colanders held into position with an old-fashioned apron. It looked vaguely familiar. Isabel's, maybe.

'Redman, where the bloody hell have you been?' she yelled, hands on her hips, pretend cigarette hanging out of her bright red mouth. 'Don't tell me you've been up the pub this whole time, it won't wash. Your dinner's in the bin.'

For good measure, she stood well back and slammed the door in his face. Inside, he could hear James crying and Patsy remonstrating with their weird and wonderful daughter. He had to knock again, feeling a fool.

'Are you not going to have a word with her?' Patsy said. 'She's turning into a brat and she doesn't take a blind bit of notice of me.'

'No,' he said wearily. 'I want to tell both my children I'm sorry about their fucked-up parents. I want to tell them I love them. I want to laugh with them and make them happy.'

Patsy looked sullen but allowed him into the sitting room, where he forced himself to watch TV with Lottie and James while she cooked pasta in the kitchen. The whole scene felt weird and the sooner it was sorted out the better. First on the agenda was the fact that Lottie didn't get the part she'd auditioned for. On the one hand, it was good she'd had a knock-back, although it would have lent some serious relevance regarding the move to Chester, but he ploughed on regardless with the news he needed to impart.

'Look, you two, Anna has been really poorly and I had to look after her. I didn't want you to catch it as well.'

Both children were mostly disinterested in this information but he could sense Patsy's antennae on full alert. He began to tell them about Claymore's house, how big it was, and more importantly, how big the garden was. So big that he'd agreed to them having a dog if they'd like to go and live there. Of course their reaction was a guaranteed hit. James didn't really understand the hullabaloo, but joined in the yelping and barking with Lottie.

Patsy came to the door, wiping her hands on a towel. 'Is that right?'

'Yeah, that's right.'

While the children were eating spaghetti Bolognese in the kitchen, she followed him outside to his car, her eyes flashing, mouth pursed. 'And you didn't think to discuss this with me?'

'Nope. Anyway, what's not to like? Big shops, city life. You'll have to get a job though, because you'll be responsible for a quarter of the rent, same as me.'

'How do you mean? Who's paying the other half?'

'Claymore's tenants.'

'You can't do this, Jack! I'll get on to my solicitor and the child support agency.'

'You do that. I expect it'll wipe out all that money you've got stashed away.'

She folded her arms, chest heaving indignantly while he did his best to ignore her.

'Why are you being so nasty?' she said. 'Have you had a visit from Simon? He was round here on the night of the launch, banging on about that bloody letter. So I put him straight. It *was* Anna, wasn't it? Is that why she didn't turn up at the gallery?'

'Banks?' Wary of his reaction, he kept his eyes firmly on the glove box, selected a CD, and started the engine. 'Nope, we've not seen him, he's obviously got the message. I'll be in touch about Chester.'

The window glided back smoothly and the rest of her reaction was muffled by glass. It was quite possibly the best performance of his life. Lottie would have been impressed had she understood the full extent of his acting skills. Anna would have been impressed just by his sheer restraint. He floored the accelerator and roared down the A55.

Monday morning in the office.

'I need two dogs,' he said to Tabitha. 'One of them needs to be fierce. Ex-military would be good. And another one, one that doesn't mind being dressed-up.'

She shot him the usual look, the sort reserved for madmen and estate agents on the hypothetical run. He opened the blinds wide in his office, removed the stapler and the box of paperclips from the drawer, and placed them on top of the desk, ready for action.

Clare was hot on his heels. 'I need to speak to you.'

'Fire away,' he said, switching on his laptop. He pulled up the sales spreadsheet first, pleased to note that his team had done exceptionally well in his absence with regard to sales. Well, Clare had.

'And not only that, he's continually late,' Clare was saying. He let her run on, something about how hard they'd all worked the previous week except Oliver, who'd taken advantage of Jack's absence and seen fit to play loud music upstairs in the flat during business hours. And then there'd been a semi-naked girl pressed against the upstairs window on Saturday morning for the whole of Wilmslow to see.

'She was wearing some sort of bridle. Tabitha reckoned it was a cat harness.'

'Clare, sit down.'

She pulled out a chair and he gave her a minute to cool off. 'Clare. I'd like you to be branch manager. If you want to be, of course. You get a much bigger salary. And the use of my office, including my highly-coveted, leather swivel chair.'

'What?'

'Think about it. Let me know end of the week?'

'Oh! Well, I wasn't expecting that.'

'No, neither was I. Thing is, I'm going to be living at the farm pretty much full-time.'

Her mouth dropped open a bit more. 'Oh, you mean you're retiring?'

'Um, I'm not sure about that part, but staffing obviously needs a re-think.'

Was he retiring? What would he do all day, take over from Gina at the Taffy branch, making coffee and arranging viewings? Now he'd got what he wanted with Anna, it threw everything else into a state of flux.

Despite his award-winning performances on the public stage of life, it was more difficult when he only had his conscience to account to. His mind ran over and over everything he'd done and said. What if someone had seen him circling the quarry, the campsite, and the car park? He'd made sure he had the dogs with him on each occasion, but it was hard to disguise that overwhelming fear, guilt, anger. Hopefully his masked expression and body language hadn't given him away, but his guts were in a terrible state.

He kept telling himself it had been a suicide. It wasn't even manslaughter, although on the strength of his raw emotions it felt like he'd committed cold-blooded murder. He'd never get the images of that place out of his head. Even in the cold light of day, it had a haunted atmosphere. Other than the water in the reservoir, which had taken on an opalescent jade hue, the entire place was grey. The rain hammered down, spiking the surface of the water and adding several more inches. He'd trudged through the quarryman's cottages, through the stacks of slate and the rusted machinery until he came to the church wall. Please, God, let this be an end to it all.

He called Anna, a lot. 'You OK?'

'Same as an hour ago, distracted.'

He pushed a hand through his untidy hair and spun his swivel chair round to face the window. When he ran through his plans for the business, she made him repeat it all. 'Hold on, I was going to suggest I named you as co-owner of the farm on the deeds?'

'No! Don't do that, there's really no need. It belongs to you and Josh.'

An intake of breath and a sigh. 'You are still going to live here?'

'Anna, I can't wait. Just trust me on this.'

'After everything you've invested in the farm, I wanted us to be on level footing.'

'That doesn't matter. If anything happens in the future, I don't want Patsy, or more to the point, anyone else she hooks up with, having any kind of claim on us. I've a way to go with this kind of thing while the children are so young.'

'Don't you think you're being a bit over the top?'

'No, I don't. She's had me by the financial balls twice now. It's better this way.'

He had to protect his assets. He needed to consolidate what he'd built and worked for into a position where it was impossible for Patsy or, God forbid, anything else in the future, to blow it all apart. The walls and the drawbridge to his kingdom needed to be impenetrable. Raping and pillaging were still rife, even in the modern world.

Charles West, his solicitor, wasn't especially surprised by his plans but expressed severe reservations.

'Let me get this straight. You want to gift the agency business to your children *before* your death?'

'That's it, yeah. I want a yearly annuity from the business, but on paper I won't own anything.'

'This is both premises, yes? And Quay Cottage, and the flat?'

'Both properties need to belong to the business, not to me personally. And any rental collected from the properties goes back into Redman Estates.'

'I see. Leave it with me, let me work out a long-term plan so you won't incur gift-tax.'

'Long-term? No, it needs to be short- to medium-term.'

'Alright,' he said slowly. 'I'll work out two plans, one fast and expensive and the other sensible, then you can compare.'

Since when had he ever done sensible?

It took Clare only a couple of days to accept the branch manager position, with the proviso that Oliver was warned to tow the line. Or she'd sack him. With Tony as lettings manager and Tabitha moving into Clare's old shoes they all had happy faces, except Oliver who'd done nothing but complain about Clare being in charge during his absence.

It wasn't going to work. No matter how many warnings Oliver received, the status quo would be compromised.

It was his turn to cook dinner.

'This will cheer you up. I'm moving out of the flat,' he said, tossing steaks into the frying pan. Oliver was in the sitting room with his feet up on the coffee table, throwing nuts into his mouth. Everything that ran off electric was switched on: laptops, televisions, lamps, all buzzing away. There was even a row of gadgets getting charged on a bank of six sockets sitting on top of the windowsill, sticky and covered in dust. Normally, this bugged the hell out of him but he decided to take a different tack.

'Yeah, I'm moving in with Anna, full-time.'

'Seriously?' Oliver shouted back. 'Does that mean Amy can move in here?'

'Sure. I'll get you both sorted out with a rental

contract. You'll need to change the utilities into your name.'

The silence was absolute, followed by the sound of huge pennies spinning through space and looking for a slot in Oliver's brain. He materialised at the kitchen door with a deep frown, can of lager in hand. 'Amy hasn't got a job.'

'Problem then. Let me know what you want to do.'

'Are there any options?'

'Always. Let's see, pay for it all yourself? Or find someone who can share and pay for their half.'

'What if I can't find anyone?'

He shrugged and chopped up some mushrooms, pretending to contemplate Oliver's dilemma with as much sincerity as he could muster. 'Here's another cheaper option. You could live in Quay Cottage, get Josh to share with you, and work at the Conwy branch. Gina's leaving to have a baby, did I tell you?'

A beat of indignant panic. 'No way! Mum's at the cottage, I'm not living with her and my creepy little sister.'

'Not for much longer. She's got to move to find a job. And here's another thought. Amy might get some work down there, you could at least do some gigs.'

'But I hate the Taffy branch.'

'Your problem then. Let me know what you want to do.'

He could feel the scowl land like a physical blow between his shoulder blades.

The staff wanted to celebrate their respective promotions and this predictably took the form of a Friday night booze-up. Jack promised to open up on Saturday morning with Oliver, who had a face like a wet week.

'How come everyone's had a massive wage hike

except me?'

'You need some fine-tuning. Like turning up on time.'

They were in the Dirty Duck. Clare and Tabitha were sharing a bottle of wine. Tony came back to the table with two pints of Cheshire Totty and a bottle of designer beer for Oliver. While the others were talking about office politics, he took his son to one side and told him about the changes he was working on with Charles West before Oliver got too addled to understand what he was talking about.

'So, everything you do with the regard to the business will impact on your own investment, do you get that?'

'That's kinda cool ... I'm a company director!'

'Only technically, but in theory, if you were to stay here you'd still be the tea-boy. Although if you wanted to move to Conwy you'd be a much bigger fish, only in a smaller pond.'

'Eh?'

'Assistant manager.'

He lowered his bottle of lager slowly. 'No sweat?'

Tim waved his copy of the *Financial Times* and made his way over. 'Sorry I haven't collected my trousers. I've just seen Clarissa and she says they're in your office. I thought I'd never see them again. I've had nightmares about where they might turn up.'

'Clarissa's here?'

'Talking to her henchmen at the bar.'

'Right, I'll get another round in,' he said, getting to his feet. His palms were suddenly sweaty. He had no idea what her boys had done with Banks' car. One day it was there, stuffed to the gills with camping equipment, and the next it was gone. A phone call, that was all it had taken. At the bar, Dum and Dee barely acknowledged his existence, but Clarissa more than made up for their professional disinterest.

'Jack, how lovely to see you. How's business?'

'Good. Can I get you a drink?'

'Always. A large Chardonnay.'

She shimmied her way round to his side of the bar and manoeuvred half her ample backside onto a vacant bar stool. 'I believe the boys have been helping you out again with that bad debt,' she whispered into his ear, boobs pressing in close, a hand travelling over his back. 'I hope it's all resolved now? I can't bear people who don't honour their debts.'

'It's sorted.'

'Faaaabulous! I rather think, by my calculation, this could possibly have you back in *my* debt, Mr Redman.'

'I can't come for dinner if that's what you're thinking. I'm out with the staff.'

'It'll wait, a little added interest won't do any harm,' she said, winking. 'Ciao.'

In October, he took the contracts round to Chelsey's house when they were ready for signing. She was scooping up icing and filling a piping bag then writing something in squiggly loops across a chocolate cake. 'Is this to do with Mum?'

'Only a bit. I've wanted to do it like this for ages, and now I'm moving to Conwy it just makes sense.'

She glanced at the papers on the table, not reading anything but signed it anyway, leaving a smudge of cake mix behind.

'I know you'll have been over it with a fine-tooth comb.'

'Yeah. Chel, are you alright?'

'Oh, you know, work, work, work,' she said, lifting the bowl off the cake mixer and wiping her hands on her jeans. 'I know that's not what you mean.'

'It takes a while to get used to it.'

'Do you know anything about him?' she said suddenly, then looked skywards. 'Sorry, I swore I wasn't going to do this.'

'Then don't. Believe me, he's not worth another thought.'

She came to him and put her floury hands around his face, and smiled. 'OK.'

Driving away, he felt sick with the twisted deception. His daughter's father was at the bottom of a reservoir in a disused pit in North Wales. And that was where he'd stay. Where he had to stay, for all their sakes. Once in the car, he called Anna and told her, simply because he had no one else to sound off to.

'I can't help thinking that it was her father, and I beat him up. Jesus, I'm going mental.'

'I painted it today. The quarry, I mean.'

'What the fuck for? Anna, you can't put that in the gallery, everyone will *know*.'

'Know what? It was quite cathartic. I'm working on some of the miners now.'

'Oh, well, that's good. Good that you're painting again.'

'I'm working in the gallery too. I'm enjoying it more than I thought.'

'Is that because you're scared in the house?'

'I don't know. All I know is I want you to be here.'

'Listen, I've been offered a big dog.'

She laughed. 'What kind of dog?'

'Labrador Rottweiler cross. He's been beaten up and abandoned in the past but I think he'd be a good guard dog. Shall we give him a chance? He's too big for most places.'

'I guess so. I hope he's alright with the ducks and geese though, and the sheep!'

The dogs' home were only too pleased to re-house

Lonsdale. They'd looked at Jack's pictures of the farm and listened patiently to Lottie's elaborate descriptions of the garden and mountains. The dog had only lived in a builder's yard on a chain, and so had never experienced the countryside, but the kennel maid said this would probably work in their favour. 'If you warn him off the sheep and the fowl the minute he gets there and be firm and consistent, you should be fine. He's very biddable.'

He looked enormous in the car and left slobber on every available surface. Both children were so excited he left the choosing of their own dog for another time, until they'd settled into Chester. They'd been to look at Claymore's house and it reminded him of The Links, when he'd been happily married to Patsy in Prestbury all those years ago. That seemed like another lifetime, or someone else's life entirely. The children loved the huge, rambling space and the equally huge, secure garden. The move to Chester went ahead with hardly a ripple on the surface of his life. Since 19 Church House Way was fully furnished, they managed the whole evacuation in just two cars, with Oliver driving the Fiat. In the end, Patsy was shifted with two suitcases and a box to her name.

'I want to take the sculptures and the throws and the sofa from Harrods!'

'Problem. You see, I can't have Quay Cottage empty, you shouldn't have slung out all my old stuff.'

Thankfully, he didn't have to endure the forty-minute journey with her in his car. Lottie and James were a lot more cheerful. When they arrived at the property, Claymore's sister was already in situ and ready to issue Patsy with a list of rules. He left her to it and grinned for another forty minutes all the way to Wilmslow.

In the office, he moved out of the chair he'd

occupied for some twenty years, and Clare moved in. Within days it was clean and tidy and full of plants. 'I won't let you down,' she said, removing the porno calendar off the back of the door and stuffing it unceremoniously into the bin.

'Clare, I've known you for fourteen years. I trust you completely.'

She frowned at the computer, adjusting the height of his chair. 'I'm still unsure about some of these spreadsheets and the payroll.'

'I'm not going anywhere just yet, and when I do, I'm always at the other end of a phone.'

'I don't want to keep bugging you.'

'You won't be, you'll be helping me to merge into the hemisphere of the partially retired.'

He felt like a spare part though. When Tony went out for lunch, he sat in the back office and googled dog-training with a super serious face. Oliver appeared at the door, flicking a pen top on and off.

'Yo, Dad. Amy's like, totally made up about living in Conwy. So can we do it?'

'Uh-huh. Leave it with me,' he said. He barely lifted his eyes from the screen but once Oliver had gone, he had to turn to face the wall in case anyone saw him grinning. Later, he called Josh, not surprised that his stepson was more than happy to share Quay Cottage.

'No, that's fine. I mean, the flat's been great but the cottage is even better.'

'It's been tenanted a lot so it's got an electric meter in there, but don't let on to Ollie.'

Josh laughed. 'Better get saving the pound coins. Hey, good news about you and Mum finally getting it together.'

'Yeah, yeah it is.'

They started packing up the flat in earnest. Every

weekend he went down to the farm, he took another case of clothes, a box of books, or a stack of files. Ironic that he was in much the same position materially as Patsy. Then on the weekend of Bryn and Hilly's wedding, he took the final step. The staff had wanted to give them both a proper send-off but he'd declined. A leaving party felt much too final. The empty flat, stripped bare of their personal belongings, was enough to deal with. Tony was busily measuring up and taking photographs.

'Bear in mind, whoever you get as a tenant needs to be compatible with the business premises.'

Tony smiled and rolled his eyes. 'He's a handful, that lad of yours. He has potential though, he can sweet-talk.'

'Yeah, well, he'll be where I can keep an eye on him, like a work in progress.'

He informed Clare to go ahead and advertise for a junior, and this was the moment he felt truly redundant, all bases covered. All that remained now was his own life to live. He slipped away quietly, with no fuss. Oliver had already gone ahead and taken a week's holiday, setting up house with Amy in the cottage. He was on the phone in no time.

'Dad, can we take this electric meter out?'

'No!'

'It sucks. Can you tell Gran to stop tapping on the window and peering in?'

'No.'

It was the end of an era when he pulled off the drive one Friday morning in November. He was to meet Anna at the Mountain Hotel at noon. Hilly and Bryn were finally tying the knot. He had no doubt that the money had facilitated this and at first he'd been anxious that they'd maybe gone overboard and people would ask questions, but when he arrived, he knew this wasn't the case at all. The hotel wasn't the most salubrious of locations, and Anna had assured him that it was a simple civil ceremony and there would be only the four of them in attendance.

Every time he passed the yard, he saw another small improvement. The Irish horses, Heather, and the caravans had gone and the land had been raked and rolled, the fencing repaired and painted. This time, there was a new sign swinging at the end of the drive – Hopkins Livery. This filled him with tremendous satisfaction, and he paused for a moment, taking in the square of looseboxes and the barn bursting with bales of summer hay. The contrast was acute on such a drab day, with the clouds scudding high above Conwy Mountain, grey on grey. Not the best weather conditions for a wedding: mostly wet with flashes of cold, reluctant sun.

What the hell, it was the most amazing day ever!

It was the day he'd finally come home, home to the Land of My Fathers. What sweet irony was that?

He pulled in to the hotel and she was waiting for him, this extraordinary woman with violet eyes and unruly raven hair. They clung together in the shabby reception area like long-lost lovers.

'I love you so, so much,' he said.

'*Cartref croeso.*'

The registrar came out to say hello and explained that she had instructions to ask them both to please wait in the car park for the arrival of the bride and groom. She even issued them with a huge white umbrella.

'What's all this about?' he said to Anna, but she just shrugged.

'No idea, honestly.'

Huddled outside, they waited. Presently, rounding the bend in the road, a small tableau of figures emerged through the mist, the sun shining on the wet hedgerows like a token of goodwill. A horse and rider in Victorian garb being led by a man in a top hat. There was a teenage girl walking behind, waving fluorescent paddles in an effort to slow down the traffic, which was slightly out of place but somehow it didn't detract from the main event. A school coach rumbled by, full of swaying kids pressed up against the windows and they had to back the horse into a field entrance so it could pass.

As the procession moved closer, it became clear it was Hilly on the horse, wearing something long, and hopelessly impractical and fussing with a veil. Bryn, in an equally historic morning suit, walked alongside with a silver-topped cane.

'It's *Blue*,' Anna gasped eventually, a tissue pressed to her eyes. 'The stupid woman's riding Blue in a side-saddle.'

She looked emotional, so he didn't say anything, just kept one arm firmly around her shoulders while the other did battle with the umbrella in the wind.

'Jack, put the umbrella down, she'll freak out.'

'Who will? Hilly?'

'No, Blue!'

She smiled and explained, but despite his lack of equine knowledge he saw for himself the magic in the prancing Arabian mare, its white mane and tail flashing like snow on gunmetal. The horse seemed to float above the ground like a creature of some higher order. Whether it was merely mortal or touched with some other unknown spirit, he knew for certain that it belonged irrevocably to this land of misty mountains.

They turned into the car park and Bryn helped her to dismount.

'Thank God that's over,' Hilly said, hitching her long skirts above the pools of water. 'She's been a bitch over that saddle, she *hates* it.'

Anna ran to embrace the horse, then Hilly. Both women laughed, then cried.

The marriage ceremony was short and sweet. They went through a colossal amount of tissues. The men were allowed one each, which did the job sufficiently. Lunch was late and lavish at a country house fifty miles away from prying eyes.

Much later, they left Hilly and Bryn to enjoy the bridal suite and travelled back to Gwern Farm in comfortable silence. Lonsdale barked loudly and authoritatively the minute he put his key in the lock, and they took a moment to grin at each other. Inside, they were less joyous at the state of the kitchen bin and the hearth rug, but it made them laugh and that was more important. He unbolted the back door, let the dogs out, and lit a cigarette. Life was almost perfect.

It was curious to think that on paper he owned nothing, but none of that mattered because in his heart, he had everything.

EPILOGUE

It was a foul day for a school field trip. The coach collected them from the youth hostel and brought them along the pass. They had to wait for a moment on a narrow section for a horse, ridden by a woman in Victorian dress, to go safely by. A stable-girl bringing up the rear waved them almost to a stop. Some of the nicer children were interested in not only the striking horse but the side-saddle and the authentic outfit, and this made for an interesting and appropriate discussion. There was always a hard-core of naughty kids to spoil it though, the kids who found it more amusing when the driver had to employ the air brakes, and the girl with the traffic paddles had stuck two fingers up. A couple of them even returned the gesture through the back window.

'Darren Jones! Sit back down and put that mobile phone away or I will confiscate it.'

She'd be hoarse before the end of the day at this rate. Really, for a thirteen year old he liked to push boundaries. He was a right ringleader, with his mock tattoos and earring. Hopefully the climb up Conwy Mountain would wear him out a bit. It looked like the rain would hold off. There was more forecast, so she'd arranged to do the indoor activity later. She and Barbara, the art teacher, could have a cup of coffee in Conwy while the A-level biology students supervised slate mine research in the information centre.

They filed out of the coach at the top of the pass and she clapped her hands for attention. The children shuffled and wiped runny noses, packed lunches in rucksacks, brightly coloured waterproofs flapping in the wind.

'Right, listen to me, no climbing on *anything*. And please stay together, don't go wandering off. Some sections of the old mine workings can be extremely dangerous. I don't want to have to inform your parents that you've fallen into the pit and we can't find you.'

Some of them were stunned into silence and some laughed and larked about. Darren Jones mimicked her voice and his little crowd fell about laughing. They started the assent, the two older students bringing up the rear and controlling the stragglers. It wasn't really dangerous. The local council had seen to that – imagine the flak she'd get taking twenty children to accidentally plunge to their deaths down old mine shafts. She joked with Barbara about losing Darren Jones.

At the top, they divided the children into four groups.

'Red team go with Mrs Thomas. You'll be drawing some of the buildings. Blue team go with Samantha, you'll be answering questions one to five on your worksheets. Then yellows with Chrissy, questions six to ten. White team are with me and we're going to walk the site and try to imagine what life must have been like as a quarryman in Victorian times.'

The moaning started straight away. It was always the same, no one was ever happy about the group they were allocated to, the name of the group, or who was leading them. She set off at a brisk pace, Darren Jones meandering behind, already tampering with his white name badge.

'So, this is the old site of Penmaen Quarry. The slate industry in Wales began in Roman times and it's still operational today, but not on such a grand scale.

Now, who can tell me what slate is mostly used for?'

''Eadstones, innit,' Darren piped up.

'Headstones. Well, yes, that's one of the uses, well done.'

They continued to throw answers at her as they walked towards the cottages and reservoir. After a while, she became aware of a sweet, cloying smell. It wasn't there all the time, but it caught the back of her throat now and again and she noticed a couple of the children holding their noses. She could see Barbra wafting the air under her nose as she attempted to explain how the slate was split into thin slices for tiles. After a moment, her colleague trotted over.

'There's a really terrible smell near the water. Like something's died in there.'

'Yes, I keep getting a whiff. Probably a sheep fallen in. It must happen.'

They both turned instinctively at a shriek.

It was Samantha, the biology student. 'Oh my God!' she kept repeating, pausing to retch.

'Oh, for heaven's sake, she should be studying drama, not biology.'

'I'll start walking back the other way, should I?'

'Yes please, Barbara. I'll go and sort out Samantha.'

Barbara rounded up both groups of children and headed them back towards the mounds of slate, while she strode purposefully towards the young woman, who was now sat in an undignified manner on a rock with her head between her knees.

'What on earth is the matter?' she said.

Samantha looked up, her face devoid of colour and swallowed hard. 'There's something in there, in the water.'

'It'll be an animal.'

Her head moved slowly from side to side. 'Wearing

an identity necklace?'

She steeled herself to look over the rusted iron fence where there was a gap in the coiled barbed wire. Why did she look? She should have called the police and risked getting a ribbing for wasting their time. Like Samantha, she saw the necklace first, floating intermittently and catching the light, but then her eye was drawn naturally to the mass hovering beneath the surface of the water. It was a human body – or it *had* been a human body.

It was the most hideous thing she'd ever seen. The water blurred it to some extent, but the white, bloated flesh was like over-cooked pasta, black orbs where the eyes had been. Part of the face had been nibbled away. The necklace was twisted around the neck, and there was a name on it, she was sure. God rest the poor soul, at least they'd be able to identify this person, trace the relatives, and give whoever it was a proper burial.

She turned away, holding onto a post to catch her breath.

'Call the police,' she said.

THE END

Jan Ruth writes contemporary fiction about the darker side of the family dynamic with a generous helping of humour, horses and dogs. Her books blend the serenities of rural life with the headaches of city business, exploring the endless complexities of relationships.

For more about Jan Ruth and her books:
visit www.janruth.com

SILENT WATER
PART THREE OF WILD WATER

BY
JAN RUTH

The tragedy and comedy that is Jack's life; a dangerous web of lies concludes a bitter-sweet end.

Jack Redman, estate agent to the Cheshire set and someone who's broken all the rules. An unlikely hero or a misguided fool?

In this sequel to Dark Water, Jack and Anna must face the consequences of their actions. As the police close in and Patsy's manipulative ways hamper the investigations, will Jack escape unscathed?

With her career in tatters and an uncertain future, Anna has serious decisions to make. Her silence could mean freedom for Jack, but an emotional prison for herself. Is remaining silent the ultimate test of faith, or is it end of the line for Jack and Anna?

CDIDNIGHT SKY

BY

JAN RUTH

Opposites attract? Laura Brown, interior designer and James Morgan-Jones, horse whisperer - and Midnight Sky, a beautiful but damaged steeplechaser.

Laura seems to have it all, glamorous job, charming boyfriend. Her sister, Maggie, struggles with money, difficult children and an unresponsive husband. She envies her sister's life, but are things as idyllic as they seem?

She might be a farmer's daughter, but Laura is doing her best to deny her roots, even deny her true feelings. Until she meets James, but James is very married, and very much in love, to a wife who died two years ago. They both have issues to face from their past, but will it bring them together, or push them apart?

WHITE HORIZON

BY
JAN RUTH

Three couples in crisis,
multiple friendships under pressure.

On-off-on lovers Daniel and Tina return to their childhood town near Snowdonia. After twenty-five years together, they marry in typically chaotic fashion, witnessed by old friends, Victoria and Linda who become entangled in the drama, their own lives changing beyond recognition.

However, as all their marriages begin to splinter, and damaged Victoria begins an affair with Daniel, the secret illness that Tina has been hiding emerges. Victoria's crazed and violent ex-husband attempts to kill Daniel and nearly succeeds, in a fire that devastates the community. On the eve of their first wedding anniversary, Tina returns to face her husband - but is it to say goodbye forever, or to stay?

SILVER RAIN

BY
JAN RUTH

*Alastair Black has revealed a secret to his wife in
a last ditch attempt to save his marriage.*

A return to his childhood family home at Chathill Farm is
his only respite, although he is far from welcomed back by
brother George.

Kate, recently widowed and increasingly put upon by
daughter, sister and mother, feels her life is over at fifty.
Until she meets Alastair. He's everything she isn't, but he's a
troubled soul, a sad clown of a man with a shady past. When
his famous mother leaves an unexpected inheritance, Kate is
caught up in the unravelling of his life as Al comes to terms
with who he really is.

Is Alastair Black her true soulmate, or should Sleeping
Beauty lie?

57365945R00186

Made in the USA
Charleston, SC
11 June 2016